The Subsequent Proposal

Joana Starnes

ISBN: 1492874884
ISBN-13: 978 - 1492874881

There is a rose
that grows in a secluded garden,
beginning life as a small, ungainly yellow rosebud,
tentatively tinged with hints of orange.

Yet, as it blooms,
the tones of jealousy slowly lose ground
before the vibrant red of love everlasting
as it spreads into the petals, until they open fully
into a gloriously perfect
fire-rose.

By happy coincidence,
this is precisely what this story is about!

Prologue

Droplets of dew glistened on the shrubs that bordered their path, as the pair strolled in companionable silence. They had met again, on their morning ramble – by accident rather than design – but the gentleman was not sorry for it.

Her company was soothing, which was a great deal more than he could say, at this point in time, of everyone else of his acquaintance. She made no demands of him, and it was only in her presence that he felt neither watched, nor pitied.

They very seldom talked, in fact – but when they did, there was a gentleness about her and a sort of quiet wisdom that belied her years and her withdrawn nature. They had been discussing poetry a while ago, and he could not fail to smile as he recalled her all too pertinent advice.

"I venture to hope, Sir, that you do not make poetry your steady diet," she had sweetly told him, with a kindliness of manner he had, by then, grown accustomed to associate with her. "I, for one, have observed that it is the misfortune of poetry, to be seldom safely enjoyed by those who could respond to it completely. Indeed, those animated by strong feelings – and thus most likely to estimate it truly – are the very ones who ought to taste it sparingly…"

She had proceeded then to recommend Dr. Johnson's writings to his attention, along with other works of the same bent, all calculated to rouse the mind and fortify the spirit, and though she did not venture to speak further of any notions she might have harboured of his inner turmoil, her very gentleness was in itself uplifting, giving the clear impression that she fully understood.

He shook his head. He could not fail to see that the young woman who now walked beside him deserved a better lot than the one Fate had dealt her.

A father who ignored her – too engrossed in the illusion of his own importance, and thoroughly determined to care for nothing but his name, his lineage and his eldest daughter. An elder sister who did not fail to treat her more deserving sibling with nothing but the strongest and least merited contempt.

Why would they treat her in this abhorrent fashion the gentleman could not pretend to know but, with his senses sharpened by his own unremitting wretchedness, he had come to feel the wretchedness of others in ways that he had never experienced before.

She did not deserve it. She was kind and amiable, her unassuming manner and the warmth of her nature strongly reminding him of a dearly loved sister. *That* was probably the reason why he had begun to feel so protective of her over the intervening months, and so incensed on her behalf by the ill-treatment she constantly received from her relations.

She deserved a great deal better and, while thoroughly persuaded *he* did not, all things considered, the gentleman could not quite discard the thought that, if happiness in marriage was no longer in his reach, then calm contentment and the satisfaction of having made the happiness of others might perchance suffice.

He took a deep breath.

"I am very fortunate to have encountered you this morning, Miss Elliot," he finally began, "as I had hoped for the opportunity of a private interview. I shall leave these parts in a few days' time, and before I left there was something I most particularly wished to speak of."

He paused and swallowed. He was not ready for this, he ruefully determined, as the familiar pain twisted in vicious knots within him. He fought the urge to close his eyes and once again allow it free reign over his heart. Instead, he stopped and turned to his companion.

"Miss Elliot," he resumed, with another steadying breath, "I sincerely hope that what I have to say will not offend or pain you, but throughout the course of our acquaintance I could not fail to see that your constant kindness is hardly ever met with its just reward. I cannot claim the right to speak further of it, other than assure you that Lady Russell is not the only one sensible to your sterling qualities, nor the only one able to appreciate their worth. I have had the pleasure of your acquaintance for long enough to know that your society can be the warmest blessing to anyone around you and, while I scarce deserve the honour, I wish you would allow me to make it my life's work to safeguard your happiness."

Her eyes, fixed on his countenance since he had begun speaking, opened wide at this, so wide that they appeared to consume her thin, pale features.

"Miss Elliot," her companion said with great gentleness, "would you do me the great honour of accepting my hand in marriage?"

She gasped – a sudden, audible gasp and, without warning, her countenance was suffused with the deepest sadness. In visible distress, she looked away, but did not resume walking. She cast around instead, searching for something that could not be found, then fixed her eyes upon her small gloved hands. She had released his arm as soon as they had paused in their slow amble, and was now twisting her fingers together, in something that appeared nothing but the severest discomfort.

He sighed. *What* had he done? He had no wish to pain her – there were plenty of others who seemed determined to do precisely *that* and, by Jove, he would not swell their number!

"Forgive me – " he began, but could not finish, as his young companion laid a quelling hand on his arm.

"Nay, Sir, 'tis *I* who must beg your pardon. I have not imagined… You see, I have not known that you could possibly be harbouring such feelings!"

He made to speak again, but before he could think of the right words to frame the apology he knew the circumstance required, the young lady's raised hand gave him pause.

"You must allow me, Sir, to express my deepest gratitude for your kind offer. You… speak of my worth. Allow me, pray, to return the compliment. I too have had the pleasure of your acquaintance for long enough to know that you deserve a great deal better – "

He forcefully shook his head at this, but the lady would not permit the interruption.

"Nay, hear me, pray! 'Tis a long time since I have enjoyed the benefits of a warm companionship such as your society has provided, and had I known your feelings, I would not have allowed it… that is, I had no notion… I have not the slightest wish to pain you, Sir, and pray believe that I am deeply honoured by your sentiments, but…"

She raised her eyes to his at last.

"You deserve the courtesy to know, Sir, that I cannot return them. I know you well enough to be persuaded that I can safely share this with you… You see, eight years ago my heart was touched by another… Nothing came of it, and through my own wretched fault I lost my chance at happiness. So you see, you cannot safeguard it," she added with a wistful smile that filled him with compassion, "and it would not be fair to let you try. It would be but a poor return for your unprecedented kindness," she quietly finished, and finally looked down.

It was his turn to gasp, as her words suddenly revealed the enormity of his misjudgement. He had been selfish. Even in this mistaken notion of doing a good deed, he had been selfish.

Over the past months, he had found her presence soothing, had found her quiet kindness a welcome balm to the constant ache in his heart. He had sought her as an antidote to his loneliness and anguish, and told himself that he could repay her by taking her away from hurtful kin to a place where she could safely flourish. And it was only *now* that he realised he could have inflicted a worse wound than them all, if she had come to love him.

For all he had to offer was warm compassion. That, and some sort of calm affection. Not love, nay – neither love, nor passion. They belonged to another, who would never claim them now. Compassion was a bitter fruit, though, when one hungered for love…

Yet – she had just told him – love was for her an equally tormenting recollection. With some effort, he restrained a rueful chuckle. Perhaps… He bit his lip. Perhaps there was hope for them after all…

"Forgive me," he said again, and although he saw her draw breath to speak, this time he would not let her stop him. "You have just made me see how wrongly I have acted and that, to all my previous misjudgements, I very nearly added yet another one!"

"I fail to catch your meaning, Sir," she replied softly, "but I am quite certain you need not apologise."

"And yet I do," he quietly retorted. "I have misled you – unwittingly, 'tis true, but that does not excuse it. You see, Miss Elliot, what I have to offer is my hand, an honourable name and the deep respect your person could not fail to command in anyone disposed to do you justice. As for my heart…"

He bit his lip again. To say that he, too, had loved another would be nothing but a pale reflection of the tormenting anguish that consumed him. He winced – and to his surprise and fleeting pleasure, a small gloved hand was laid comfortingly on his arm. Their eyes met once more, and Miss Anne Elliot whispered with the greatest compassion.

"You need not speak of it, if it gives you pain."

He nodded and exhaled, soothed by her kindness, her warmth, her healing touch.

"Be that as it may, it must be said," he resumed at last. "I cannot offer you my heart, Miss Elliot. I wish I could, for you are worthy of the deepest affection. Everything else I have, though, is yours if you care to have it. Nay, do not answer now!" he swiftly added. "There is no need for haste, no need at all. Just… think on it, this is all I would ask you, and if you can find reasons to accept my offer, I can only promise I shall never give you any cause to repent."

She made no answer, but stood there before him, her eyes intent on his. Wide brown eyes, full of that sort of pity that does not grate or injure, but soothes the deepest wounds. What she saw in his, he could not tell, but a moment later her gloved hand squeezed his arm again, then settled around it as she wordlessly indicated that she was ready to resume their walk.

"I thank you, Sir," she whispered and nothing more was said, for a long time.

Again they ambled, and again the silence settled around them, not as a laden curtain but a warm, comforting garment at the end of a heart-wrenching day.

They circled the small pond, watching dragonflies dart over the reeds towards the silvery surface and, from someplace behind them, an early bird arose to greet the day with cheerful song.

As though awoken from the deepest of reflections, Miss Elliot gave a little start, then squared her shoulders and looked up towards him.

"I wish to thank you for escorting me this morning," she said, with some sort of quiet determination, "and… I thank you for the offer of your hand. I *have* thought on it and, if the companionship of a kindred spirit is what you are seeking, then I would gladly give it, Mr. Darcy. I am pleased and honoured to consent to be your wife."

Chapter 1

Three months ago, in April…

"How *dare* she?" he burst again with vicious fury, driving back the stopper of the port decanter with such unreasonable force that it was a wonder how it did not break.

The shock and grief had by now given way to anger – and Darcy welcomed it with savage pleasure, for anger did not hurt anywhere near as much!

Who did she think she was, this country Miss of meagre stock, no fortune, no connections, to spurn the Darcy name? To cast aside his offer as though it were a peddler's worthless heap of rags?

The blasted neckcloth would not come undone, and Darcy tugged again with renewed fury until the cursed knot gave way at last – and he could breathe. He drew a ragged breath and took the cut-glass goblet up again, the ruby liquid swilling dangerously as he spun around towards the bed to cast the crumpled piece of linen atop the counterpane. With another oath, he struggled to unfasten the small buttons – awkward to handle at the best of times – and took the goblet to his lips for a long draught.

Was she perchance oblivious to the fact that ladies of vastly higher birth would have been honoured to follow in Lady Anne's footsteps – and rightly so?

The Darcy name went back to the Norman Conquest but nay, it was not good enough for Mrs. Bennet's daughter, with her mighty connections who lived above the shop!

He took another gulp, then slammed the goblet down upon the oval table, not noticing the drops that splashed and marred the perfect surface. He strode up to the bed and spun around again, thrusting his hand beneath the open collar of his lawn shirt to furiously rub at his aching neck.

Offended and insulted! *She* had the audacity to claim herself offended and insulted by the honest confession of the scruples that had given him pause in offering for her!

He snorted as he ran his hand over his face. It was perhaps a mercy that the shock had stunned him, otherwise he might have had a vast deal more to say about exactly *which* one of them had just cause to feel insulted!

He spun around again to pace the blasted strip between his four-poster bed and the large windows.

Pemberley's succession! Georgiana's comfort! He had been willing to put *all that* into her hands! To entrust her with everything that mattered! And she had thrown it in his face without a second thought!

What did *she* have to offer? The priceless connection with a country-town attorney, his vulgar wife and a selection of shopkeepers! Oh, and of course, the genteel side as well, let *that* not be forgotten! A father who would castigate his kin in public, all for the sake of a witticism, and a cheap one at that, when frankly he would have been better advised to give himself the trouble of taking a birch rod to the back of his youngest, before it was too late and she was fully grown into a mindless hoyden! And as for the parson, heaven help us! *What* had she been expecting? That he should be *delighted* to align his name with theirs?

Well, at least he had told her *that*, Darcy all but spat in vindictive fury and ran the back of his hand over his lips, refusing to acknowledge the sudden flash of guilt at the recollection of her turn of countenance, and how she had flinched, when she had heard those very words.

"Well, what did she expect?" he said aloud, less viciously this time.

Ungentlemanly, she had called him and, despite the surge of anger at her sheer presumption, he could not fail to own that he had *not* been raised to belittle his inferiors in this fashion, regardless of what he privately thought of them. It was, in truth, a conduct hardly befitting of a gentleman to point out the obvious difference in their stations, and having been spurred on by anger was but a poor excuse!

"What of *her* conduct, though?" he retorted darkly, in like-for-like response to the uncomfortable thought.

Was it befitting of a lady to champion another in the midst of a proposal, and to his face as well? And not just any man, but *Wickham!*

"*Wickham*, of all people!" he burst out in fresh anger and walked back to the table to pick the goblet up again.

He tossed down the remains of port and strode up to the windows, then swiftly back again. The thought of the wretched scoundrel twisted his insides into a savage knot. It was not enough that he had wreaked havoc in Georgiana's kind and trusting heart! That he had schemed to take her away from him, to blight her very life for his own ends, all devils take him! Nay, he simply had to crawl back out from some repulsive hideout to spread his malicious poison over *his own* life as well!

He gripped the goblet in his hand until his knuckles whitened, oblivious to the small mercy that the glass was thick enough to withstand it, rather than shatter into shards in his unconscious grasp.

Did she believe him? Did she give credence to the letter?

Or was she determined to still be taken in?

Surely she could not imagine he would concoct a story such as that, involving his own sister! Surely she was not still unprotected in the face of that devil's lies and schemes! She *would* believe him, would she not? Or was the abhorrence he inspired too strong for her to credit a single word he wrote?

"Heavens above!" he whispered, as fresh pain cut through him.

For six months now, she had commanded his heart beyond sense, beyond reason. She had made him forsake all duty to his lineage, his name, his very self, to the point of making her the most honourable offer! And yet abhorrence was all that she had ever felt for him!

The crushing thought bore down with such unyielding force that everything else faded for a moment, even fury and righteous indignation.

With another ragged breath, Darcy dropped down in the large winged chair standing in the corner of his chamber and closed his eyes as he leaned his head against the backrest.

'You could not have made me the offer of your hand in any possible way that would have tempted me to accept it.'

The words pierced through him, mercilessly stabbing deeper into the gaping wound.

She, who was everything, regarded him as nothing.

Worse than nothing!

The vicious pain propelled him out of his chair again and he resumed his pacing, raking his mind for thoughts that would bring back the anger, to help him through the searing pain again.

It did not come. Despite his utmost efforts, for many sleepless hours, the anger would not come.

~

"*I do not require it, Lydford!*" he heard himself thunder, and was not surprised by the fleeting look of dismay that crossed his man's features as he turned to dispose of the offending breakfast tray that he had brought, against his master's express wishes.

Passing a hand over his unshaven face, Darcy allowed that an apology was in order.

"Think nothing of it, Sir," Lydford evenly replied and although his man said nothing further, Darcy could almost feel his practised eye slide with even more dismay over his attire.

He had dismissed him early the previous night, long before Lydford could perform all the duties he deemed necessary in order to assist his master to retire. He had not changed for bed, nor had he slept, and the wrinkled shirt bore the marks of the brief slumber in a high-backed chair and the excruciating hours spent pacing in his chambers. The dressing gown and nightclothes still lay spread over the untouched bed, along with the crumpled neckcloth and a discarded coat, and Lydford walked up to retrieve the latter, shaking it gently into place, clearly unable to restrain himself from shaking his head as well, when he noticed the deep creases set in the fine cloth.

Darcy swallowed.

Having served him faithfully for five years now – over and above the decade of diligent service to his father – Lydford could justly lay claim to some degree of freedom of expression, not to mention a great deal better treatment than he had just received. But if his man was about to launch into any remonstrations about how difficult it was to remove creases from such cloth, he would not vouch for his temper, nor the consequences!

Thankfully for everyone concerned, Lydford *did* know better, and nothing more was said as the older man removed the crumpled articles to the dressing room and remained there to go about his business. Darcy could hear him sharpening the razor, and felt compelled to cast over his shoulder:

"I shall not require your services, Lydford, I thank you. You may leave me now!"

"I fear I shall have to disagree, Sir," Lydford quietly observed, and Darcy could still hear him continuing with his preparations. "I believe some exertion is in order before you can greet – "

"I have clearly told Weston that I wish to see *no one!*" Darcy forcefully interjected, but his man was equally unperturbed.

"Weston sends his deepest apologies, Sir, but he could not bring himself to say as much to Lady Malvern."

Darcy groaned, and before he could extract further intelligence from his valet regarding the unwelcome arrival, the door to his bedchamber was opened wide with utter nonchalance, and his cousin entered.

"Aye, Fitzwilliam, make yourself at home, pray – and indeed why not?" he shot with biting sarcasm, but his cousin did not see fit to acknowledge Darcy's remark.

Nor did he apologise for the intrusion.

"Good morning, Darcy – or should I say *'good day'?*" the Colonel replied with the same nonchalance, and dropped unceremoniously onto the seat at the foot of the bed. "I would make haste to dress, if I were you. You know full well that my mother will not take kindly to being kept waiting."

"I was not expecting Lady Malvern – or you," Darcy retorted darkly but, in lieu of any response, Fitzwilliam walked over to the dressing room and poked his head in.

"You will excuse us for a moment, Lydford," Darcy heard him say and was riled in no small measure to see his man complying without question to his cousin's request and quietly abandon his employment to move past them – swiftly, for his age – and close Darcy's bedchamber door behind, as he stepped out.

"If you have quite finished ordering my people about, I would appreciate it if you left me," Darcy all but growled. "Make my excuses to your mother, pray – "

"I shall do nothing of the sort!" Fitzwilliam replied with sudden sternness. "I will say my piece, and then I shall summon Lydford, and *you* shall take no time at all to ready yourself for company. And then, Cousin, you will come down with me and let Lady Malvern know you are delighted to accept her invitation to join us at Audley, to celebrate her sister's birthday."

"I am barely acquainted with Lady Wrotham and I have no intention to – "

He did not get to finish. In two long strides, his cousin was by his chair, towering above him.

"Darcy, you *will not* drag Georgiana through this – or else I might have something to say to you as well about your selfish disdain for the feelings of others!"

The look of devastation on his cousin's countenance gave him pause and the Colonel looked down in deep remorse as he retracted.

"Forgive me, that was uncalled for. I should not have – "

Before a full apology could come, Darcy burst out:

"How did you know of this? Have you seen her? Has *she* told you…?"

"Of course not! Heavens above, man! What on *earth* are you thinking?" Fitzwilliam retorted with obvious impatience, not needing to inquire whom did his cousin speak about.

"Then… *how?*" Darcy whispered.

His forceful manner suddenly abandoned, the Colonel leaned to lay a comforting hand on his cousin's shoulder.

"*You* did," he replied gently, giving his cousin's shoulder a light squeeze. "Three nights ago, when we returned to town. You do not remember…"

It was not a question, and Darcy made no answer. No, he did not remember having revealed quite so much on the night when, unable to bear the crushing grief any longer, he had begun to tell his sympathetic cousin methodically plying him with drink just *why* he looked as though the world was at an end.

Because it was… She would not have him!

She would not have him. Five simple words that spelled the very end.

He made to speak – to ask Fitzwilliam just how much more he had disclosed the other night, but all that came out was a tired sigh. It mattered not. Presumably he had revealed all there was to it, or just about enough, in any case.

He shrugged. If there was anyone alive to whom he could entrust his deepest secrets, it would be his not much older cousin. And if *he* chose to make full use of his disclosures and torment him with them, at least Darcy knew that they would go no further – just as well as he knew that the torment was in every way justified.

"I am distraught to have given Georgiana more cause for concern" he sighed again. "Do you know what exactly did she say to Lady Malvern?" he tiredly asked after a while and looked up to his cousin, only to see him shake his head in mild reproach.

"I should have thought you knew your sister better than suspect her to have gone tattling to my mother," Fitzwilliam smiled at last. "Nay, it was Henrietta who let the cat out of the bag, in a manner of speaking, and I for one am rather glad she did."

"What has your sister got to do with this?" Darcy asked, not really caring, but he was about to hear all there was to know, nevertheless.

"She was surprised to hear that you would receive no one, not even her, and then proceeded to wheedle out of Georgiana as much as could be got. The poor child knew nothing, other than that you had returned from Kent in such a state as she had never seen you – and was distraught there was no way for her to find out what had caused it, or find the slightest means to help."

Darcy shook his head.

"Forgive me," he muttered, and his cousin pressed his shoulder again in sympathy.

"It is not my forgiveness you should be seeking, and perhaps not even hers. She would understand. But you *must* see that you cannot continue in this fashion," he urged with sudden energy.

His cousin, however, merely shook his head again, more despondent than Fitzwilliam had ever seen him – so he urgently added, his voice betraying all his affection and concern:

"Darcy, if there was a way to take this off your shoulders, I would, in a trice. There is not, though, so all I can offer is to carry the burden with you, if you would allow me. But spare your sister all the pain and anguish! For her and her alone, you *must* exert yourself!"

It was testament to Fitzwilliam's wisdom and powers of perception that he had not urged his cousin to exert himself for his own good. He knew full well that it would carry little weight, in his present state. It was only the thought of Georgiana's blameless suffering that stood a chance to reach him – and, in the end, with great difficulty, reach him it did.

Lydford was summoned back, and his refreshed master was eventually able to join his relations in the drawing room, to shock them with his haggard countenance and make his aunt mutter something no one could discern.

It was beyond him to make civil conversation, but thankfully Fitzwilliam and Georgiana took *that* upon themselves. All that was required of him was to take some of the refreshment Lady Malvern decreed should be placed before him – that, and consent to join his relations into Somersetshire, before the month was out.

It was at Audley that he had met Miss Elliot.

Miss *Anne* Elliot, that is to say.

He had, of course, become acquainted with her older sister as well, and her father, but any reference to the elder Miss Elliot made him recoil in nothing but disgust. Her air and manner he would have found repugnant, regardless of his own frame of mind. There was a great deal of self-consequence about the pair, father and elder daughter alike, in their dealings with their perceived inferiors, and *that* was only surpassed by their eagerness to fawn upon those who, in either wealth or title, stood noticeably above them.

More familiar with the local worthies and rarely in town, they were distracted for a while by the need to pay court to others. Before too long though, they were eager to express their gratification at renewing Lady Malvern's acquaintance, and clearly show an interest in stronger ties with those of her party.

The ties they sought were not merely those of friendship, and Darcy was soon to find Miss Elliot vexingly alike Miss Bingley, and as determined to court his attention – but it was only when he had heard her addressed as *'Elizabeth'* by a quiet, thin girl with mild dark eyes and even milder manner that his temper had flared, beyond common sense and reason.

That anyone as different from *her* as nature and manner would allow it should bear the same name! That he should have it spoken in his hearing with misplaced pride by Miss Elliot's vexing father, quick to extol her non-existent virtues and thinking they held sway!

That she would, as many before her, attempt to court his favour by noticing his sister and insisting that, to *'dear Georgiana'*, she should not be Miss Elliot, but Elizabeth at once! To hear the name on his sister's lips and know that, had his dreams been answered, another Elizabeth would have by now shown her kindness and genuine affection, rather than empty flattery with an ulterior aim!

His cousin must have sensed the full extent of his displeasure – and perhaps its cause – and had taken pains to preserve him from the Elliots' notice, so that he would not be provoked into a full display of deliberate incivility towards two of Lady Wrotham's guests.

He seemed to have enlisted his elder brother's willing aid and thus, gratified by Leighton's interest, Miss Elliot was quick to transfer her relentless attentions away from Darcy and upon a better catch.

"I find myself greatly indebted to your brother – and to yourself, I'd wager," Darcy had muttered dryly over his cup of coffee some evenings later, when Miss Elliot had left them as soon as Lord Leighton had walked into the room.

The Colonel had laughed.

"The least we can do, Coz, and you are more than welcome. I would hate to see you turn tail and hasten back to town – and I daresay you do not need more prompting! Besides, I can scarce justify making you bring Georgiana here for nothing more than the pleasure of Miss Elliot's attentions! Henrietta can weather them better, the dear soul, she is made of sterner stuff!"

He had teased, as was Fitzwilliam's way – a strategy he had employed from their earliest childhood and which had never failed him, at least where his cousin Darcy was concerned.

Yet, beneath the banter, the helping hand was there. Fitzwilliam did not attempt again to make him drown his troubles – he would not have dared, not in his aunt's house or in his mother's presence – but he steadfastly persevered at his side, and often sought him out, wherever he was hiding.

That night, Fitzwilliam's trained nose led him to the gardens, where his cousin had retired when the gentlemen had at last decided to forsake their port and rejoin the ladies.

A brief spell in the drawing room had assured Darcy of his sister's comfort, ensconced as she was with the younger Miss Elliot in quiet conversation over a book of poems, in a secluded alcove. He had no wish to interrupt them and an exchange of glances, as well as Georgiana's animation, was enough to persuade him that she fared a great deal better with Miss Anne than Miss Eliz… *Miss Elliot!*

His retreat was discreet and quick, and Darcy descended the stairs at some pace, then made his way through the vast glazed doors into the gardens.

It was very quiet, but for the buzz of laughter and conversation from the open windows above him, and darkness was stealing swiftly upon the grounds.

A footman came to ask if there was anything he desired – a drink, or perhaps a lantern? – but Darcy chose neither. The man bowed and withdrew and Darcy walked further away from the house into the shadows.

He took a deep breath, relishing the quiet. He had always found it hard to tolerate large company, with all the mindless chatter, and even more so now – though, to own the truth, bar from Miss Elliot and her vexing father, the rest of Lady Wrotham's guests were pleasant enough. Still, they could not raise his interest. Nothing could. Bland, aimless conversation, devoid of all excitement, of sparkle and of hope…

He winced again as snippets of former conversations, so long ago, at Netherfield, returned to haunt him with empty promises of a life that now could never be. The jagged knife twisted once more and then delved deeper at the excruciating recollection of merry eyes and the most tempting lips curled up in an arch smile.

Flirtation, he had thought it, and a clear sign of interest! Fool, ten times a fool and worse than a fool! Was he so thoroughly devoid of understanding? Or had he only seen what he had wished to see?

He heaved a long sigh of vexation as he heard the door open behind him, and then slow footsteps. The same obliging footman must have returned to ply him with heaven knows what else, he assumed, wishing the man would have the sense to see that all he wanted was to be left alone!

However, it was Fitzwilliam's voice that broke the stillness.

"Do you wish to talk?"

"No. I do not," Darcy replied, without turning.

"You need not hide out here, you know," the Colonel remarked, sipping his brandy, as he slowly walked forward until they stood shoulder to shoulder. "You are quite safe from Miss Elliot at the moment. Leighton has just asked her to play for him."

Darcy sighed again.

"I thank you, Cousin, but you need not keep watch. Go and amuse yourself. I am quite well."

It was, of course, a falsehood, and Fitzwilliam presumably knew it.

He was *not* well. He was wandering about like a lovelorn fool, and sooner or later he would *have* to rally! For Georgiana's sake, if not his own, he could not spend his life moping about in such a dreary, self-indulgent fashion! Fitzwilliam had the right of it. There were others entrusted to his care – and, unlike Bingley, he had a duty to uphold!

The sudden thought of his former companion gave him pause.

He could not have failed to notice the drastic changes in his friend's demeanour – nor could he reassure himself that they would be short-lived. Even before Christmas, Darcy had determined that *this* was significantly different from all the other times when Bingley had thought himself in love. On previous occasions when Bingley had declared himself enchanted by some angel, the fascination had ceased fairly soon after its object had disappeared from sight.

It had not happened this time, that was plain to see, but it was only *now* that Darcy had a grasp of what his friend must have been going through. Now that he knew *precisely* how it felt to be told that the object of his deep affections did not return the sentiment in any way.

Darcy winced again. Perhaps *she* knew him better than he knew himself! Perhaps he *did* have nothing but selfish disdain for the feelings of others – otherwise it would have crossed his mind by now that Bingley ought to be informed, in some way or other, of that dreadful day's disclosures!

As part of the litany of his manifold faults, she had taxed him with ruining, perhaps forever, the happiness of a most beloved sister. It had emerged that Miss Bennet *did* care for Bingley after all, and that his own interference had caused the deepest heartache.

Bingley would have to be informed of this – the sooner the better – and, if there was any justice in the world, Miss Bennet would forgive him his temporary desertion and his friend would be happy.

The thought stabbed through again, in the same wound.

If that should come to pass, his close association with Bingley must come to an end – there was no other way! Heavens above! Was he to sit and dine with her at Bingley's table? Dance with her at Bingley's Christmas Ball? Was… – merciful Lord in heaven! – was he to stay within Bingley's circle for long enough to see her married to another man?

Fitzwilliam could not have failed to hear the groan but made no comment, merely turned sharply to cast a glance towards him.

Nothing was said for a long time and silence reigned around them until the Colonel brought himself to speak.

"Will you join us on the morrow, Darcy? There is a scheme in place, I hear, to visit Cheddar Gorge, a few miles to the north. Lord Wrotham tells me that the sights are quite astounding, and Georgiana has expressed a great deal of interest to see them. 'Tis a small party, I am told. Merely myself, your sister, and six or seven others. Miss Anne Elliot is one of them – but thankfully none of her relations – and Langford, I think, and Montrose and his sisters."

"I thank you, Cousin," Darcy quietly replied, and they both knew that the gratitude he was expressing was not for the invitation to see the delights of Cheddar Gorge.

"Georgiana seems quite taken with Miss Anne Elliot," the Colonel remarked, his eyes upon the brandy he was swirling in tight circles in his glass. "A very pleasant lady, is Miss Anne, and uncommonly kind to your sister. I have never seen Georgiana quite as much at ease with anyone as she is with her. There is a sort of gentleness about her that seems to draw your sister. Raise her confidence and cheer her up, you know… after all that mischief in the past…"

The unwelcome reminder was not of a nature to kindle Darcy's spirits. Nor was the implication of his cousin's words.

"I sincerely hope you are not about to turn matchmaker, Fitzwilliam! I assure you, I have no interest at the moment in the marriage mart!"

"No, I should imagine not," his cousin offered quietly, returning to his brandy. "May I ask," he said after a while with obvious hesitation, "if you have formed any sort of plans? That is to say, what will you do, after your visit here?"

Darcy's features tightened. He had no plans – no notion whatsoever. There were no plans. Just duties, reins to pick up again. Pemberley. Georgiana. *Those* were his anchors – and there was nothing else to sustain him now.

"I believe I shall return to Pemberley for the summer," he offered at last, only to see Fitzwilliam shake his head.

"Not the best of notions, if you do not mind me saying. Just you and Georgiana, left to your own devices…"

"I was not planning to bring Georgiana," he tiredly replied. "Lady Wrotham had invited her to extend her visit, and escort her and her relations to Bath, sometime next month."

Fitzwilliam grimaced. This solved but half the problem, to his way of thinking.

"And you?" he pointedly asked, but his cousin merely shrugged, then squared his shoulders.

"Do not concern yourself on my behalf. I am well – or I shall be, in a while. I have to conquer this, I know – and it *will* be done, one way or the other. You will excuse me now, there is an urgent letter that I have to write. To Bingley," he rather reluctantly added in response to his cousin's inquisitively raised brow, and Fitzwilliam nodded in sudden comprehension.

"Aye, it must be done," the Colonel concurred, then sought his cousin's glance again, remorse clearly written in his countenance. "In case you have forgotten, in your befuddled state, the night when we returned from Rosings, let me apologise again for the mischief I caused – "

"I *do* remember," Darcy interjected. "Think nothing of it," he added with some effort.

Fitzwilliam's inadvertent disclosures regarding his involvement in Bingley's affairs could not have come at a worse time and, lividly angry as he had been with his cousin for his loose tongue and wretched timing, Darcy could not fail to own that blame should be affixed to its proper place at last.

"It was not your error, Fitzwilliam. It was mine," he brought himself to utter.

And it was high time to atone for that!

Chapter 2

True to his word, Darcy set about to write the long and very awkward letter, and the missive was dispatched at first light. He disclosed nothing of his own affairs to Bingley – no good could possibly have come from *that* – but a full account of his own errors was candidly provided, as well as the intimation of Miss Bennet's sentiments regarding his close friend.

It had not been an easy task to supply that delicate piece of information without disclosing *how* exactly such a topic might have been brought up, but Darcy trusted that his friend could not care less how did *he* come to speak of Miss Bennet's feelings with the lady's sister, and all that he could think of would be to see his heart's desire at last.

The very notion made him ill. His own heart's desire despised him and abhorred the very mention of his name!

'I had not known you a month before I felt that you were the last man in the world whom I could ever be prevailed on to marry.'

The molten wax dripped upon the letter and, with a ragged sigh, Darcy pressed his seal into the dark red pool that looked a lot like blood.

He did not hear from Bingley. Not during the remainder of his stay in Somerset; not even later on when, as he had told Fitzwilliam, he returned to Pemberley, leaving Georgiana behind.

The notion saddened him, but could not surprise him. It would have been a miracle indeed if his friend had forgiven him for his interference. Darcy knew full well that, had the situation been reversed, he could not have forgiven any man who would have presumed to part him from Elizabeth.

The fact that, unlike Bingley, he would *not* have taken his marching orders from anyone but the woman he loved carried little sway. Bingley was unaffectedly modest, with too strong a dependence upon Darcy's judgement rather than his own.

In *that* respect at least, it was just as well that Bingley would not wish to have anything to do with him in future. It was high time for him to grow into being his own man. Besides, the rupture would have come in any case, once Bingley and Elizabeth's eldest sister had reached their understanding.

The pain was by now a familiar companion. He carried it to town, and then to Pemberley.

In many ways, he was truly glad that Georgiana was not there to see it, despite her unwillingness to remain in Somerset – mostly out of deep reluctance to leave him to his own devices, Darcy surmised, for otherwise she seemed quite happy at Audley, with Lord and Lady Wrotham, their family and friends.

He had to own, Fitzwilliam had the right of it – as always. Miss Anne Elliot's company was a good restorative and her mild nature, so similar to Georgiana's, coupled with a much better understanding of the world, could not fail to be of great benefit to his sister, so Darcy was assured of Georgiana's comfort while he was away.

As to his own comfort, *that* was something he clearly could not vouch for. There was no comfort for him, anywhere he went – and least of all at Pemberley, as he soon discovered.

Great many duties awaited him there, and his steward had no difficulty in occupying most of his waking hours with estate business that had to be addressed, but as soon as the diligent Mr. Hatherley left him, the empty halls of Pemberley would do nothing but painfully remind him of what it was that he had lost.

He had long dreamed to bring her there, to have the glory of her presence brighten the old halls, and the thought that it would never come to pass brought on a deeper anguish than all he had endured – and the sleepless nights spent in aching loneliness in his bedchamber drove him away to roam the moonlit halls like yet another of Pemberley's forlorn ghosts.

He could not bear it for longer than a fortnight.

Long before May was out, he travelled back to Somerset to rejoin Georgiana, having determined that loneliness at Audley was at least slightly less painful than most.

She was not at Audley anymore, he soon discovered. The family had travelled to Bath earlier than previously planned, and Darcy saw no reason why he should not follow. The fine old place was not so busy now as it would soon become later in the summer and the quiet town, old as the hills despite the modern buildings, held far greater attraction than the vexing bustle around St. James's Square.

Lord and Lady Wrotham's party had greatly diminished. It was only immediate family and a few intimate friends that had followed them to Bath. Sir Walter Elliot, thank goodness, was not amongst them but, for Georgiana's sake, Darcy was pleased to see that Miss Anne Elliot *was*. She was not staying at the Wrotham townhouse, but very close to it, in Rivers Street, at the house of Lady Russell, an old friend of her departed mother's and her own godmother, Darcy soon found out.

It was not surprising that they were thrown into company together nearly every day, over the following month. Nor was it surprising, now that he had come to know her better, to see that her society had visibly worked wonders, making Georgiana flourish. There was a warmth about her that could not fail to soothe an ailing heart. Her own spirits oppressed by her relations' selfish neglect, she must have known how to bring comfort and soothe the broken spirit of another, with gentleness and care.

What came as a surprise was that, in some small measure, she had even succeeded to somehow soothe his own. Not his heart – nay, his wasted heart could not beat to her kindness any more than it could leave him altogether, go back to Hertfordshire where it belonged and take the pain with it, leaving him at peace at last. Yet some measure of peace slowly settled within him as they sat, all three, discussing books and music, or ambled together around the old city of Bath.

She had read the same books as he, and apparently they had inspired her with more or less same feelings. The notion could not fail to stir the muted anguish, as he remembered how *another* had refused to discuss books with him at the Netherfield ball – so he was glad to silence the painful thought, if only for a moment, and attend Miss Anne as she warned him against the dangers of a steady diet of melancholy poems upon a broken heart.

It was not surprising that, towards the end of their sojourn in Bath, faced with Georgiana's mournful reluctance to part with her new friend, he had accepted Lady Russell's gracious invitation to spend some time at her house, which was separated only by a lane from Kellynch Hall, Miss Anne Elliot's home. Nor was it surprising that, in his early morning ambles, he had encountered their lovely neighbour often and joined her on her walks. And lastly, it had come as no surprise that he had brought himself to make her an offer, as much for her sake and Georgiana's as for any other reason.

The fact that she had seen fit to accept him *did* bring a measure of surprise, particularly in view of her stilted disclosures about her broken heart – but also brought some sort of mild contentment, at the full knowledge that, in Miss Elliot's kind and capable hands, Georgiana's future would be safe and well guarded.

And so was Pemberley's. And perhaps his own.

Darcy could barely suppress a huff of vexation at the sight of Sir Walter Elliot pausing in his discourse to stop before the enormous looking-glass that graced the drawing room into which he was admitted a short while earlier, when he called at Kellynch Hall to ask for the baronet's consent.

Sir Walter studiously rearranged his neckcloth, then brushed his lapels for an imaginary spec of dust; he smoothed the front of his very elegant vest, briefly considered the effect, then tugged at both his cuffs.

"Ah, indeed, Mr. Darcy," he recommenced at last, turning once more towards him. "Indeed, my daughter and I are most gratified by your kind offer! I take it that Anne has consented, has she not?"

"Miss Elliot has done me this great honour," Darcy replied curtly, endeavouring to give as little indication as possible of his impatience to be gone – and of his disdain.

"Well then, I am only too pleased to welcome you into this family, Sir. Your connection to the Earl of Malvern and, by marriage, to the ancient line of de Bourgh speaks highly in your favour. I have taken the trouble, you see, to consult the Peerage, once we have been honoured with your acquaintance. There is but one matter that I would like to bring to your attention," Sir Walter added before lowering himself upon one of the sofas, with the greatest care for the tails of his grey coat. "Pray, Sir, be seated. Can I offer you some refreshment?"

"I thank you, no," Darcy swiftly declined, and took the seat the baronet had indicated. "This matter you were speaking of, Sir Walter?" he then prompted, and his host steepled his fingers before him, as he chose his words.

"Ah, yes," he murmured, clearly having come to some conclusion. "I see no impediment to my younger daughter's marriage, Sir, none at all, except, that is to say, its timing."

"Timing," Darcy repeated, as a statement rather than a question, and finally the other chose to elaborate.

"Timing, aye. You see, Mr. Darcy, I have another daughter – "

"Indeed, I have had the honour of making Miss Elliot's acquaintance," Darcy interjected dryly, failing to see where would the lady fit into the present conversation – unless the foolish baronet was entirely lost to all sense and reason so as to offer his *other* daughter to him as a possible life companion!

"You have, of course, and I must say, I am rather surprised –… Well, be that as it may! The material point, my dear Sir, is that my eldest daughter has already experienced the extreme discomfort of seeing a younger sister marrying before her, and I would not wish to assist another in compounding the offence – "

"*Offence*, Sir?" Darcy enunciated in a tone of voice that would have given pause to those who knew him better.

The baronet, however, continued unperturbed.

"Of course, you understand that it cannot be a comfortable feeling to lose one's precedence before not merely one, but *both* one's sisters! It mattered little when my daughter Mary was wed to Mr. Musgrove, as we held high hopes at the time of a most eligible match, but in the present circumstances I would consider it a favour, Sir, if you would have the goodness to consent to a long engagement."

It was with a great measure of self-restraint that Darcy neither clenched his fists, nor shared his true opinions. The man had now sunk in his estimation beyond anything he had ever thought Sir Walter capable of!

To think that he had inwardly censured the master of Longbourn for teazing Miss Mary out of the notion of performing yet another ill-chosen and ill-delivered piece! The lack of parental support and consideration that his chosen course of action had implied paled before the magnitude of Sir Walter's selfish contempt for his second daughter. That he would be prepared to risk her happiness and future for no good reason other than his eldest daughter's sake revealed to him the true extent of Miss Anne's mistreatment. The time when he could take her far away from them could not come soon enough!

"How long?" he asked, for no other purpose but to sound the depths the man would choose to sink to.

"A twelvemonth, shall we say? That would provide more than ample time!"

"How so?"

"We have been quiet and confined at Kellynch, Mr. Darcy, and the society the country offers cannot boast of great variety. This will, however, change. We are to remove to Bath and settle there in a month or so. In such extensive and superior society, I do not doubt that Miss Elliot's worth will soon be recognised."

Darcy forbore to share his views on the matter; instead, he coolly retorted:

"A year's engagement is not something I am prepared to consider. Besides, if I may be allowed to point out, Miss Anne Elliot is of age, from what I understand."

The words had barely left his lips, before Sir Walter drew himself up in his seat, his countenance testament to his acute displeasure.

"Anne would not marry to disoblige her father. She has not done so at nineteen, and I very much doubt she would make a beginning of it at seven and twenty!"

So *that* was the backdrop of the story! He had not asked her for details, of course, on the day when Miss Anne had chosen to make her disclosures, but Sir Walter's outburst had suggested that the attachment she had spoken of had not been sanctioned by her parent.

A better acquaintance with the said parent was proof enough, in Darcy's eyes, that the match he had not deigned to sanction must have had its worth – yet the gentleman's daughter had bowed to the parental request. *That* must have been the wretched fault she had referred to – and although less convinced than Sir Walter that she would repeat her youthful error, Darcy had no wish to make her choose. A mutual agreement with the lady's father was the better option, he determined, which was why he suddenly spoke up.

"Six months is all I am prepared to offer – with Miss Anne's concurrence, needless to say!"

"I am persuaded that a twelvemonth would serve a great deal better, but I *am* prepared, Mr. Darcy, for my daughter's sake, to consent to eight months if – "

"Six months, Sir Walter!" Darcy enunciated with an air of finality, tired of bargaining his betrothed's happiness with a man he thoroughly despised. "Now, if you would excuse me, I would like to rejoin your daughter. I hope I can tell her that you have agreed to six months' engagement."

"*I* will tell my daughter that I consent to have the engagement announced in six months, with the wedding to follow after a reasonable time," Sir Walter declared crisply and stood, as though to indicate that the interview was at an end.

Riled in no small measure by the entire business as well as by the manner of his summary dismissal, Darcy offered a perfunctory bow and, Sir Walter's pronouncements be damned, he went to seek his betrothed in the gardens.

He found her walking in the shrubbery behind the house and lost no time to acquaint her with Sir Walter's restrictions. In lieu of any answer, Miss Anne gave a little wistful smile.

"Should you prefer to be married in a fortnight, Mr. Darcy, I shall raise no objections and neither will Lady Russell," she quietly assured him and her dark eyes drifted up to his.

He could not fail to smile at the sweet yet determined manner in which she had declared her future allegiance.

"It shall be your decision, Miss Elliot," he offered gently, as he carried her hand to his lips. "If it would please you to remove to Pemberley sooner rather than later, I would gladly tell your father as much, in a trice!" he added, and the smile that graced his countenance bore a hint of boyish mischief she had never seen before. "If you would choose to honour your father's wish rather than work to disoblige him, I will support you in every way I can – though, if I may say so, he does not deserve you, and I am eager to take you away from such affronts as soon as I can!"

She gave a little tinkling laugh.

"I hardly notice them these days, Mr. Darcy, those actions that you call affronts – yet it is not for my father's sake that I am prepared to consent to his request. They will remove to Bath soon enough, in any case."

"And you will not go with them," he stated with some satisfaction.

"I will not. It would give me pleasure to spend my last unmarried months with Lady Russell, and perhaps with my sister Mary, at Uppercross, in that valley beyond."

"I hope Lady Russell can be induced to travel into town. To London," he felt obliged to clarify, suspecting that, in that part of the country, *'town'* – with all the delights and beacons of fashion – would mean Bath, or perhaps Cheltenham. "If that can be arranged, my sister and I would be delighted to join you, although at this time of year the customary amusements may be rather thin on the ground."

"I am persuaded you do not care for such amusements," Anne smiled widely, laying a hand on his arm, and Darcy pressed it with his own.

"You know me well. Nay, I do not care for them. But it would please me to be able to squire you through town, and have you visit us in Berkeley Square as well. As you can imagine, Georgiana would be utterly delighted – and I can scarce wait to share the news of our engagement with her. As I am sure you know, she thinks the world of you! Your father need not be concerned," he added with well-concealed distaste. "The engagement will not become public knowledge before its time. My sister can be trusted to keep it to herself. Or rather," he amended with another smile that made him look at least five years younger, "she can be trusted to let it go no further than Fitzwilliam, and his devilish good skills at wheedling out other people's secrets!"

"I shall not scruple either to share it with at least one other person," his companion assured him in response. "Lady Russell must not be kept waiting for six months before she can rejoice at our engagement. I would not on any account trifle with her affectionate solicitude, or allow her to hear it from anyone but myself."

The two announcements were independently made that very day, and the recipients of such uplifting news were as delighted as the couple had expected.

For her part, Lady Russell was more than delighted – she was vindicated in the advice she had given her dear Anne eight years ago when, at her persuasion, Anne had consented to break her engagement with the dashing Captain Wentworth. Dashing he had been, yet the young man had no prospects, no fortune and belonged to a most dangerous profession, and Lady Russell had long congratulated herself on her success in showing Anne the lack of wisdom that such a scheme entailed.

In the eight years that followed, the lady's conviction in her own opinions had begun to wane. The darling child had lost her bloom, and clearly her father's wilful ignorance of her many virtues was not a soil upon which the dear girl could flourish.

But *this!* Oh, *this* was what Lady Russell had been hoping for, when she had persuaded her goddaughter to draw back from the lot of a sailor's wife. An honourable name, a worthy husband who could give her the station in life that Anne, darling Anne, deserved. And she, for one, could not heap enough blessings on that sweet girl, Mr. Darcy's sister who, by eagerly seeking Anne's society, might just have been the means through which they would soon be united.

Chapter 3

Darcy blotted the paper and put his pen down, then cast another glance over the long list of instructions he had drawn for his attorneys, so that they could start the necessary preparations pertaining to his future marriage. All appeared in order, and Darcy abandoned the paper on his desk and walked up to his strongbox.

A brief search revealed the item he was seeking. A dark blue velvet case, bearing his mother's initials upon the lid.

The greatest part of his mother's own jewellery was bequeathed to Georgiana, when she came of age, yet this box, preserving the headdress and necklace she had worn on the day of her marriage had been destined to go to the unknown woman who would become her son's wife.

A. D. Lady Anne Darcy. And now the small box would pass to another Anne Darcy, before the year was out…

With a flick of his fingers, Darcy opened the lid. Nestling in velvet folds, the intricate design encrusted with glittering diamonds revealed itself in its old-fashioned splendour. Darcy swallowed hard, his hand tightening into a fist and he closed his eyes to banish the vision of the headdress glittering from amongst unruly auburn curls…

This would not do! *She* did not want him – and impossible as it might be for him to cease wanting her, he would do well at least to refrain from encouraging fruitless recollections, empty wishes and all manner of dead dreams!

He slammed the lid shut and locked the diamond set back in the strongbox, but before he could return to his papers, his real life and his senses, the strangest commotion reached him from the great hall.

He made to walk up to the door to inquire about the cause of the disturbance, but before he could reach it, the door flew open and Bingley burst in, with Weston on his heels, clearly put out by the strange reversal.

"I thank you, Weston, you can leave us now," he instructed the vexed butler, who bowed and closed the door, whereupon Darcy turned to his friend with a mixture of disbelief, pleasure and confusion. "Bingley – …" he began the awkward greeting, but before he could continue, his guest interjected with utmost impatience:

"I trust you will forgive me for bursting into your study in this fashion, but would you mind telling me what is the meaning of *this?*"

A piece of hot-pressed paper was thrust into his hands, and Darcy did not need to unfold it to know that it must have been the letter he himself had sent. He forbore to state the obvious, so he offered simply:

"What should you wish to know?"

"*Everything!*" his friend exclaimed, and nervously waved off the silent offer of a seat. "Everything, from the very beginning – I daresay, from the ball at Netherfield!"

Darcy sighed.

"'Tis all in the letter," he tiredly retorted.

A full confession to an irate Bingley who should by now have a good notion of everything there was to know was not a welcome prospect – but presumably no less than he deserved.

Seemingly of the same mind, Bingley cast him a baleful glance.

"I beg to differ! There is a vast deal that you seem unwilling to disclose – like the trifling fact that they had been at Pemberley! I had to gain this charming piece of news from Mrs. Bennet, Darcy! *Mrs. Bennet!*"

"Of what are you speaking?" Darcy all but stammered. "*Who* has been at Pemberley?"

"Pray, do not play the fool, Darcy, it hardly suits you!" his friend burst with such vexation as he had never displayed towards anyone, to Darcy's knowledge, and least of all him.

"Bingley, let us sit," he soothingly offered.

There was no way of garnering anything from his visitor until their tempers settled, and nothing could be gained from storming at one another in this fashion.

"You must believe me when I say I do not understand you," Darcy resumed. "I have just returned from Somerset two days ago. I have not been at Pemberley since May."

Bingley did not sit, but seemed rather more disposed to give his friend some credence.

"So you have *not* been there to welcome them?"

"Welcome *whom?*" Darcy forcefully prompted, heartily tired of Bingley's incomprehensible charade.

"Miss Bennet, Miss Elizabeth and their party," Bingley enunciated, then added something more – but Darcy was no longer listening.

He seemed instead to have forgotten how to breathe.

Elizabeth at Pemberley. While he had been in Somerset, Elizabeth had been at *Pemberley!* She had strolled through the same halls that he had haunted, missing her dreadfully, to the point of acute physical pain – and he had not been there!

"Why had she come?" he whispered, and it was only when his friend began to answer that he realised he must have voiced his thought aloud.

"Mrs. Bennet told me that her sister by marriage hails from Lambton," Bingley supplied with a gesture of impatience. "They all travelled there to see the sights and seek some old acquaintance that was still residing in the area and, before moving on towards Dove Dale, they stopped at Pemberley, for Mrs. Gardiner remembered it fondly, from the times she used to tour it with her parents, as a girl."

"So it was *Mrs. Gardiner's* wish rather than… the Miss Bennets'?"

"That is what I gathered. Why should you wish to know?"

"No reason. Pray, continue!"

Of course there was a reason! A feeble wisp of hope of having been forgiven was stirred by the notion of Elizabeth wishing to visit his home. But surely, even if it was somebody else's wish, she would not have consented to set foot inside it, if she still resented him and his very name!

Caught in his own thoughts, Darcy failed to notice that his friend *did not* continue but, a few moments later, a glance at Bingley's darkened countenance warned that the confrontation could scarcely be avoided.

"Would you care for a drink?" he asked, despising himself for his evasive tactics.

It was barely midday, but neither stopped to consult a pocket watch. At Bingley's nod, Darcy poured for both. Still, neither sat, but faced each other, one leaning against the dark panelling, the other – the large desk.

"I am glad at least to have the opportunity to apologise in person rather than merely by letter for my misjudgement last autumn – and the pain I have caused," Darcy began at last but, to his surprise, his friend waved the matter aside.

"I have not come here to reproach you for my own errors, Darcy!"

"*Your* errors?" his friend interjected and, at the sound of surprise in his host's tones, Bingley looked away with a wry grimace.

"*You* have not courted her, Darcy – *I* have. *I* should have known her feelings, and not allow myself to be persuaded to walk away from the best of happiness!"

It was not easy to argue with that notion – and Darcy did not. In truth, it was a rather welcome statement from his callow friend.

"I can only assure you it was not done with malice," Darcy earnestly retorted. "I did not believe Miss Bennet to be indifferent because I wished it. I believed it on impartial conviction. A conviction that, however amiable she may be in temper, her heart was not likely to be easily touched."

Bingley pursed his lips.

"As I said before, *I* should have known better. *I* was the one supposed to understand her, and her wishes and feelings – not you. What I fail to see though, Darcy, is how can you reconcile your claim at best intentions with the deception in the spring? Worse still, the collusion with my sisters! *They* knew that, had I known she was in town, I would have called upon her. You must have seen it also – and, much as it vexes me, I can see *why* my older sisters would treat me as though I was still unbreeched and in leading-strings, but devil take me if I understand why would *you* presume to do the same!"

With that, Bingley emptied his glass in one draught and left it on the small table beside him.

"I did not wish to see you pained by an attachment that was not returned," Darcy offered, but his tone lacked conviction, for he knew full well that there had been vastly more than *that* spurring him on.

His friend arched a brow.

"Did you, now!" he shot back. "And there was I thinking that it was your prejudice against the family that carried the most weight!"

Darcy sighed.

"Bingley, all I can vouch for is my regret at having interfered," he tiredly offered. "I have long thought that I could not forgive anyone who tried to put me in the same position. Yet here I am, begging your forgiveness for treating you as a child rather than an equal," he added simply, "and for all the suffering I have caused to you and… those you love."

At that, Bingley's eyes narrowed.

"You know that, for my part, I could have forgiven you the worst of transgressions, but to think that *she* had been injured also – …"

He bit his lip.

"You wrote there," he nodded at the letter, "that her sister hinted she had suffered because of my abandonment – and I was rendered livid by the thought! Last week, as soon as I read your letter – "

"Forgive me," Darcy interjected, "are you saying you have only read it *last week?*"

"Aye, to my misfortune. I have just returned from the North. I left town in March – did you not get my note? Could not stand the blasted place and everybody! But be that as it may, as soon as I read your letter, I came to see you, and found the house shuttered. Then I set off to Longbourn – and you may imagine my distress and anger when I could not see her, and learned she was in Derbyshire and touring *Pemberley!*"

"When will they return?" Darcy asked in a ragged whisper, then cleared his voice and gulped some of his drink.

"A se'nnight. Maybe more."

"And did she – Mrs. Bennet – tell you more about the family?" Darcy pressed on and, impossible as that might have seemed a moment earlier, Bingley's countenance darkened even further.

With all the ease of a *habitué* in the house in Berkley Square, he walked over to the selection of decanters and refilled his glass, without the need of an invitation. He did not drink though, but spoke without turning, and his voice was low and hard.

"Oh, aye! Mrs. Bennet had a vast deal to tell me – and I can only pray she meant to torture me with falsehoods for my previous desertion, for if she spoke the truth, Darcy! If she spoke the truth…!"

He broke off and took a long draught from his glass, then suddenly spun around to face his host.

"If she spoke the truth," Bingley all but spat with uncommon bitterness, "then thanks to my own weakness and to your deception, I have walked off from Miss Bennet's path just in time to make way for another!"

"I do not understand you. What exactly are you saying?"

Bingley made a sharp gesture of impatience – so sudden that he nearly spilled his drink.

"Merely that, had I not walked away from Netherfield last autumn, or had I been *informed*," he added, with harsh emphasis, "that she had been in town in the spring, "by now we might have reached an understanding – and I would not be seething in your study at the thought of Miss Bennet touring Derbyshire in the company of a charming captain!"

"*What* charming captain? Did you not say just now that the Miss Bennets were at Pemberley?"

"They *were*. With a large party of friends, comprising their aunt and uncle Gardiner, Mrs. Gardiner's friend, her husband and her charming brother, recently returned from the high seas!" Bingley poured out with biting sarcasm – and Darcy could scarce tell if his friend was unable to speak sense, or whether it was *himself* who had lost his senses. Whose friend? Whose husband? And whose charming brother? Was Bingley *determined* to be vexing, or was he just unable to string two words together?

With some effort, Darcy forbore to ask that precise question. Instead, he worked to steady his voice, when he asked another:

"Would you explain, pray, of whom are you speaking?" he inquired, his voice slow and measured and, as poor reward for his effort at a semblance of calm, he received Bingley's clearly impatient huff.

"I fail to see what you can find so difficult to understand! Mrs. Croft is a friend of Mrs. Gardiner's, a former school companion, or something in that vein, and this lady, her husband and her naval brother have decided to accompany the Gardiners and their nieces on their northern tour," Bingley proceeded to enunciate, as though he was requested to clarify an obvious matter to a rather dim, or purposefully awkward child. "If you must know all the details Mrs. Bennet gave me, it appears that Admiral and Mrs. Croft have leased a property, where they aim to settle later in the year. As the owners were yet to vacate the place, the lady chose to spend some time in town. While there, she came across Mrs. Gardiner and, having nothing better to do while they were waiting for the house to become available for their occupation and pleased to continue their resumed acquaintance, Mrs. Croft persuaded her husband and her brother to join the Gardiners on their tour. Mrs. Bennet took great pains to tell me, when I called at Longbourn, that the lady's brother showed little inclination for the scheme, but his views altered once he learned that Miss Bennet and her sister were to be of the party. As we both know – some of us for a vast deal longer than others," he interjected darkly, "Miss Bennet had been staying with the Gardiners since Christmas and, as of mid-April, so had her younger sister. Thus, they had frequently encountered Mrs. Croft and her relations – and I tell you, Darcy, when Mrs. Bennet dropped that titbit of information, she was positively smug! As I said before, I hold great hopes that she was merely determined to punish me for my desertion for, when Miss Kitty joined us, she seemed shocked by her mother's intimation. Before too long, Miss Kitty was sure to point out that her Aunt Gardiner said it was *Miss Elizabeth* whom Captain Wentworth appeared to be courting, not Miss Bennet, and that *she* formed the same opinion, when they stopped at Longbourn, on their way to the North. Mrs. Bennet seemed exceedingly vexed by Miss Kitty's interference and I could not fail to see that, when she disclosed as much, her mother shot her a dark glare and rolled her eyes. In any case, there is no time to lose. I am determined to set off to Netherfield at first light on the morrow and I was hoping..."

But Bingley's swift words, tumbling one after the other in anxious haste faded from Darcy's hearing, as wave after wrecking wave of shock turned everything around him into chaos and he could sense nothing but blinding, crushing pain.

It was bound to happen, he had always known it. He had fully expected that, if Bingley renewed his connection with the Bennets, he would arrive one day on his doorstep to deliver news that would tear his world apart! And yet no prior preparation was likely to defend him against the vicious grip that ripped him into pieces, nor would it stem the tide of shards that coursed through him, racing through his veins to tear into his heart.

'And was she welcoming his courtship?'

The searing question that he could not ask burned in Darcy's throat. He chased it down with the burn of brandy, and squeezed his eyes shut. And yet the image branded into his mind's eye would not vanish. Elizabeth smiling up at some dashing, sun-tanned naval captain. Elizabeth at Pemberley, walking through what should have been her home, on this Captain Wentworth's arm.

The gripping vice twisted his insides into another knot, as Darcy failed to heed Bingley's second prompting. By the time he had felt compelled to prompt his host for the third time, there was not a shred left of the younger man's proverbial good-humour.

"Darcy? I say, *Darcy!* I would have thought that, all things considered, you could at least give me the courtesy of an answer!"

The angry tones forcefully reverberating through the study brought Darcy back from the excruciating stupor.

"Forgive me. I was not attending," he said at last, his gravelly voice that of a man who had long lost the habit of speaking.

"Indeed! And there was I thinking you were seeking an excuse to refuse me!" his guest retorted, heated antagonism in his countenance and manner.

"Refuse you what? Forgive me, Bingley," the master of the house offered once more, as he passed a hand over his face. "I shall have to ask you to repeat your question."

"As I just *said*," Bingley complied with visible vexation, "both my dratted sisters have refused point-blank to be of any assistance in the matter, and shall not, under any circumstance, travel to Netherfield with me. As such, I will of course be able to ask the family from Longbourn to dine with me at Netherfield once Miss Bennet returns, but my hands are tied, were I to aim for anything less formal. Believe me," Bingley added with unprecedented sternness, "given the present state of our connection, I would scarce be asking this of *you*, if I had anybody else to turn to. As it stands, you are my only option. So, what is your answer? Will you come to Netherfield and allow your sister and Mrs. Annesley to join you, so that there is suitable female company in residence, to draw upon?"

Were it not for the new shock Bingley's words engendered, Darcy would have felt heartily ashamed by his friend's implication, when he had spoken of the current state of their association, and even more so by his hesitation in making the request. As matters stood, Darcy could only gasp.

"You cannot be asking this of me!" he exclaimed swiftly, and this time could not fail to notice the extreme coldness of his friend's reply.

"I see! Well, at least I know how much reliance I can place on the strength of our friendship, and indeed how much credence on your professions of regret, in that letter yonder!" the younger gentleman bitterly observed. "With another man, I would be graceless enough to remind him that he owed me this, by way of retribution, but I find myself too sickened by the mere thought of having to tell *you* as much. You will excuse me, Darcy, I have matters to attend to!" Bingley all but spat and made to drain his glass, his countenance a clear indication that he wished for nothing better than stride out of the house in Berkeley Square and never return.

He did not, though. His former friend's anguished exclamation stayed Bingley's hand, and the younger man turned towards his host again.

"For God's sake, Bingley!" Darcy had burst out, "Believe me, would you, when I say I would do *anything* to help you – anything but *this! I cannot* **do this**, Bingley!" he fiercely repeated, a raw edge to his voice that the other had never heard before.

Nothing was said for a long moment, as Bingley's better nature held him in place, yet would not let him pry. For his part, much as he regretted his own outburst, Darcy suddenly came to see how fruitless it must be to struggle further to keep his friend in the dark. The truth of what had happened would be made known to him before too long, once Bingley and Miss Bennet reached their understanding…

"I daresay you shall be told, sooner or later," Darcy tiredly voiced his thoughts aloud, "so you might as well hear it from me now. I cannot do what you require of me because…" he took a deep breath before forcing the truth out. "Because last April I have made Miss B– … Miss *Elizabeth* Bennet an offer – and she has refused me."

The words sounded odd, outside of him, ringing in his hearing rather than silently tearing through his soul, and Darcy's countenance contorted in another wave of pain.

"She –…? Oh. *Oh!*" he heard his friend exclaim and, with comprehension dawning, anger was wiped clean off Bingley's countenance, to be replaced by the deepest contrition.

There was every chance he would become incensed again, as soon as he remembered that his far from impartial advisor had brazenly warned him in the strongest possible terms against a connection with the very same family, Darcy thought and sighed, wishing for the anger, as it would be far easier to bear than his friend's compassion.

Whether the notion had occurred to him or not, Bingley did not speak of it, though. Instead, he offered quietly:

"I am *that* sorry, Darcy! There you are, with *this* on your chest, and I come to plague you like the very devil! I would not have – you know that, do you not? – if I had the slightest notion! Well, then! *Of course* you have no wish to come to Netherfield, with or without the ladies! Forgive me for asking. Will you – …? That is to say, I hope you know you are most welcome though, should you change your mind…"

Darcy made no reply, other than nod his silent thanks. His friend could not imagine just how much he *did* wish to avail himself of the invitation. How much he craved to see her. Hear her voice again. See her full lips curl up in that bewitching smile.

The old wound bled, torn open by the thought that another claimed her smiles, her laughter and perhaps her kisses. That someday soon she would give her hand in marriage. Her heart, her mind and her every allegiance given to another. Her love and constant presence another man's blessing. Her lovely form in another man's arms.

"Good heavens, Darcy!" Bingley exclaimed in horror as this time the much thinner glass *did* shatter into pieces in his best friend's grip. "Here, take my kerchief!" he anxiously offered and, hastening to Darcy's side, he abandoned his own glass on the desk, to free his hands and better assist his friend in stemming the blood that gushed from a long cut just under his fourth finger.

Carelessly set upon the desk behind them, the glass toppled over, spilling its contents in a honey-coloured rush that seeped, unheeded, into some sheets of paper covered in even script.

Neither noticed, as Bingley clumsily endeavoured to tie the kerchief around his best friend's hand, repeatedly advising that he should seek more competent assistance from Mrs. Herbert, the housekeeper.

"I would have thought –… No matter!" Bingley retracted swiftly, unwilling to point out that his companion should have had more sense than breaking glasses in his fist!

He turned instead to retrieve his own – only to notice the extensive damage.

"Oh, damn and blast!" he gasped. "Just look at what I have done! I am heartily sorry, Darcy! You would be right in thinking I have come here to cause nothing but trouble!" he mumbled as he frantically looked around him for something he could use to rescue the unsalvageable papers, all the while searching through his pockets – a fruitless endeavour, as his sole kerchief was now tied haphazardly around his friend's right hand – and it was only when his eyes fell on the ruined papers that, for the first time in over a half-hour, Darcy remembered he was now a promised man.

"Nay, leave them! Leave them, Bingley, do not concern yourself!" Darcy urged, laying his hale hand on his friend's arm to forcefully restrain him from his efforts, then reached to take hold of the already illegible instructions.

Single-handedly, he crumpled the three dripping sheets and cast them to one side.

"Do not concern yourself," he quietly repeated, then took a deep breath. "No matter. It shall not take long to draw them up again."

Chapter 4

"That will do, Lydford, do not fuss!" Darcy muttered, as his man busied himself with changing the dressing on his cut.

It had bled profusely for some time and, after Bingley's departure, he had seen some wisdom in following his friend's advice and summoning his efficient housekeeper.

Shaking her head at the unfortunate mishap, she had promptly fetched several slices of agaric and placed them on the bleeding wound, then covered them with lint, above which a tight bandage was applied, to keep everything firmly in place. The slices of agaric had fallen off some three days later, revealing the unsightly gash, which Lydford had just cleaned and expertly bandaged.

"The post has just arrived, Sir," the man said as he removed the bowl and the old dressing. "Shall I have it brought up to your chambers or –… "

"The study will do fine, I thank you," Darcy interrupted, and forbore to remind his man to cease treating him as a convalescent.

'Tis but a cut, by Jove, and not an amputation!', he all but huffed as he allowed Lydford to ease his arm into the coat sleeve with more than the necessary precaution.

The lapels were smoothed, the corners of his collar straightened and with a discreet nod, Lydford silently declared him ready to face the day.

Fresh coffee awaited in the study, along with the post, and Darcy took a sip of the scalding brew as he proceeded to sift through the neatly stacked pile. The morning paper lay at the very bottom, beneath several envelopes and, as he picked them up, one by one, the hand on the third one from the top gave him pause. There was no blot of ink on the direction for once, but the sender's identity was as clear as can be, and Darcy weighed the sealed envelope in his hand before casting it aside with a long sigh.

He took another sip of coffee and began to open the others.

Five from his business agent, three of which required immediate attention.

A brief note from Lady Russell and, enclosed within it, a concise page from Miss Anne, both relating more or less the same – namely that Sir Walter Elliot had finally settled upon a residence that would befit his station; that he planned to remove to Camden Place before the month was out, escorted by Miss Elliot of course, as well as her companion, a Mrs. Clay, and that, as previously settled, upon their removal from Kellynch, Miss Anne would go to spend some time with her godmother.

A letter from Fitzwilliam was opened next, revealing sundry accounts of country life at Leighton Hall, Lord Malvern's seat in Cheshire and requesting, in Lady Malvern's name, full details of the enthusiastic madness with which the Czar Alexander and King Frederick of Prussia had recently been welcomed wherever they had chosen to show themselves in town.

The next one was from Kent and stated in no uncertain terms that a yearly visit at Rosings was a great deal less than what her ladyship expected, and that the pleasure of Darcy's company was requested in July. A cursory glance over the rest of the letter, as he finished his coffee, informed him that, on the following visit, he was expected to bring Georgiana – and, with a scowl, Darcy folded his aunt's missive and relegated it underneath the furthermost pile.

For perhaps the sixteenth time, his glance drifted towards Bingley's letter, still watching him from the corner of his desk, with the bright red eye of its carelessly applied seal.

With an impatient huff, Darcy gave in at last and swiftly tore it open to extract the pages covered in large, uneven script. He took a deep breath and steeled himself to read.

She has come, Bingley had begun without preamble. *The party had returned to Longbourn five days ago. I have instructed my people to inform me, as soon as they got wind of it, and I was told that they had arrived on Thursday and that the aunt and uncle had remained with them for yet another day. There was no mention of other members of the party, and only one carriage was seen returning them to Longbourn.*

I called upon the family the day after their relations' departure, and I confess myself unsure of my reception. Mrs. Bennet was as effusive as ever, but there was a steely glint in her husband's eye and as for Miss Bennet… Darcy, I know not whether she will forgive me for my transgressions! She barely spoke a word to me beyond what common civility required, and I doubt she looked in my direction more than thrice!

I could not stay long, as they appeared to be in the midst of preparations for Miss Lydia's departure. She had been invited to accompany Col. Forster's wife and she will leave tomorrow morning, when the regiment removes to Brighton, for their last assignment.

I could scarce exchange a word with Miss Bennet – or indeed anyone – as Miss Lydia was very vocal in her excitement, and so was Miss Kitty, though it was disappointment rather than excitement that spurred her on. Miss Kitty has informed me that, although older, she has not been invited and I was left in no doubt that she was not best pleased!

I had to take my leave, it seemed the only option, but I was invited to join them for dinner the following day. The party was not large, which was a pity, for in restricted company it was very plain to see that Mr. Bennet is not regarding me with a friendly eye – not that I blame him! – and neither does his second daughter…

Forgive me if I pain you now. Should you very much prefer I made no reference to Miss Elizabeth Bennet in my subsequent letters, pray say so and I will comply. For now, I shall assume you will be pleased to know that she is in good health. I have not seen her at all on the day of my first visit, as she had set off on a walk before my arrival, but yesterday at dinner I sat between Miss Bennet and her second sister and we have had several opportunities for conversation.

I really cannot tell whether Miss Elizabeth spoke to me a great deal to mask the fact that Miss Bennet would not, or whether the reverse was true, and she was endeavouring to protect her sister from having to converse with me.

I am rather disposed to believe it was the latter, especially after this morning's events. I have called again at Longbourn this morning and it was plain to see that Mrs. Bennet would not be at all averse to allowing me the opportunity to converse privately with her eldest daughter – but it was equally obvious that her second daughter did not share her views.

I am distraught to say that she does not trust me, Darcy – and I cannot fault her any more than I can fault her father – though I am at a loss as to how can I regain their trust, if they persist in their endeavours to protect Miss Bennet from my society. Protect her against **me**, *when I would give my right arm to keep her safe and happy!*

There was a rather large inkblot beneath the last sentence, where Bingley must have forcefully punctuated his exclamation, and Darcy lifted the letter closer to the light, so that he could read the words it partially covered.

He needed not have given himself the trouble. The next line was nothing but a profuse apology for ranting on in this thoughtless fashion about troubles he had brought upon himself, in a letter to someone who was not even bolstered by his own tenuous hope.

Darcy let the letter drop before him on his desk and closed his eyes as he leaned his head against the backrest.

Devoid of any hope – how dreadfully fitting!

He did not have the smallest hope of finding the fulfilment his younger friend was seeking. He did not have her hand, and he would not have love. *Her* love, the greatest prize for any man! How had he not seen it, before it was too late? Would she still have refused him, had he not openly disdained her world and everybody in it? Had he not worked to separate her sister from his friend?

He frowned. It would behove him to remember it was all in the past. She had refused him, and now he had offered for another, who had graciously accepted his hand in marriage, as well as his offer of a helping hand. He could not dwell forever on matters that could not be changed!

And yet…

Insidious, and with strong, honourable arguments to support it, the thought crept in – advanced – took hold.

Did he not owe Bingley a helping hand as well, in his predicament? Would it not help his innocent friend's case to assure

Miss Bennet's sister that it had been *his* fault, not Bingley's, that his friend had not sought her sister out?

Her eyes would flash in anger to hear such disclosures but, unlike the anger she had displayed at Hunsford, would this not abate, once she learned that he was keen to make amends?

Would this be too much to ask for – to part with kindness, or at least in peace?

It would further Bingley's cause and it would injure no one. Not the family at Longbourn, none of them; not Georgiana; not Miss Anne Elliot and his promise to her. It would injure no one – except perhaps himself.

But that was a risk he was prepared to take!

Leaving his papers in careless disarray for once, Darcy left his study and went in search of his sister. He found her in her private sitting room, curled up with a book.

"Fitzwilliam!" she exclaimed in obvious delight. "I had not expected you would conclude your business so soon! Shall I order tea – or would you care for breakfast?"

"Breakfast would be good, if you are ready to join me. But first, dearest, I have a question to ask."

At his young sister's eager invitation, Darcy proceeded to give her a vastly abridged version of Mr. Bingley's troubles, though he did not omit to mention his own role in the affair.

"To my way of thinking," he concluded, "as I had a hand in mistakenly steering him away, the least I could do is attempt to redress the wrong. So my question is, dearest, would you be willing to travel to Netherfield with me?"

"Oh, Fitzwilliam, would I just!" the young girl clapped with obvious excitement. "Poor Mr. Bingley! Such a kind, generous man! *Of course* I would be delighted to come and assist you in any way I can! If only we could work together to help Mr. Bingley find as much joy as you have found with Anne!"

Her brother swallowed hard and made no reply. He looked up to find his sister's eyes lovingly fixed upon him – so, with the greatest effort, he turned up the corners of his lips into a valiant smile.

With a measured step, Darcy walked to one of the large windows.

So! The deed was already done!

That very morning, while the Darcy carriage was still making its way towards Netherfield, Bingley had called at Longbourn, had found the opportunity to open his heart, had proposed and had been accepted – and there was no need for him to be here now.

No need at all!

Returning to town would be by far the most sensible option, yet even as the thought occurred, Darcy knew that he could not. He could not leave without having laid eyes upon her, even. Without hearing her voice once more.

Besides – he chose to hide behind more manufactured reasons – what would his sister think, or her companion, of being dragged all the way here, merely to travel back the very next day? Nay, they *had* to stay, if only for a short while, and take the opportunity to show that he had reconsidered his untenable position and that, little as it mattered to the principals, he was giving his full support to the match.

"Are we to travel to Longbourn now, Mr. Bingley?" Darcy heard Georgiana ask. "I was so very glad to hear your happy tidings, and I can scarce wait to meet the lovely lady who has claimed your heart."

To his mild surprise, Bingley did not answer – and Darcy turned away from the window, only to see his friend's hesitant glance directed at himself. Knowing full well what was required of him, he took a deep breath and advanced towards his sister with a fairly convincing smile.

"And so you shall, dearest!" he offered with great determination. "The future Mrs. Bingley is one of the worthiest ladies of my acquaintance, and I should be delighted to introduce you to her," he concluded, as Bingley's grateful glance increased his guilt tenfold.

He did not deserve his gratitude any more than he deserved Elizabeth's love, all things considered, and no amount of belated contrition could set it all to rights!

The journey to Longbourn seemed dreadfully long – and at the same time the work of a moment. Bingley had talked to Georgiana incessantly throughout, as they rode abreast, leaving Darcy to follow close behind, paying no heed to his friend's nervous chatter – too overcome by what would soon come to pass.

The walls of Longbourn, of warm yellow stone, were suddenly before them, tall windows watching their approach like as many eyes.

With a deep, steadying breath, Darcy dismounted, left the reins in the hands of a young lad, then walked up to assist his sister.

Moments later, they were following Bingley and Longbourn's housekeeper down the corridor which, he vaguely remembered, led into the parlour. Ahead of them, the housekeeper opened a door and bobbed a curtsy.

"Mr. Bingley and his party," she announced and stepped out of the way to allow their entry.

With another deep breath, Darcy followed his companions, squinting at the transition from the dark corridor into the sunlit room. As soon as his eyes adjusted, the anticipation – anxious to the point of pain – gave way to the sharpest stab of disappointment.

She was not in the parlour. It was Miss Bennet and her sister Mary who stood up to meet them.

With a vast deal of effort, he struggled to recollect his duty. Civil words of greeting were promptly offered, before he requested permission to introduce his sister and, once Georgiana had curtsied to their hosts, Darcy advanced towards Miss Bennet.

"I hope you will allow me to congratulate you on the happy tidings Mr. Bingley had shared with me this morning!" he said with the warmest smile he could school his features into. And he *would* smile, by Jove! Force his own pain into some quiet corner and paste a smile upon his countenance for the duration, lest she thought he still disapproved of his friend's choice! "As you can tell, my friend is overjoyed, and all of us who care for him must thank you, Miss Bennet, for making him so happy! And indeed, how could he be otherwise? My friend is a great deal more fortunate than most – for he has found and secured his perfect counterpart as his life companion!" he added with feeling and bowed to her again.

Miss Bennet's glance was full of kindness and her voice gentle as she replied to him – but Darcy could scarce hear a single word, suddenly aware that, to his right, the door into the adjacent music room stood open, framing a slender figure that had yet to step in.

He almost did not dare turn to look, lest she was proven to be a figment of his over-taxed imagination, yet every fibre of his being told him that it was not so.

Had she stood there, then, the entire time? Had she heard the words he had spoken to her sister – feeble surrogate of an apology as they might have been?

"Lizzy! Do come and join us," Miss Bennet softly prompted, her kindly tones now registering in his hearing, as they affectionately called *that* name and, his senses reeling, Darcy turned.

The deepest blush suffused her beloved face as she walked to him and, had his own life depended upon it, Darcy could not bear to look away. The very sight of her soothed wounds too deep for healing; painful wounds, which time would never heal.

Oh, he knew full well that, when he walked away, every comfort he had received from her mere presence would only serve to tear through him again, but the thought of future pain could not detract from the glory of the moment, when his every sense rejoiced in beholding her once more.

He could not speak. He could merely offer the deepest bow as she curtsied, her own eyes cast down.

A brief touch on his arm reminded him of the world around him, and he acknowledged Georgiana's silent reminder of his duty with a nod. He cleared his voice, hoping it would not fail him, and was relieved when the right words came out:

"Miss Bennet, would you allow me to introduce my sister to your acquaintance? Georgiana, this is Miss Elizabeth Bennet."

It was not merely his own impression – Bingley's telling glance confirmed that his voice *had* faltered upon the name, but there was nothing to be done about it, and he watched with anxious restraint as the young ladies hesitantly greeted each other.

"Will you not sit down?" the eldest sister urged, and they all complied in silence.

And silence reigned still, broken at last by Bingley as he suddenly asked his betrothed how she was faring. Proper response was duly made, the glance that passed between them adding warm feeling to the dull commonplaces.

Darcy's glance was rooted to the floor – to be precise, rooted to the spot where *her* pale yellow slippers peeped from under the hem of her skirts, as he cursed the folly of not having chosen a different seat, from which he could observe her without being too conspicuous about it.

She would not say another word, which in itself was staggeringly alien to her nature, leaving Darcy to torment himself with the thought that she probably resented his further intrusion upon her family circle. Yet there was no anger in her eyes when, a few moments later, she flashed a glance towards him, only to catch him staring – and they both hastily looked away again.

The opening door served to show that the housekeeper at Longbourn was attuned to her duties, for refreshment was brought in without the need to ask – and Darcy had the joy to see Elizabeth move and walk up to the table that stood right before him to busy herself with preparing the tea, as her elder sister was serving the coffee.

She asked for Georgiana's preference first, then took a cup to her. Her unease visibly mitigated by the simple fact of having an occupation, with a brimming heart Darcy heard her speak warmly to his sister and urge her to try some sweet concoction, allegedly something their cook most particularly prided herself for.

"I did not have the heart to tell her I have tasted nearly as good or perhaps even better in St. Albans, but I trust the secret is safe with you, Miss Darcy," she offered with a smile that made the young lady's brother wonder how was he to bear it when he would have to leave this room again.

She turned to him then, and everything else faded before the vision of her lovely lips forming his name and asking if he would care for tea, or perhaps coffee.

"Tea, I thank you," he hastily replied, alighting upon the first choice offered, since it hardly mattered, his eyes drawn to the slender fingers busily at work, pouring the milk into his cup, and then the steaming tea.

"Sugar?"

"I thank you, no," he answered and stood as she approached him, eyes lowered upon the liquid in the cup.

Her eyes shot up when she stopped before him, so very close, perhaps closer than ever, and he saw hints of amber and specs of golden light in their mesmerising depths, before the lashes fluttered, screening them from him again.

"I thank you," he repeated, this time in near whisper, raising his hand to take the cup from her.

A sudden shock coursed through him, as his fingers curled over her own, underneath the saucer. The touch of her cool skin, for the first time unhindered by the lifeless barrier of gloves, sent spikes of white-hot fire through his fingers, and white-hot spikes shot like shivers through his spine as her eyes flew up to his again and her lips parted to release the faintest gasp.

He could not tell whose fingers trembled first, but the cup shook and rattled – and some of the scalding liquid splashed out and spilled over his palm, onto the still raw cut, no longer bandaged.

A sharp intake of breath through his teeth was all that he permitted, but even so, she could not fail to notice. She gasped again, this time in utter horror.

"Mr. Darcy! I am *terribly* sorry!" she exclaimed with feeling and, in a flash, the offending cup was set aside. "Your injury! Nay, Sir, pray allow me!" she added with determination when she saw him attempt to shake the liquid off his hand.

A swift glance around her revealed a useful item and she picked a napkin off the table, before promptly availing herself of his injured hand and ever so carefully pressing the piece of linen down upon it.

The others might have been watching them or not – but, as far as Darcy was concerned, they might as well have been the only two souls alive in the world. His upturned hand still resting on her palm, he saw her keenly search for signs of worsening in his injury, then dry the cut again with gentle, ever so careful dabs.

If the earlier brief contact with her bare fingers had sent a shock wave through him, this sent all his senses swimming, with all the powerful effects of a fine wine. He could not bear to consider how, in a perfect world, they would not step apart, nor could he grasp exactly *why* was she showing him such generous compassion. Unheeded, the disjointed wisps of thought swirled and faded as he immersed himself in dangerous, intoxicating depths.

She was still holding his hand, and her gentle ministrations healed a great deal more than a scalding burn on a fresh cut. A moment later, she must have seen no point in dabbing it further, and the napkin was tucked out of place, held only between palm and thumb. As though without deliberate intent, the tips of her fingers fluttered in a semblance of a very light caress over the hale skin below the cut and then, presumably to remove every remaining droplet, she bent her head and blew ever so softly over it.

Heaven and hell exploded in him at that moment – and later on, he could never tell *how* he had kept enough control over his shattered senses. How he had not crushed her to his chest, his lips on hers, feeding the hunger he had carried with him everywhere he went. Not stopping, never stopping, not even to draw breath, until she understood they could not be apart – in this life or the other – any more than they could live if they were cut in half!

Goodness knows how, he remained frozen. Only his fingers violently twitched as the warm puff of air sent his pulse drumming wildly. He did not close his hand, nor did he withdraw it but, suddenly and inexplicably self-conscious, she withdrew hers and clasped them both behind her back.

"Would you prefer coffee instead, Mr. Darcy?" Miss Mary offered from the other end of the room, clear censure in her eyes, though whether for himself or her own sister, or both, Darcy could not tell.

"I thank you, no," he said at last, his voice gravelly and, with a bow towards Elizabeth, he retrieved his cup of tea from the small round table where it had been abandoned and regained his seat.

He did not dare look in her direction more than once, and all that he could see was that her complexion had turned a shade of scarlet and she was again determined to not speak another word.

"I must say, I think we have been particularly fortunate lately, with this stretch of good weather!" Georgiana suddenly interjected, to Darcy's gratitude and enormous surprise at her readiness to help relieve the almost palpable tension. "I can only hope it lasts a little longer for – have you heard, Mr. Bingley? – there are great plans for lengthy celebrations next month, to honour the peace."

"I have indeed heard a great deal about it," Bingley willingly assisted. "Great celebrations at St. James, fireworks in the park. There is even a rumour of a small-scale naval battle to be staged on the Serpentine," he added, providing enough fuel for further conversation, and Miss Bennet and Miss Mary promptly began to ask for more details.

Darcy took the cup of tea to his lips. It had cooled sufficiently by now and he took a long sip, followed swiftly by others, his throat all of a sudden intolerably dry.

"And as for His Imperial Majesty The Czar Alexander–..." Bingley began, but before he could finish, the door to the parlour burst open, under a bold hand.

"Gentlemen, you do us great honour! And particularly *you*, Mr. Darcy! 'Tis a long time since I have had the pleasure," Mr. Bennet called out in his habitual tones, which left his more discerning listeners to wonder whether he was in earnest – or whether they were being very subtly mocked. "Now, my dear spouse is gone abroad this morning, to share some particular good tidings with our friends and neighbours, so I fear it falls on *me* to ensure you are suitably entertained! Well, then, let it not be said that I neglect my duties!" the gentleman declared, surprising nearly everybody present by taking a seat amongst them – and making Darcy wonder if perchance Mr. Bennet was versed at reading minds.

Glass in hand, Darcy walked to the fireplace. There was no fire – the mild weather certainly ensured it was not required – but he could not stand still, nor could he sit down.

They had returned from their call at Longbourn some two hours earlier, then they had sat at dinner and, throughout that time, Darcy had been unable to quell the violent disturbance that held him in its grasp.

"Would you allow me, Mr. Bingley, to say that I have found your betrothed utterly delightful?" he heard Georgiana say, a smile in her voice. "I wish you could have made the lady's acquaintance, Mrs. Annesley," she added to her companion. "Perhaps you can join us when we call again, or maybe Mr. Bingley will ask the family to dine here soon."

Bingley was all too happy to declare his intention to invite them thither as soon as it could be arranged, and shortly after, Georgiana turned towards him.

"I comprehend your meaning now, Brother. It is indeed an honour to have made Miss Bennet's acquaintance. And her family – they appear very pleasant people, especially the father…"

Darcy made no answer, unwilling to express the view that perhaps his sister would have formed a different opinion of the family, had the lady of the house been at home – then promptly chastised himself for the ungenerous thought.

"But, may I ask," Georgiana hesitantly offered, "do you have any particular objections to me furthering an acquaintance with the second Miss Bennet? Forgive me, but I felt it would be safer to ask, since you appeared to… well, you seemed very uncomfortable in her presence. I trust you do not… disapprove of her?"

Suddenly aware that he was gripping yet another glass in his uninjured hand, Darcy felt it prudent to place it on the mantelpiece. Somewhere behind him, Bingley seemed abruptly pestered by a bout of cough – or perhaps he had choked on his own drink.

There was no doubt in his mind that, of the entire party, it had been only Georgiana, in her sixteen-year-old innocence, who had misread the signs. Miss Mary had already expressed her censure at his unguarded behaviour and as for Miss Bennet, she was so close to her second sister that she, like Bingley, must have been sufficiently well informed to know that his discomfort had *not* been a sign of disapproval.

"Would you care for a ride tomorrow, Darcy?" his friend called, unnaturally loudly, and proceeded to rattle some decanters on the drinks tray.

"I thank you, yes, I believe I shall join you," Darcy found his voice at last then, conscious it could not be avoided – nor should it be – he turned to Georgiana.

"Nay, dearest, I have no objection to your association with Miss Elizabeth Bennet." Thankfully, the name rolled of his lips without a hitch this time and his voice did not shake when he quietly added, "I have no reason to disapprove of her."

"Oh, I *am* glad! She seems a very pleasant lady, although quite shy, from what I gathered – which, as you can imagine, suits me very well indeed," Georgiana concluded with a conscious little laugh.

An odd sound, promptly smothered, came from Bingley at hearing Elizabeth's unease misconstrued as shyness – and then he coughed again.

"So, then! Whereabouts would you care to ride, Darcy?" the younger man cut in, and his friend could hardly fault him for his determination to be of assistance – he merely wished his friend would not be quite so conspicuous about it! "I am told there are fine woods towards Bramfield. Perhaps Miss Darcy would be induced to join us? You are one of the most confident riders I have ever seen,

Miss Darcy, so I daresay you must have had a fair amount of practice galloping with your brother over the fields of Derbyshire!"

"I thank you, Sir, but riding is a pastime I can indulge at any other time. For my part, I would rather pay another call to the ladies at Longbourn, and introduce them to Mrs. Annesley's acquaintance – that is, Brother, if you do not object?"

"I have no objection," Darcy replied curtly. "You will excuse me now, I wish to retire. Good night, dearest, and pleasant dreams."

He offered Mrs. Annesley a bow as well, followed by a nod to Bingley. He refused to acknowledge his friend's compassionate glance in any way and strode out of the drawing room towards the stairs and thence to his chambers, cursing the moment when he had chosen to disclose his torment to his friend. Bingley, with all his kind and supportive nature, lacked subtlety in everything he did and his inexpert efforts to protect him were as misguided as Georgiana's wrong assumptions.

"I thank you, Lydford, you may leave me now," he told his man and the habitual refrain, heard far too often in the last few months, made the old valet discretely shake his head.

"Are you quite certain, Sir?" the man dared offer, and Darcy sighed.

"Aye – go. You may rest easy though, I *do* intend to sleep," he replied with a fleeting smile, allowing some degree of familiarity which, given his longstanding service to the Darcys, Lydford undoubtedly deserved.

He did sleep, though not for long, and only in the early hours. And his dreams were welcome – disjointed, impossible, exquisite dreams of Elizabeth Bennet – despite the savage pain they caused when he awakened, and was dragged back into a life devoid of hope.

Chapter 5

"Oh, Fitzwilliam, look! Miss Bennet is come!" Georgiana exclaimed, and promptly released his arm to hasten to the slender form clad in yellow muslin that had just emerged from one of Netherfield's glazed doors leading into the gardens.

He had seen her, even before his sister did, her sudden appearance sending the old torrent of ice and fire rushing through his veins.

She looked towards them with a start when she heard Georgiana call her, clearly not expecting the encounter, and her glance flitted to him for a moment, before she turned to his sister to apologise for having intruded on their walk.

"Think nothing of it! We are happy to see you, are we not?" Georgiana spun to him to affectionately prompt him into concurring with her, to set her new friend at ease.

"But of course!" he hastened to reply, his eyes upon her, even though she would not look at him again.

"I think perhaps I should rejoin my mother and sister," she quietly offered. "Mr. Bingley had invited them this morning to have a detailed tour of Netherfield, and I thought at first I ought to leave them to it…" she stammered, her blush deepening, as she almost unwillingly cast another glance towards him.

He winced, the tenor of her thoughts painfully clear. She had not wanted to witness her mother's raptures at the prospect of the eldest daughter becoming mistress of all the luxuries of Netherfield – and she undoubtedly remembered each and every one of his own strictures on the very subject.

Darcy pursed his lips. An open conversation could not be had with Georgiana present and he was certain that some things *had* to be left unsaid, but he simply could not let the moment pass without conveying his regrets at his intolerable conduct!

"Nay, do not leave us!" Georgiana interjected, to his immediate vexation, for she had spoken up before *he* could find his words.

Her visible determination to alleviate Elizabeth's disquiet could not fail to please him though – nearly as much as her aplomb surprised him – as his sister eagerly continued:

"Will you not walk with us? Come, you must see the rose garden at least! It is delightful at this time of year. Do you not think so, Brother?" she purposefully enlisted his cooperation again, and Darcy was only too ready to comply.

He offered his arm and ventured to add earnestly, willing her to understand:

"Aye, pray walk with us, Miss Bennet, and perhaps we might have a chance to speak of comments which, although beyond forgiveness, might at least be forgotten, in the fullness of time."

She could not fail to catch his meaning, and apparently she did not. To his astonishment and boundless gratitude, she quietly offered in her turn:

"Those who have erred themselves must surely grant forgiveness, as they too might wish that unwarranted aspersions had not been cast so thoughtlessly, and so wholly without foundation!"

Breath caught in his chest at her words – so welcome, and so unexpected – and Darcy bit his lip.

"I thank you..." he brought himself to whisper. "That is... very generous! Undeservedly so."

"Not at all, Mr. Darcy, I assure you – 'tis not generosity at all. Merely a question of justice!"

She took his arm then and, having cast him a puzzled glance, Georgiana took the other.

Not in the habit to question his words, and hardly ever his opinions, his younger sister let the strange exchange pass without comment – and Darcy was left to the painful pleasure of feeling Elizabeth's gloved hand resting in the crook of his arm as they made their way towards the much-praised rose garden, bitter-sweet thoughts swirling through him, unconfined.

He could scarce believe that she was willing to pardon his unpardonable conduct – yet it *was* so, she had just declared it!

He bit his lip again. She had believed him then, about Wickham – and had perchance forgiven his presumptuous interference in Bingley's affairs as well, in the face of his readiness to support his friend and finally make amends. Her visible discomfort in his presence notwithstanding, she *was* prepared to let them part with kindness, and he blessed her for it, as well as for everything else!

He took a deep breath. For better or worse, nothing more could be said on the subject of his insulting comments and ill-worded letter – it was impossible, in Georgiana's hearing – and he struggled to think of anything else that *might* be safely said.

She was also silent, just as she had been at Longbourn, and though it pained him to see her so altered from the cheerfully teasing, delightful impish creature he had verbally fenced with last time they had been at Netherfield together, Darcy knew that it could not be helped. The ease had gone from their interactions – but, heaven be praised, at least the open conflict seemed to have gone as well.

"I trust you are keeping well, Miss Bennet," he ventured quietly at last, as they ambled forward, the gravel crunching under their slow footsteps. "And… hm!… all your family, of course…"

"We are, I thank you, Sir," Elizabeth whispered – and nothing more was said.

"I am so glad my brother brought me here, Miss Bennet! I have never visited in this part of the country and I am so happy to have done so at last! Such pleasing scenery, so serene and beautiful! You are very fortunate. Hertfordshire is delightful!" Georgiana suddenly offered, mildly surprising Darcy yet again with her readiness to cast her own reserve aside and help maintain a conversation when none of the others would – or could.

He wondered briefly at it, until comprehension dawned, bringing with it a flash of gratitude, uncomfortably tinged with guilt.

It must have been Anne's influence that had brought about the change. It must have been the time spent with *her* that had bolstered Georgiana's confidence, making his young sister brave enough to attempt assisting someone whom she mistakenly considered as shy as herself.

At his other side, Elizabeth seemed to rally.

"No more so than Derbyshire! There is such breathtaking beauty in the rugged majesty of the peaks…" she began – but then stopped abruptly.

Darcy could not tell whether she had been silenced by uncomfortable associations with his own wretched proposal or, worse still, whether she was unwilling to discuss Captain Wentworth with his sister – and him. Neither thought was welcome and Darcy held his peace, unable to find any words that suited.

"Oh, aye! Mr. Bingley told me that you have travelled to Derbyshire last month, and that you have also stopped at Pemberley," Georgiana exclaimed in sudden inspiration, but the topic she had chosen had no greater success in alleviating Elizabeth's unease.

She merely offered stilted words of praise to Georgiana for her lovely home, then declared herself taken with Mrs. Reynolds and her firm reliance upon the family she served.

"Her commendations were of no trifling nature, for indeed what praise is more valuable than that of an intelligent dependant?" she quietly observed, before swiftly deciding to change the subject by asking Georgiana whether she might allow her the pleasure of hearing her play. "I have heard reports of your great proficiency at the pianoforte, Miss Darcy," she earnestly added and, as Georgiana began to shyly protest against such encomiums, Elizabeth asked instead what music she favoured.

Grateful for the opportunity to talk of something other than her skills, Georgiana hastened to let her new friend know of her delight in Mozart, and the subject was canvassed by the ladies with great determination, until they passed under the leafy arches that led to the rose garden. All sorts of shapes and colours flourished there, filling the air with heady scent. The narrow path no longer admitted three and Elizabeth released his arm to walk ahead through the fragrant confusion of colour.

His heart lurched again to see her draw up to a tall, heavily-laden stem and bend one of the flowers towards her, closing her eyes as she inhaled the scent. The colours of an English rose upon her cheek… Softer and more luminous than any one of them!

Unconsciously, Darcy tightened his fist. What in heaven's name was he *doing?* What purpose did it serve, to torture himself so?

Life had parted them – through her choice, later confirmed by his. She would not have him, and he would soon be wed to another! *What* was he doing then in this rose garden, breathing in the heady air of temptation, branding this picture of achingly beautiful perfection upon his very soul and heart and mind?

Oh, he should turn and leave! Every sense of self-preservation clamoured for him to bow and bid his adieus – and yet he would not stir, eagerly taking in the sight, the intoxicating potion. And every fibre of his being welcomed it, as it cleansed away the tormenting picture he had left behind, when he had stormed out of the parsonage at Hunsford.

A vision of an English rose in a summer garden. The only recollection that would remain untainted by misunderstandings, or by the bitterness of former strife.

The only one to treasure, of all the ones he had…

Darcy shifted in his seat on the narrow sofa as the strains of music, instead of bringing the delight and comfort they once had, grated on his every nerve as *that man* leaned towards her to timely turn the pages.

Heavens above, *why* had he not called at Longbourn the previous day to take his leave, before he left the country? Had he done so, he would have been spared the excruciating torture of seeing the woman he loved openly courted by the dashing Captain Wentworth. And dashing he was, devil take him, with his good looks, tanned complexion and affable manner!

And now, the picture he would take with him on the morrow, when he left Elizabeth behind, would be of him sitting on the piano seat beside her, turning her pages, only to receive her fleeting smile.

Violent hatred, such as he had not experienced for any man, not even Wickham, coursed through him as the song finished and, in a warm feeling voice, Wentworth assured the fair performer that he had never heard this particular piece played with such vivacity and spirit. Damn him to the fiery pits of hell and into the arms of Hades, did he imagine for a single moment he was the only one to unquestionably adore her vivaciousness and sparkle?

A slashing pain cut through him at the thought that now he was perhaps the only one entitled to tell her so. She was at ease with the blasted Captain Wentworth, *that* was plain to see, whereas there had been nothing but awkwardness and short, stilted exchanges in all her recent interactions with himself!

"Would you not play again?" Georgiana softly urged from the seat beside him. "You have played that song so beautifully!"

"Not faithfully, I fear," Darcy heard her differ, her eyes fleetingly alighting upon *him* at last, only to look away with visible disquiet.

Great Scot! Did she think him so devoid of every proper feeling that she imagined him inclined to *criticise?* Much as he recoiled from having to endure the torture of seeing her continue at Captain's Wentworth side, he could not give her the impression he had not enjoyed her playing – so, despite his every inclination, Darcy brought himself to add his entreaties to his sister's.

"It was flawlessly done, Miss Bennet," he quietly offered, "and I hope you will favour us with another song."

"Aye, Lizzy, sing that aria you are so very fond of. You have practised it so often of late that you must be able to play it without notes by now, if you so wished! The one with the sweet sorrow that nothing can dispel," Mrs. Bennet interjected, then hummed a bar or two, surprisingly in tune. "A very pretty little song it is, my dear, is it not? The gentlemen will be delighted, of that I do not doubt!" she added, her speculative glance travelling from one eligible visitor to the other.

Her daughter, however, briefly pursed her lips at her mother's comment and stood from the instrument, at which point Wentworth was prompt to spring to his feet as well.

"So, Mr. Darcy!" the lady of the house turned to him. "You are to leave us now, I hear! Do you have any plans to return in the near future?"

"I fear I cannot say – not at this juncture," was all that Darcy could offer in good conscience.

He could not disclose that Bingley had asked him the other night to return and stand up as best man at his wedding. Yet – much as he owed Bingley, and touched as he had been to be asked, in view of his past transgressions – Darcy's every sense recoiled at the prospect.

The very notion brought to mind the most heart-wrenching picture he could think of. Elizabeth walking down the aisle in the small Longbourn church, flowers in hand, ribbons in her hair. Elizabeth walking towards him, to join him at the altar as her elder sister's bridesmaid, achingly beautiful and forever lost.

Did Bingley think him made of stone to stand there and bear it, knowing that she would not walk up to him to be his bride?

Or was he lost to any shred of reason, now that he had his own felicity in sight?

The thought was unkind, and well he knew it, but Darcy was past caring. He cleared his voice, then shifted in his seat again.

"I hope my sister's home is as welcoming as yours, Miss Bennet," the dashing Captain offered, and Darcy seethed again, particularly as he could not fail to detect genuine warmth in the man's address. "You cannot imagine the lure of home and kin to those of us who have not had the right to claim them anywhere but aboard their ship, for so many years!"

He smiled at her as he said that, the plague upon him! – and before he could disgrace himself with word or gesture, Darcy forced his eyes to look away. They must have developed a will of their own though, for they would not. His gaze fixed upon her, Darcy could register every play of unreadable emotion in her countenance, every sigh, every blush. She glanced in his direction one more time, for a fleeting moment, before casting her eyes upon her folded hands, and Darcy gripped the armrest as he shifted in the cursed seat again.

"Well, then, Lizzy, if you would not play, why do you not take our visitors to see our pleasant little corners? Aye, *follow Jane's example*," she added with an emphatic nod, "and show our guests around the different walks. I daresay they will be pleased with our little wilderness – or the hermitage!"

The hermitage was nothing but a contrived arrangement of rocks; one of the follies so favoured by his parents' generation. Darcy knew as much, for he had once escorted the Bennet daughters through their gardens, and they had chosen to walk to it and rest awhile on the stone bench it sheltered.

The mere thought of Wentworth secluded there with Elizabeth in exquisite intimacy made his insides turn, even more so when he had to forcibly remind himself that wherever she would choose to go – and with whom – was, she had determined, none of *his* own affair.

"I should be delighted to see the wilderness, Miss Bennet!" Georgiana interjected and, for some unfathomable reason, Elizabeth looked up to *him* again, before she stood to comply with her mother's instructions.

They walked out together – and it brought no surprise, merely sharp anguish, to see Wentworth giving Elizabeth his arm, and her quietly taking it.

"There is something quite wonderful about an English garden, particularly here, in the south," the Captain wistfully remarked. "I daresay the rain, much as we rant against it, nurtures the gentle verdure into something more pleasing to the eye than any exotic riot of colour in the world! I beg your pardon, Sir!" he suddenly retracted with an apologetic smile towards Darcy. "I understand from my host that you do not hail from these parts. May I assure you, I intended no disparagement of whatever corner of good old England that you would call home."

"You need not mention it!" Darcy retorted coolly, hoping he did not sound as gruff as he feared he might have.

"So, where do you hail from, if you do not mind me asking?"

"Derbyshire," he replied curtly, riled in no small measure by the fact that he truly could not fault the man for his willingness to make amiable conversation.

"Pemberley is Mr. Darcy's country home," he heard Elizabeth elaborate in his stead, very quietly, without a glance in his direction, leaving Darcy to wonder how was it that, at every turn, he could do nothing but further attract her censure.

Had he *not* learned any of his lessons?

"Pemberley? Sir, I must – "

"My friend Bingley has informed me – " they began at once, in Darcy's case in earnest endeavour to make amends for his earlier ill-humour. "Pray, continue, Sir," he invited, with a slight gesture of his hand, and the other obliged.

"I was about to beg your pardon. I have not made the connection, when we were introduced. Pemberley, of course. We have been privileged to visit your beautiful home earlier this summer, when we were touring in the north with Mr. and Mrs. Gardiner. A truly remarkable part of the world, Derbyshire, and I cannot wonder at your attachment to it," the Captain civilly added. "Very little can compare with the untamed beauty of the peaks – although I *have* found a different sort of rugged beauty in certain parts of the West Country."

"Have you often visited in the West Country, Captain Wentworth?" Georgiana endeavoured to play her part in furthering the conversation.

"Not often, nay. A short trip only, in the summer of 1806, while I was staying with my brother, who had the curacy of Monkford at the time, in the parish of Kellynch."

"Kellynch! With such a singular name, it must be the very same place *we* have visited, during our stay with Lady Russell, is it not, Brother?" Georgiana turned towards him, then looked away again, before he could advise caution with a telling glance.

He truly could not fathom why he feared the prospect of Georgiana disclosing his as yet unannounced engagement. It would be of no concern to anyone if it *was* made public, save for Miss Anne's foolish father! It would be of no concern to *Elizabeth*, in any case. His eyes narrowed as he endeavoured to force the thought aside, along with at least *some* of the anguish it engendered.

To his surprise, Wentworth's interest flared beyond the requirements of common courtesy.

"Lady Russell of Thorngrove, near Kellynch Hall?" he asked.

"The very same! Are you acquainted with her ladyship?" Georgiana inquired.

"Briefly," Wentworth replied, then turned towards Elizabeth again. "So, Miss Bennet, what is the history of your lovely hermitage? I must confess myself quite curious about it."

"You should not raise your expectations, Sir, 'tis none too exciting," she smiled. "A mere fancy of my father's great-uncle. The wilderness holds much more attraction, to myself as well as my sisters. In effect, you can see my sister Catherine availing herself of its pleasures at this very moment," she indicated and indeed Darcy could spot Miss Kitty Bennet strolling though a delightful and deceptively wild-looking arrangement of shrubs and meadow flowers interspersed with Michaelmas daisies, lavender and a particularly attractive variety of poppies.

"Such a fortunate association! Miss Bennet, I can see why you would favour this delightful spot!" Georgiana remarked, walking ahead of them to follow in Miss Kitty's footsteps.

Wentworth did not budge, and Darcy clasped his hands behind his back. If the Captain held hopes of visiting the hermitage with none but Elizabeth for company, on this occasion he *will* be disappointed, Darcy thought grimly with almost childish petulance. The other man, however, seemed unperturbed by his visible determination to persist at their side and they strolled together, their number down to three, along the sandy path than ran by the side of the wilderness towards the tall structure that Darcy easily recognised.

"There," Elizabeth indicated with a smile, as the path curved around it, leading to the stone bench sheltered in a skilfully contrived alcove. "Nothing too remarkable – but a very pleasant spot to come to, if one is keen to read in some peace and quiet," she added and Darcy's eyes softened at the conjured picture of *her* reading here, curled up on the seat.

"Do you often come here to read?" he asked without thinking and his heart did a strange little twist when she turned to him and smiled.

"'Tis my favourite hiding place," she declared with the old sort of impish archness he so adored and had not seen in such a length of time. "It appears that others have discovered it though," she remarked as she sat down and finally noticed a few sheets of paper tucked between the moss-covered wall and the corner of the seat. "My sister Kitty must have misplaced her letter," she said and retrieved the sheets, with the obvious intention to return them to their rightful owner.

As she did so, she casually gave them a cursory glance. Something must have caught her eye though, for a moment later she all but tore the top page aside and avidly began to read the next one.

"Miss Bennet?" Captain Wentworth prompted with visible concern. "Is there anything amiss?"

She did not reply. Indeed, it appeared that she had not even heard him.

"This cannot be!" she whispered with utmost distress. "It is in every way horrible! But the date!" she suddenly exclaimed and both gentlemen started, eyeing her in mystified incomprehension. "The date! The date! What is the date?" she cried again, feverishly searching through the pages until she finally must have found the first, tucked away out of place between the others, for she gave a breathless *"Oh!"* that could have signified both relief and utter horror. "There is not a moment to lose!" she gasped, not to them but to herself, and stood up with the visible intention to pick up her skirts and break into a run.

She had stood up too fast though, and a dizzy spell must have overcome her, for she swayed and sought the rocks behind her for support. She did not need them. At the same instant, her two companions reached to steady her, supporting an arm each.

"Good God! What is the matter!" they both cried at once, with more feeling than politeness, then looked away from her to glower at each other.

"Miss Bennet, would you not sit down?" Darcy advised, speaking over the Captain, who desired to know if there was anything he could do.

"Do sit down!" Captain Wentworth urged as well, scowling briefly at Darcy. "You are very ill!"

For his part, Darcy all but snorted. That was hardly helpful!

He lost all interest in Wentworth's comments though, helpful or otherwise, when Elizabeth began to speak in a low, trembling voice, visibly making every effort to recover herself.

"I thank you," she replied to both. "There is nothing the matter with me. I am quite well!" she added with determination – a valiant falsehood. "I am just distressed by something dreadful I saw in this letter! You must forgive me, gentlemen! I have not a moment to lose! I must send word to my father!"

"I will ride to fetch him!" Wentworth offered, before Darcy could say the same and, ignoring the look of pure hatred that was shot his way, he hastily inquired: "Do you know where he could be found?"

"At the parish meeting – 'tis always held at the *Red Lion*, the first inn you will see, as you ride into Meryton."

Wentworth nodded, then leaned to take her hand.

"I know the place! Now… Miss Bennet… is there any message you would wish me to carry, or do you merely want me to bring your father home?" he asked, very gently, with an obvious concern for her comfort that Darcy would have found more than commendable, had he been able to spare a thought from the urgent wish to rip the sailor's hand apart.

Under his very eyes, Elizabeth paled even further, if that was possible.

"He must be told the truth, otherwise he might not treat the matter with all the haste and seriousness it warrants," she whispered through unwilling, stiff lips – and Darcy knew her father well enough to comprehend that her fear was perfectly justified. He also knew how hard it must have been for her to openly admit it. "Much as I would like to conceal it from you both and from any man of honour, the truth is that, in two days' time, my youngest sister is contemplating leaving all her friends; she means to elope – to throw herself into the power of… of Mr. Wickham!"

"Wickham!" the two gentlemen cried at once, yet again – and this time they did not glower at each other, but exchanged looks of extreme surprise.

Before they could question one another as to their acquaintance with the man, Elizabeth spoke first, and to Captain Wentworth.

"This name is too well known in these parts – but I had not thought *you* would have heard it…?"

Her remark sounded very much like an inquiry, and Wentworth hastened to reply.

"Oh, I have heard it often enough! In effect, if he is indeed the Mr. Wickham I am thinking of, I should be most eager to renew his acquaintance – for I owe this man a debt that *begs* to be repaid!" the Captain added fiercely. "I will leave you now, Miss Bennet. Once your father is informed, we shall decide together on the best course of action!"

He bowed over her hand and, with a curt nod to Darcy, he was gone, the parting glance leaving the other in no doubt that he would *not* have decamped so readily, were it not for the highly irregular circumstance.

"Would you like me to escort you back to the house?" Darcy quietly asked as soon as Captain Wentworth left them. "Or would you like a moment to recollect yourself?"

"I… I have to return… speak to my mother, my sister…" she faltered, then suddenly burst out, wringing her hands: "When *my* eyes were opened to his real character! Oh! Had I known what I ought, what I *dared* to do! But I was afraid of doing too much! Wretched, wretched mistake!"

She looked up then, and her eyes fastened upon his.

"*You* know him too well to doubt the rest! She has no money, no connections, nothing that can tempt him to –… If they are not stopped in time, she will be lost forever!"

"I fear you may have long been desiring my absence!" Darcy suddenly said, her words forcibly reminding him of the frightful urgency of the situation. "Would to heaven that anything could be either said or done on my part, that might offer consolation to such distress. But I will not torment you with vain wishes! I must away! May I escort you back to the house," he offered again, "before I go in search of my sister?"

He got no immediate reply – merely a long, steady look suffused with the deepest sadness, as though she knew they might not lay eyes upon each other again. Her glance tore through each and every one of his reasons and defences – as did the wistful smile that fluttered on her lips.

"I thank you, no. You must away, of course. I understand," she concurred with no emphasis, just some sort of quiet determination. Godspeed, Mr. Darcy," she said at last, and her voice *did* falter.

She smiled that wistful smile again, and offered him her hand.

His heart in wretched turmoil, Darcy took it in both of his, cradled within them, tenderly protected, just as he would have wished to protect *her*, for the rest of her life.

There was no sharp shock of desire this time, even though her bare hand was clasped between his palms, firmly in his grasp.

There was nothing but the raw need to ensure, in any way he could, that no harm could ever touch her. If only she knew this! Then perhaps, one day, she would understand…

He bowed to press his lips against it – the first time he had ever kissed her hand – his heart breaking, piece by crumbling piece, with every moment that was bringing the dreaded separation from expected future sorrow into excruciating fact.

Chapter 6

His lips still upon her hand, he rose from his deep bow and kept it, pressed against his cheek, and she made no motion to withdraw it, just stood watching him, her eyes dark and very wide. He turned her hand, so that it was the palm that was held against his face and this time she *did* move it, though still not to withdraw it, but to caress his cheek with her fingertips.

He swallowed hard at her light caress and almost did not dare stir, as though she were some untamed elfin creature who might take flight if frightened by some incautious gesture. Ever so slowly, he turned his cheek against her palm until it rested on his lips, and he pressed the lightest kiss upon it. Her eyes widened, darkened even further, and her own lips parted in a faint, barely audible gasp – and he was thoroughly undone. She was in his arms before he even noticed he had moved and, gloriously, incredibly, her hands went to his shoulders, then about his neck.

The thrill of her acceptance sent molten fire through him and his lips found hers with a hunger of two hundred and thirty-three excruciating days without her – with all the hunger of two hundred years. Her lips trembled under his and the molten fire rose to his very scalp to spread like lightning through his veins again when he could not doubt that, instead of rejecting him in shock or dignified decorum, she was responding to his kisses, as hungry for him as he was for her.

Her hands shot up to tangle in his hair and she drew him closer, as though the separation was as dreadful to her as it was to him, as though she could not bring him close enough. With a fierce gasp, he *did* bring her closer, his hands spread over her back, her warm, pliant form fitting so perfectly against him, so undeniably right, that it was a wonder how neither of them had seen they were each other's match, from the very first day that Fate had brought them together. Her lips parted, her sweet scent overpowering, and his hunger rose, consuming him – warning him that *this* could never be enough.

"Elizabeth… Elizabeth… Elizabeth…" he murmured against her lips, her skin, her hair, and then her lips again. "I cannot forsake you! I cannot! I cannot lose you! I cannot bear to think of a life without you – 'tis not worth living, 'tis but a slow death! I cannot lose you! I beg you, do not send me away again! I love you! Elizabeth, *I love you!*"

"And I love *you!*" she whispered back, her hands bringing him closer, and joy exploded in him as he heard the words.

The kiss grew deeper, fiercer, more demanding – clamouring to make up for all of the lost time – and yet he had to stop, he had to ask, he had to *know* that she will not fade away like the empty promise of a dream in the cold light of day.

"Then marry me! Elizabeth, marry me! Do not leave me to go through life without you!"

"I *will* marry you – it seems I have little choice in the matter!" she playfully retorted, her laughter warm upon his lips, his face – and his mouth hungrily found hers again before he noticed that, despite her laughter and light-hearted teasing, there were tears in her eyes, tears running down her lovely cheeks, running so freely that his own cheeks were wet. And cold. Suddenly cold. Painfully cold…

His hand moved up to wipe off the cold dampness. It was not mere dampness – his face was all but drenched. A rumbling ache and frightful confusion was all that he could register for a few brief moments – until the crippling blow hit him with such vicious force that he groaned, in physical pain.

A dream. A dream. Nothing but a dream. She had *not* said she loved him. She had *not* promised herself to him in marriage – nor could he offer for her now, in any case.

He groaned again and dropped his head in his hands, not caring that the rain that was verily pouring in through the open carriage window was now soaking his hair just as it had earlier drenched his face.

The depth of misery was beyond anything he had ever lived through. The cruellest torture, nothing less! He had been tortured by dreams of her before, but none so real. None so perfect – so vivid and so achingly right!

A long sigh racked his chest as he ran his hands over his still damp face and then his hair, shaking the cold rain from it. He sat up and reached to slam the window shut.

The carriage thundered at great speed on the dark road to Brighton and Darcy leaned back into the seat, pressing his eyes shut to banish – or perhaps to keep – the vision of her standing in the Longbourn hermitage with that long, wistful look upon her face, as he had bowed once more and left her.

He had hastened to collect Georgiana, bade his adieus to Mrs. Bennet and hurried back to Netherfield. He had forgotten, in his haste, that Bingley was not to be found there, but blissfully roaming somewhere through the Hertfordshire countryside in the company of his future wife. Thus, he had been unable to ask for Bingley's support in person, and charge him with Georgiana's comfort until his return. He had put all that in writing to his friend, and entrusted Georgiana to Mrs. Annesley's care, before embarking on preparations for a swift departure.

He had not told Georgiana much. It would have served no purpose to distress her. He would not conceal though that his unexpected change of plans had something to do with the need to foil Wickham's. She *had* been distraught at this, but it could not be helped. She *had* to be informed that Wickham stood at the origins of the disturbance. It was to be expected that she would often visit at Longbourn while he was away, and he would certainly prefer she did not hear it from Mrs. Bennet's lamentations.

And then he had set off, with no one but his coachman and a footman in attendance, the speed his team was travelling at doing nothing to quell either his anger or his violent impatience.

He had not settled upon the best course of action. Not yet, not quite. To begin with, he had no notion what he was to do with Miss Lydia Bennet, when he came upon her. He could not very well take her under his protection, without a member of her own family present, nor did he imagine that she would willingly be separated from the scoundrel – and bodily carrying her off was not an option he could reasonably consider. He could only hope to garner the support of the Colonel of the regiment, and his wife's. They were, after all, responsible for their young guest's safety and comfort, and they might be expected to provide some consolation when it became apparent that her best-beloved had been run through or even better, shot!

For that was his immediate intention. Stop Wickham in his tracks, by any means available, and pay him back for the distress that he had caused the Darcys in the past!

The vastly rewarding picture of the scoundrel standing before him at dawn at twelve paces made Darcy's lips curl in a savage smile. Oh, aye! At least in *that* the blasted Captain Wentworth had the right of it. Wickham had accrued some debts that *begged* to be repaid!

The carriage slowed a fraction, and then slowed even further, and Darcy could see a cluster of lights ahead. He could not tell how far they had got to, having fallen asleep on the journey to dream excruciating dreams, but every roll of the wheels was bringing him closer to his purpose, and he was violently glad of it!

The carriage slowed to a snail's pace and finally stopped before a sprawling and dimly lit structure that bore a sign making it known as the *Royal Oak* at Patcham. The name of the village was spotted with grim satisfaction. It was, he was quite certain, the last stage before Brighton, and it was reassuring to see they were nearly there at last.

Darcy checked his pocket watch in the vague glimmer of the carriage lights. It showed almost an hour after midnight. At this rate, he could be in Brighton by two.

The thought gave him pause. There was little to be gained from arriving at that hour – not the best time to begin seeking the encampment, or Wickham's lodgings, or Colonel Forster's home. A couple of hours' rest and a brief repast might be the better option, and then set off again, to begin his searches at first light.

It was just as well that he had made his decision. Thus, he could inform his footman of it a moment later, when he appeared at the door to ask whether his master would prefer to merely change horses, or to stop.

It was not long until a sleepy-looking wench opened the doors in response to the footman's forceful knock and stepped aside to let the stern gentleman enter. Half-asleep as she might have been, she was sufficiently astute to notice that this was not a customer to be led into the taproom, where the best part of a dozen weary travellers were sleeping in motley heaps upon the floor, and some on the wooden benches. She motioned him to follow down a narrow corridor to one side and ushered him into a small but decent looking private parlour, then walked up to the table to light the candles from the one she still held in her hand.

"I'll be sure to start the fire, Sir, in a jiffy!" she informed him, then asked if she could bring him anything by way of sustenance.

She nodded at Darcy's swift instructions, bobbed a clumsy curtsy and was gone, leaving him to divest himself of his great coat and his hat and cast them on one of the hard-backed benches that faced each other, down the long sides of the table.

He was not left to his own devices for more than a few minutes. A sharp knock broke the stillness, and Darcy bade the newcomer enter. It was the girl, bringing more firewood and everything she needed to kindle the fire, and also the hosteller himself, who bowed deeply to the fine gentleman who honoured his inn, before coming up to lay a good spread on the table.

"There's a jug of our best ale, Sir, unless ye'd favour porter, an' cold meats, bread an' cheese, an' some of me wife's best game pie! I trust ye'll find it to yer satisfaction. Is there aught else ye might require?"

"Just that you look after my men – that is all."

"They're down the hall, Sir, and Hannah'll see to 'em directly. Well, I'll leave ye to yer supper. All ye 'ave to do is call if ye'll be needin' aught else."

Darcy nodded his thanks and the man left him, shortly followed by the girl, once she had set the fire burning under the wide arch, then carefully spread his coat before it, so that it would dry.

Thankful for the silence, Darcy sat, elbows on the table, resting his face in his hands for a moment, before rubbing his eyes and turning to examine the several offerings.

The pie looked good – in effect, so did the other fare, and he availed himself of a selection and began to eat.

He had not noticed until now that he was very hungry. The last meal had been an early breakfast, curtailed by the impatience to ride towards Longbourn. With a frown, Darcy helped himself to a glass of ale then, as soon as he had finished eating, poured himself another and took it to one of the large chairs that stood before the fireplace. He drained it soon enough – the man had been in earnest, the ale was not bad – and it was only when he was startled by the sound of activity and voices ringing in the hallway that he realised he must have drifted off to sleep.

Darcy sat up and checked his pocket watch again. No more than an hour had passed since his arrival at the inn, so he could allow himself to slumber further in his seat – but not before instructing the innkeeper's people to rouse him in another hour, he determined.

He stood to walk to the door and call them, but there was a knock before he had taken a few steps.

It was the innkeeper, humbly begging his pardon for disturbing his rest, but there was another party just arrived, and as this was the only private parlour, would the gentleman greatly object to company?

"Whose company?" Darcy asked, morose without particular intention. He had no wish for company, and particularly not of the chatting sort.

"A naval man, Sir, travellin' with an older gentleman who might be 'is father. The older gent took hisself to bed for a few hours, but the young 'un said that a seat by the fire'd do just as well."

Darcy all but scowled. Now that would be a fine to-do!

"Did any of the gentlemen give their name?"

"Nay, Sir, but I 'eard the older gent callin' the younger 'un 'Wentworth'."

Darcy sighed. Oh, well! Needs must when the devil spits upon your supper!

"Aye, have him come in. Why not indeed!" he added with quiet sarcasm that was lost upon the innkeeper – which was just as well.

The man left, only to return at once to bow Captain Wentworth in.

"I thank you, Sir, for your – ", the newcomer began, only to stop short and exclaim instead: "*Mr. Darcy!* What brings you here, Sir?"

"The same thing that brings *you*, I'd wager," Darcy retorted dryly, before requesting that a glass and further refreshment was brought in for his unexpected guest. "Would you not take a seat, Captain?" he civilly offered and gestured to the substantial remains of his own repast. "If any of the fare should take your fancy, make free. The game pie is particularly good."

Captain Wentworth thanked him and was quick to avail himself of the refreshment. The hosteller came and went, bringing them more fare, and for a while there was silence as Wentworth ate and Darcy stood nursing his ale glass by the fire. Then the Captain refilled his own and came to join him.

The merry fire was casting a red glow over their faces and for a brief moment they more or less surreptitiously eyed each other – until suddenly Wentworth laughed.

"Well! That is a chance meeting and a half," he muttered as he sipped his drink and threw the other a good-humoured glance which, despite himself, Darcy could not fail to return as he also chortled.

"You may say as much. So, Captain, may I ask, what are your plans? I take it that you are travelling with Mr. Bennet."

"Aye. With some persuasion, he had been induced to get a wink of sleep. Not the sort of exertion that sits well upon a man his age, this!"

Darcy had never quite considered Mr. Bennet's age. He was obviously older than his wife, but his demeanour and sharp sense of humour did not bring an old man to mind, but rather a mischievous one in his middle age, who had seen a lot of the world – and did not much like it, other than as fuel for his wit and sport.

His lips twitched as he thought of the older man. Despite Mr. Bennet's failings – and the unflattering light in which Elizabeth's father seemed disposed to view him – Darcy could not help thinking he rather liked the master of Longbourn. After all, Elizabeth did not inherit many of her charming traits from her mother!

With another swig of ale, Darcy returned his thoughts to the matter at hand.

"I daresay this makes everything a great deal easier. Miss Lydia cannot very well defy her own father, although I had my doubts that she would follow *my* advice!"

Wentworth did not comment but, a moment later, he turned to look Darcy full in the face.

"You have not answered my question, though," he said quietly. "Why are you here? Or, more to the point, why would you take it upon yourself to be Miss Bennet's champion, if you do not mind me asking?"

In effect, Darcy minded very much indeed. Nor was he under the misapprehension that the question pertained to Miss *Lydia* Bennet.

"I might ask the same," he parried.

"I fail to see how that is any concern of yours," Wentworth replied calmly, without rancour, yet the words stung, for there was truth in them.

"Let us just say that I, too, owe Mr. Wickham a debt that begs to be repaid," Darcy offered, then glanced back to his companion. "May I ask of yours?"

Wentworth drained his glass.

"He has been the means of ruining the sister of a very dear friend," he quietly imparted. "My friend fell at the blockade of Toulon, before he could seek retribution. I owe it to his memory that the beast is made to pay!"

Wentworth's fierceness found its match in Darcy's breast and he nodded.

"What is your quarrel with him?" Wentworth asked after a short while.

"He had made designs upon one of my relations. They were foiled, thank goodness, but I have known him long enough to be assured that marriage to a small country gentleman's daughter does not sit well with his aim to lay his hands on a substantial dowry. This is not merely a question of an imprudent marriage that would not be in Miss Lydia's best interest," he earnestly added. "There will be *no* marriage – and he *must* be stopped!"

"He will be!" Wentworth declared grimly. "You have my word that a well-placed bullet will surely see to that!"

Darcy made a quick gesture of impatience.

"I hope you do not labour under the misconception that *you* will call him out!"

"'Tis not a misconception," Wentworth declared flatly. "I have more to avenge – and I have greater right!"

Blood rose to Darcy's head.

"Of what right are you speaking?"

"God willing, I am hoping that Miss Lydia might be my sister, before the year is out," he announced, before turning to look the other in the eye again. "Can you say the same?"

Darcy all but winced. He most certainly *could not.* He turned back to the flames – and the question came out, of its own volition.

"Have you made her an offer?"

"Again, I fail to see in what way this is any of your concern! Have *you?*"

Darcy made no answer. He will be damned before he shared the story of his loss with Wentworth! The man had more than enough reason to crow over him as it was!

They glowered at each other over their empty glasses and in the end the Captain lost his patience.

"Well, what is it to be, Mr. Darcy? Will you be my second – or will you turn back?"

Darcy's features hardened, as did his eyes, and he shot the other the sort of glance commonly met at twelve paces as he damned the man, his freedom, his alleged rights and his better chances.

When at last he spoke, his voice was low and heavy with resentment.

"Do what you will – but I *will not* turn back!"

Chapter 7

Mist swirled over the barren fields to the east of Brighton, pushed to and fro by the wind that whistled in the long grass. Two light carriages, followed at some distance by a gig, advanced at careful pace along the winding, sandy road and finally drew to a halt when they reached the predetermined spot.

The sun was not yet up, not fully, when four gentlemen emerged in pairs from the two different carriages. The owner of the gig, who had all the appearance of a medical man, kept his own counsel, as well as his place.

None wondered at it. Oftentimes before, the attending doctor or surgeon had been found guilty by association if one of the combatants lost his life on the field of honour, so it was no surprise to anybody that, in order to guard themselves from being charged as accessories under the law, medical men chose to remain out of sight, until called upon to exercise their skill.

They had little to fear if the *code duello* was observed – provided the participants were gentlemen. If the strict codes of duelling were followed, the law tended to turn a mildly complacent eye, and juries either acquitted the defendants – or charged them merely with manslaughter, for which the penalty was but a modest fine.

The same would not apply when lesser men had the audacity to ape their betters, and many men of indifferent birth have been dealt a very different portion – for they had broken the unbending, cornerstone rule of duelling: that it was a privilege of gentlemen, and gentlemen alone.

As for military men, duelling was not merely sanctioned, but positively insisted upon. Woe betide any who attempted to evade a justifiable call! Army regulations made it a court-martialling offence for an officer to fail to defend his honour for, in doing so, he would fail to defend the honour of his regiment – and that would never do!

Regardless, Darcy had decided it was best not to risk the matter. His footman and coachman, as well as a few more hired hands, had been posted around the house that Wickham shared with Messrs. Denny and Saunders, and had remained in place until the morning, when the Darcy carriage, bearing its owner and Captain Wentworth, had drawn up to the door of Wickham's lodgings, to follow him and Lieutenant Denny to the field.

As for the Longbourn carriage, it had already departed Brighton at noon the previous day, bearing a tearful Miss Lydia and her stony-faced father back towards the home which she had been in such an ill-judged haste to attempt to quit forever.

Darcy cast a glance to his left. The other two were walking side by side, some twenty yards away and – having caught his glance, Wickham looked towards them and gave a perfunctory bow.

Thirty steps more, and they all halted. In silent agreement with his principal, Darcy walked up towards the other two as Denny stepped his way to meet him. A brief nod of mutual acknowledgement made the full extent of their greeting, and then Denny asked:

"Would you care to measure the distance, Mr. Darcy, or would you be content to let the task fall on me?"

"I have no objection," Darcy replied and at that, a few more steps away, Wickham interjected smoothly:

"Fear not, Denny, Mr. Darcy will hardly be disposed to take offence to *that*. Having others do his bidding must come as natural as breathing, does it not?"

The lines around Darcy's mouth deepened and his eyes flashed with grim satisfaction. Was the dog about to imply that he had induced Wentworth to fight his battles for him?

'Oh, let him say as much!' he all but prayed, and all but smiled. Then Wentworth would have to step down, and allow *him* to be the one to teach the beast the lesson he so badly needed!

Apparently, the thought occurred to more than just him. Before Wickham could say anything further, Denny hastily intervened.

"Wickham, may I remind you that, on the duelling ground, the principals are expected to be silent, and let the seconds do their talking for them! I daresay one challenge should be enough for you to contend with this morning! As I am not prepared to be your second more than once today, I would advise you to withdraw that last remark!"

"Your scruples do you credit, my friend!" Wickham replied coolly. "Of course, if you so wish – though Mr. Darcy and I are sufficiently well acquainted for him to know that no inappropriate disparagement was implied!"

The turn of Denny's countenance gave clear indication that he was more than familiar with whatever his fellow officer had oftentimes thought *appropriate* to say about his childhood playmate. As such, it was no surprise that he promptly bade his companion to withdraw several steps further – and be sure to keep silent.

With a smirk, Wickham did his bidding, and Lieutenant Denny proceeded to measure the agreed twelve paces, of no less than thirty inches each, and set the markings in the right place upon the ground.

"Would you care to verify the accuracy, Sir?" he called to Darcy, who had followed his progress with enough attention to make any further verification needless.

He therefore waived the right and, Wentworth's pistol case in hand, he proceeded towards his fellow second to set about the next requisite task. The two sets of duelling pistols were examined and carefully compared – then, with just as much diligence, charged, smooth and single, each side giving undivided attention to the handiwork of the other, until both parties declared themselves fully satisfied.

"Are we settled upon a maximum of three exchanges?" Mr. Denny asked and, at Darcy's nod, there was nothing else left for them to settle.

"Gentlemen, would you take your places?" Darcy said evenly and, although he had barely raised his voice, it carried easily across the field, to where the principals were standing.

"May I remind you," Denny interjected, "to check your pockets for books, coins, watches or any such item that might get in the way."

"You may rest easy, Mr. Denny. Captain Wentworth had determined to remove his coat. Would the same apply to your principal?" Darcy inquired but, before he had finished speaking, Mr. Wickham had single-handedly cast off his dark cloak with a flourish, letting it fall upon the ground, several yards from his mark.

There was no coat for him to divest himself of. He was already in his shirtsleeves, and it was only then that they could see his right arm hanging in a sling around his neck.

"You might have chosen to mention your principal's condition, Mr. Denny!" Darcy observed sternly. "I had not imagined you would wait until they were on the field to request for Captain Wentworth to fight left-handed, and I would most certainly be inclined to advise him against it!"

"I saw no reason to confuse the matter, Mr. Darcy," the Lieutenant replied, unperturbed, "as Mr. Wickham had already declared his perfect satisfaction with his opponent shooting with his right, while he would use the left. Mr. Wickham has no doubts regarding his accuracy with either. It is indeed unfortunate that an altercation in *Molly's Tavern*, Monday last, has deprived him of the full use of his right arm, but I trust that under the circumstances you will see no impediment."

"I must consult with Captain Wentworth," was all that Darcy felt at liberty to say.

"I rather wish he was in mint condition," Wentworth muttered, as soon as Darcy had informed him of Mr. Denny's view on the matter, which he had been mostly able to hear for himself, in any case. "I would not have him say he had allowed me the advantage!"

"Would you care to postpone the meeting until he is recovered?"

"I daresay you would do well to make the offer," Wentworth conceded, although it was plain to see that the prospect of waiting afforded him no pleasure.

"No delay!" Wickham called from his own marking, when Denny walked up to bring the offer to him. "Captain Wentworth need not fear he has me at a disadvantage. I shall be delighted to show him I can shoot just as well with my left as with my right!"

Darcy turned to his companion.

"I daresay this is the point where my duty as a second is to ask once more if you do not see a peaceful resolution," he quietly offered. "As you well know, I am a poor choice of second, for I cannot urge that. I will ask, though, whether you may have reconsidered whose place it is to take the stand!"

"Good attempt that, Mr. Darcy – but you cannot imagine I would walk away now, and let *him* boast of my forgiveness! The honour of my friend's family is not the only one I have to defend!"

"Then have it your way – and I hope you are a decent shot! I have no notion if his own boast about his left-hand aim is founded, but I suspect it is. From what I know of him, I can assure you that valiant acts of honour are not in his nature, nor would he thoughtlessly risk his own wretched skin. I would advise you do not give him any generous chances, for he will not reciprocate – and *he will* shoot to kill!"

"I thank you for the warning," the other evenly replied and, without another word, Darcy handed him the loaded weapon, then walked away to the spot, ten yards further, where Mr. Denny stood.

"Would you care to call the shots, Sir?" the officer inquired and Darcy agreed with a solemn nod.

He cast a glance from one opponent to the other. They were both on their marks, both with their shoulders in line with their intended target, both holding their pistols with the muzzle pointing to the ground.

"Gentlemen, are you ready?" he called out and glanced to Wentworth to ascertain that he was, indeed, prepared for the grim action – but before the command to fire had escaped his lips, a loud report thundered over the field, followed a moment later by Wentworth's gasp and Denny's cry, full of unmitigated horror.

"You shot before the command!" he bellowed towards his principal, in utter shock and anger – and well he might, as Wickham's dishonourable deed was bound to smear his second's own honour.

"An error! The trigger was at fault! Is he injured?" Wickham cried, his voice shrill, seemingly in panic.

Regardless, Darcy was not disposed to believe him for a single moment. He made to run to Wentworth, but Denny's horrified cry stopped him in his tracks.

He could not tell exactly *what* the officer had shouted, but instinctively Darcy cast a glance over his shoulder – only to notice Wickham a few steps behind him, his pistol pointed squarely at his back.

~

"What are you –… *No!*" Lieutenant Denny cried in sheer horror, when he saw Wickham drop his discharged duelling pistol, produce an army one from his sling, and point it at his old enemy's back.

At his outraged cry, Wickham's would-be victim turned, standing defenceless before the loaded weapon. All he might have had was Wentworth's other pistol, already loaded for a possible second round, but it was out of reach and useless, enclosed within its wooden case.

In the whirl that followed, it was hard to ascertain exactly *what* had happened. Several things appeared to have occurred at once. Without taking his eyes off his opponent, Darcy made to open the small wooden case, but before he could do so, two loud reports ripped through the morning's silence, in such close succession that they seemed to have been discharged as one.

Splinters flew from the wooden case that housed Wickham's set of pistols. Thrust sideways into Wickham's line of fire by Mr. Denny's quick thinking and impeccable reflexes, it had not merely served to impede the aim, but to stop its owner's cowardly shot altogether. As for the perpetrator, he collapsed to the ground, brought down by the bullet fired from Captain Wentworth's weapon, that caught him in the hip. Casting aside the splintered pistol case, Lieutenant Denny drew his sword and came to tower over his former friend and companion with a murderous glare.

"I would run you through for this, if I could bring myself to soil my blade! Captain Wentworth," he called out, without taking his eyes off Wickham, "how badly are you injured, Sir?"

"A bullet to the arm," the Captain grimaced. "I have had worse, do not concern yourself!"

In some strange way, it had worked to his advantage that Wickham had shot before he could raise his arm, and thus the bullet had lodged itself in the tense muscles, rather than wreaking lethal havoc through his chest.

"The surgeon should be summoned," Darcy interjected, "but first we ought to deal with *that!*" he added with distaste, as though he was speaking of some offending piece of offal, indicating Wickham with the barrel of Wentworth's second pistol, in his hand at last. "Forgive me, Lieutenant! I have yet to thank you for your timely intervention. I owe you a life…"

"Consider it repaid by not calling me out, Mr. Darcy," Lieutenant Denny instantly retorted, "as you would certainly be justified in doing, for my association with the rat. I can only assure you that I had no notion of his character – otherwise I would *never* have agreed to be his second – "

"Lower your weapons, gentlemen! I say, *lower your weapons!*" a commanding voice suddenly rang out before Darcy could make any further reply and, through the wisps of mist that still fogged the view of the road that brought them thither, the combatants – both planned and impromptu – saw a small company of soldiers emerging, muskets at the ready, all pointing to the fallen man.

Lieutenant Saunders was amongst them, but it was the sight of his superior that made Mr. Denny promptly sheath his blade and snap into sharp salute, with all the speed brought on by years of training.

"Colonel Forster!" Captain Wentworth exclaimed in some astonishment. "What brings you here, Sir? You have not come to enforce the edict against duelling, surely!" he added with a smile, as though at a good jest.

The Colonel, however, did not smile.

"I wish you had informed me of your intention, Captain – and then I might have told you that you need not give yourself the trouble. The offence you suffered might as well have been punished by horsewhipping the scoundrel, for Mr. Wickham has forfeited his position, time and time again! You are to be court-martialled, Sir, for a conduct unbecoming of an officer and a gentleman!" he growled at Wickham. "The wool merchant you stabbed the other night in *Molly's Tavern* died this morning, Wickham – not to mention your appalling insult to me and mine!"

His hand still clasped onto his injured, bleeding hip, Wickham shot a glance of venomous hatred towards Darcy.

"Had I paid you back for taking away the life that I deserved, I would have gone to the gallows singing!" he spat with vicious fury, but the Colonel would have no more of that.

"Singing or not, that is *precisely* where you are heading!" he retorted with a scowl. "Arkwright!" he bellowed to one of his men, "go fetch the surgeon in that gig yonder! I do not wish Wickham to have the good fortune of bleeding to death before I am through with him! And your own wound, Captain Wentworth," the Colonel added, seeing blood seeping into Wentworth's shirt underneath his hand, firmly clasped on his arm. "My surgeon shall be at your disposal when we return to Brighton, but I daresay you should not wait till then!"

When applied to, the surgeon declared Captain Wentworth's injury as inconvenient rather than dangerous – provided that the scraps of cloth the bullet had carried in did not induce the wound to fester.

"I would be happy to engineer its removal, Captain, but 'tis a task best attempted when we return to town – unless of course you would choose to be attended by the army surgeon. As to the other gentleman, the bullet is likely to have fractured the head of the femur – that is to say, the thigh-bone. Allow me, Sir, to press this wad against the bleeding, it might staunch it – aye, just so. A stretcher is required, Colonel – or a cart from the village. This man will never walk again without the aid of crutches!"

"Norris, Peters – see to a cart, and be quick about it!" the Colonel barked – only to mutter as he turned his back on them, "He shall have little opportunity for walking – where he is going now!"

Captain Wentworth reached for his cup of coffee and winced as the move inevitably disturbed his other arm. A glass of brandy would have been more welcome – but his head demanded coffee, after the amount he had been instructed to imbibe during the time spent in the company of the army surgeon.

The bullet had been extracted, after a fair amount of painful probing, along with the attendant piece of cloth, but the surgeon had not been satisfied until he had matched the piece to the hole in the shirt, and thus assured himself that no other scraps ought to be further sought for. The wound was duly bandaged and the gentleman escorted to his lodgings – where he sat now, a sling around his arm.

"Would you care for dinner – or are you neither hungry, nor in the mood for celebration?" Darcy asked, and the other laughed.

"Coffee for two – champagne for one! Is that not the very essence of a duel?" he quipped, then sobered. "I daresay champagne *might* be in order, since we both had such a narrow escape! I had not known what sort of a man I challenged. It seems he had already meant to flee his creditors, and taking Miss Lydia along was merely an opportunity, a welcome diversion. With hindsight, Mr. Denny thinks that, after the altercation in *Molly's Tavern*, he must have suspected the wool merchant was not long for this world and would have disappeared much sooner, got onto some ship to flee abroad, but for the challenge – or rather, the men you had stationed at his door. And then I daresay he just could not resist the vile temptation to find a way to take you down as well before he vanished, and he grabbed his chance – in for a penny, in for a pound, I'd wager. How did he think he would make good his escape from the field though, with so many of us around him, I imagine we shall never know – but there we have it! Poor Mr. Denny! He kept apologising *ad nauseam* for not having thought of searching Wickham's sling for a concealed weapon – and indeed for agreeing to be his second in the first place. It appears that the man in question had fooled a great many!"

"He had still fooled *me*," Darcy owned, shaking his head in wonder, "and I thought I knew him at his worst! Nevertheless – he is no longer a concern of ours! What of your injury, Captain? Are you fit to travel?"

"Fit I might be," the other retorted with some nonchalance, "but I find myself devoid of transport. I daresay I shall while some days away in Brighton – I would much rather not travel by post as yet!"

"I had no intention of leaving you behind," Darcy replied, rather curtly. "As soon as you are well enough, you are most welcome to travel with me back to town – "

"But not to Longbourn, I take it," the other casually observed and, yet again, the question left Darcy's lips of its own volition.

"Is that where you are heading, then? To make her an offer?"

"And force her hand into accepting me, out of sheer gratitude?" Wentworth replied, with ill-disguised contempt. "The rest of us choose not to play so blatantly to our advantages, Darcy!" he scornfully added, emptying his cup.

For some reason, Darcy found the remark diverting rather than offending – until he recollected that, in effect, he had once done precisely *that.* He had been so convinced that no one would refuse the honour of the Darcy name and a Pemberley alliance!

"Are you not satisfied with *one* hole in your arm?" he retorted, in lieu of any other answer and, to his surprise, Wentworth merely laughed.

"I daresay I am, for a while at least! As for your question, perhaps you deserve to know the answer. I *shall* make her an offer but, for obvious reasons, the time has not yet come. Unless you aim to march ahead and ask her yourself, in which case, your arrogance be damned, I shall do so as well – and let the best man win!"

'From the very beginning, from the first moment, I may almost say, of my acquaintance with you, your manners impressing me with the fullest belief of your arrogance, your conceit and your selfish disdain of the feelings of others…'

The pain must have been chiselled into his countenance for everyone to see, Darcy determined, so he turned away from the other man.

"You need not change your plans on my account," he said at last, very crisply. "Rest assured, I am in no position to offer for her *now!*"

Chapter 8

"Mr. Darcy! A pleasure to make your acquaintance, Sir, and my thanks for returning my wayward brother to us!"

"Ah, Sophy, let the young men be!" Admiral Croft interjected, with an impatient wave of his hand. "At least he has made it home in one piece, which is more than can be said of many others!"

"Would you care for some refreshment, Mr. Darcy?" Mrs. Croft inquired of their guest as she carefully placed a cushion under her brother's arm. "I shall endeavour not to pepper you with questions regarding your acquaintance with Frederick," she smilingly promised, "nor inquire in too much detail about the source of that charming embellishment upon his arm!"

"Nay, the peppering would certainly come later," the Admiral chuckled from his corner, and his wife rolled her eyes at that.

"There really is not a vast deal to tell, Sophy," Captain Wentworth assured his elder sister. "A debt paid to a scoundrel – and that, my dear, is that!"

Mrs. Croft did not pursue the matter, but offered their guest a chair and rang the bell for tea.

"So, Frederick, what are your intentions? Will you join us when we set off to Somerset, or shall you go a-courting back to Longbourn? I do wish you would spread more canvass, and bring us home one of those young ladies, for there are more than enough to choose from! The two eldest are by far the better choice, I am quite certain, but the younger ones are both chatty and cheerful, and should one of them take your fancy, I daresay you could do far worse! Very nice young ladies they both are – though I must own, I hardly know one from the other!"

"Miss Lydia and Miss Catherine are very good humoured, unaffected girls indeed," said Mrs. Croft, in a tone of calmer praise, which could not fail to convey to Darcy that she did not consider the younger Miss Bennets as quite worthy of her brother. "As to the two eldest, I hear from Mrs. Gardiner that Miss Bennet has recently become engaged so, dear Frederick," she smiled complacently to her brother, "I fear that the Admiral has the right of it! You *should* spread more canvass, before her sister is snapped up as well!"

"Speaking of spreading canvass," her brother smoothly changed the subject, "when are you setting off to Somerset exactly?"

"This coming Monday, in effect," the Admiral informed him. "That mousy little man, the attorney – "

"Mr. Shepherd," his wife obligingly supplied.

"Aye, him! He wrote me a few days ago to let me know that Kellynch Hall is now ready for our occupation – "

"Kellynch Hall?"

To everybody else, it was an exclamation of surprise, but for Darcy, who had a full command of Captain Wentworth's countenance, it was excessively plain to see that the gentleman heard the name with much stronger emotion.

"Aye – the house that we have leased! Truly, Frederick, I wonder, do you ever hear a word I say?" his sister teasingly admonished and, in tones a great deal more sedate than previously, the Captain quietly retorted:

"I am fairly certain you have not mentioned the property by name before. So, how did you come by this place and none other?" he inquired as refreshment was brought in and Mrs. Croft busied herself with serving tea and coffee.

"A line in the paper caught my eye," the Admiral replied, "and it seemed as good a place as any. As you well know, I am not one to dally, so your sister and I went down to have a good old look at Kellynch Hall and settled with the baronet at once. A pleasant man, Sir William – "

"Sir Walter," Darcy and Wentworth corrected at the same time, then cast a surprised glance at each other.

"Aye, Sir Walter, now I *do* recall. A very good man, and very much the gentleman, I am sure, but with the most uncommon fondness for his looking-glasses! I have counted more than fifty altogether in the public chambers, and I daresay there must have been five at least in his own dressing room!"

"And is Sir Walter and his family still residing in the area?" the Captain inquired further, aiming to sound thoroughly disinterested.

As far as Darcy was concerned, he did not succeed, and the visitor was left wondering as to Wentworth's underlying reasons. In passing, he wondered also whether any of the others had been taken in.

"I have no notion," the Admiral shrugged. "This Mr. Shepherd merely told me that Kellynch Hall was empty."

There was no reason why *he* should be supplying any further information, Darcy knew full well, yet he soon found himself enlightening Captain Wentworth:

"Sir Walter has removed to Bath some three weeks previously. Maybe more."

A strange look, akin to relief, crossed Wentworth's countenance, then he cocked a brow.

"You are very well informed, Mr. Darcy," he observed. "Have you been long acquainted with the family?"

"Since this spring," was the succinct reply, then Darcy asked in his turn: "And yourself?"

Captain Wentworth shrugged, then grimaced, as the show of nonchalance merely served to disturb his injured shoulder.

"A passing acquaintance, in the year six," he blandly offered, equally disinclined to elaborate.

From her sofa, his sister glanced up.

"Was that during your stay with Edward, at Monkford?"

Wentworth confirmed with nothing but a crisp "Indeed", before turning to Darcy again. "And, may I ask, is Sir Walter settled in Bath for some duration, or is he likely to return to the environs of Kellynch?"

"I have little knowledge of his plans," Darcy rather tersely replied. "From what I understand though, Sir Walter and his daughter are in no haste to leave their current abode."

"His daughter?"

"Aye. His eldest," Darcy supplied briefly, somewhat mystified by the man's continued interest in the matter.

"I see..." Wentworth remarked; then, after a short silence, he picked up the same thread again, with some hesitation. "I take it, then, that the other two are married...?"

"The youngest is."

A longer silence this time. The Captain sipped his tea.

"And Sir Walter's second daughter?" he casually asked, turning his china cup this way and that, as though engrossed in studying the pattern.

Darcy's retort was short and sharp.

"She is not. As yet."

"Nay, I was wondering, in effect, as to her – ... No matter!" Wentworth changed his mind and waved in a show of unconcern, then straightened in this seat.

Across the drawing-room, Darcy stood from his. He could not fathom *why* was Wentworth asking all those questions but, Sir Walter's injunctions aside, the Captain – of all people – was *not* his choice of a recipient for any sort of confidences!

"I fear I have intruded for too long upon your family reunion," he offered with a bow and, despite Mrs. Croft's civil protests, echoed by her husband's far more vocal ones – so vocal, in effect, that they all but drowned out Wentworth's – Darcy took his leave.

With renewed thanks for his assistance, effortlessly forthcoming from both sister and brother, they did not hinder his departure any further, and Darcy promptly left the Admiral's elegant lodgings.

The journey to the house in Berkeley Square was too short for him to dwell either on the excruciating prospect of Wentworth *'spreading canvass'* in Elizabeth's direction – or indeed on his interest in the former occupants of Kellynch Hall.

Before too long, Darcy made his way into his own vast hallway, only to be greeted by the only sight that was likely to soothe him, at that point in time. A look of unrestrained delight upon her beloved countenance, Georgiana was verily running down the curved marble staircase. Before he could caution her, lest she tripped and fell, she was by his side and, mindless of Weston's presence, she flung herself into his arms.

"You are safe!" she whispered, close to tears. "Heaven be praised, you are safe and you are home at last!"

"Of course, little one," Darcy whispered back, quite overcome by her open display of affection, as well as by the notion of what she must have suffered while he was away.

He shook his head at his own shocking lack of common sense. *Of course* she had been fearful, everything considered! His arms tightened around his sister, and Darcy leaned to press his lips upon her brow.

"Forgive me, dearest! I should *not* have told you what I was about, and leave you with nothing to do but wait and fret!"

"Of course you should have told me!" Georgiana heatedly retorted, pulling away from his embrace only far enough to be able to look him fully in the face.

Her eyes flashed with something which, had he not known her mild disposition, Darcy might have easily taken for outright anger.

"But you should *not* have exposed yourself to the dreadful risk!" she exclaimed, forgetting herself in the aftermath of the horrific turmoil and – for the first time in living memory, Darcy was shocked to hear his much younger sister actually taking him to task: "*Why*, though, Brother? Why would you risk your life, and mine, and Anne's future happiness? Surely you knew we would be lost without you! There is no doubt about it, Mr. Wickham *had* to be stopped," Georgiana burst in the same breath – and neither of them took the time to notice that it was for the first time since the Ramsgate near-disaster that she could bring herself to mention the rogue by name – "but I never imagined, even when you left, to what extremes you were prepared to go in order to stop him!"

Darcy all but winced. He had not thought of it, and *that* was the appalling truth. For the first time in his adult life, he had not put Georgiana's interests first. He had not thought of her terror, or of her misery and despair, had anything befallen him.

Of course, once compelled by Wentworth to take second place, there was no reason why he should have, but the truth remained: it had not crossed his mind, even before that, and there was no doubt that it *should* have done!

Had he been so foolish as to think himself invincible? He winced again. For a man who prided himself for his understanding, he had been shockingly inclined to let his judgement be ruled by his passions. Fury for Wickham's vile acts of treachery, both past and present, and the fierce desire to protect Elizabeth from taint by association surely should not have been allowed to take precedence over Georgiana's best interest and comfort!

Darcy pressed his eyes shut. They should not have, but they did. And there was another truth, as shocking as it was undeniable. His first, his only thought had been of *her. Her* happiness, *her* comfort. Not Georgiana's, and certainly not Anne's.

Foolish, foolish, foolish! Self-deluded and foolish! Will he *ever* learn that it was not his place to defend and protect her? *She did not want it!* His hand, his name, his protection. Yet he was still prepared to cast everything else aside in his instinctive urge to rush to her aid!

Darcy shook his head – and even as he told himself it was high time he learned to quell those instincts, the voice of truth inside him warned that he never will.

"Forgive me, Georgiana, I most certainly should have known better – " he tiredly began, but the young girl would not allow him to continue.

"'Tis *I* who should have known better!" she forcefully exclaimed. "I am too young, too naive, too unworldly!" she chastised herself, heatedly speaking over her brother's heartfelt protests. "I had not seen it! Even as you told me that your swift departure from Netherfield was due to Mr. Wickham, I have not seen what you had in mind! Miss Bennet did, at once, and it was only when *she* had voiced her fears for your safety, and Captain Wentworth's, that I understood what you were about!"

Darcy swallowed hard, his lips firmly closing upon the burning, fruitless question.

Which Miss Bennet?

Had Elizabeth feared for his safety? Some sort of aching warmth spread through him at the thought. That she should have mentioned him in the same breath as Wentworth was painfully galling – yet the notion that she should hold him in her thoughts, that she should understand much sooner than his own sister the innermost workings of his mind was in itself a most rewarding novelty, after everything that had passed between them! Could this signify, then, that he had risen in her estimations, at least in some small part?

He had no time to pursue the useless thought – for indeed, what difference did it make, if he *had* risen a little in her estimation? Georgiana's rushed words hastened to dash the feeble hope.

"Miss Elizabeth was vastly surprised to see me, when I called at Longbourn with Mr. Bingley the following day. She said she had assumed you had taken me back to town with you, and was visibly astounded to hear that you *had not* set off to London, but in pursuit of Mr. Wickham. Her elder sister, though, had all but chided her at that, and said she had always known you had not hastened back to town, but left for altogether different reasons! Fitzwilliam, you *have* told me that Mr. Bingley's betrothed is one of the worthiest ladies of your acquaintance and she must be so, she is so wise and full of goodness – yet I cannot forgive myself that she had grasped your meaning before I could even begin to comprehend it!"

Words of comfort rolled unthinkingly off her brother's lips and the warmth of his embrace endeavoured to stem Georgiana's outburst of self-recrimination while Darcy struggled to subdue the rising tide of his own painful disappointment.

Aye, Mr. Bingley's betrothed was a remarkable lady indeed – one of the very few of his acquaintance disposed to see the best in others, against overwhelming odds. He had wronged her in every way imaginable, he had worked to thwart her best hopes for happiness – and yet it had been *her*, and not Elizabeth, who had understood that he had *not* left Longbourn to distance himself from the family, as a result of the youngest Miss Bennet's latest display of impropriety. And as for –… His tired heart twisted painfully in his chest at the thought. As for Elizabeth's opinion of him, it clearly was, in essentials, very much what it ever was…

"Mr. Bingley to see you, Sir," Weston announced with a dignified bow, once more at ease in their visitor's presence, now that Mr. Bingley seemed disposed to revert to the expected standards of behaviour and *follow* the butler to his master's study, rather than rush with unseemly haste ahead of him.

Mr. Bingley's haste had only diminished by a fraction though, and he was in Darcy's study before the latter could actually bid him enter.

"Good morning, Darcy!" he exclaimed, as ebullient as ever – or rather, as ebullient as he had been since his betrothal, nearly a month ago.

His host all but grimaced. Did Bingley *ever* aim to return to his old level of noisy cheerfulness – vexing enough as it was – or was he to swirl forever in these rose-tinted clouds, he wondered with a fair amount of ungenerous impatience.

"Refreshment? Aye, thank you," the visitor accepted Darcy's subdued offer. "Coffee, I should imagine, at this time of day. It would not do to show up in Mrs. Gardiner's parlour breathing out fumes of port wine!" he quipped, then laughed at his own sally. "I am to call upon her – them – as soon as may be, but I fear I cannot call at such an early hour!" Bingley informed his host as he perched himself on the edge of one of the heavy armchairs. "I *had* to leave my lodgings, I could not stay cooped up in the old place, but then I came to see 'tis not acceptable to call in Gracechurch Street as yet, so – here I am. I hope you will forgive me for trespassing upon your time in this fashion."

"Think nothing of it, Bingley. You are more than welcome to while away the next couple of hours in Berkeley Square," Darcy replied with the mildest sarcasm – which was entirely lost upon his friend, who took his pocket watch out and consulted it with no small amount of panic.

"Couple of hours? Nay, there is no cause for *that!*" he exclaimed in earnest. "I daresay they should not be put out if I show up at ten!"

A subdued knock announced a footman's arrival and steaming cups of coffee were poured, then duly placed before the master of the house and his guest.

Darcy took a sip of his, inwardly observing with some irritation that the other stood in no need of a stimulating beverage. He could hardly keep his limbs still as it was! With a slight grimace at his own ungenerous thoughts which – he knew full well – only stemmed from shameful envy, Darcy gestured for his friend to avail himself of the confectionery that had arrived with the coffee tray.

"So, how have you been keeping? You seem in fine fettle," Darcy offered.

The civil inquiry was, of course, unnecessary; he could easily see for himself that Bingley could not have appeared more cheerful – not within the prescribed limits of sanity, that is!

"I am, I thank you, and I am happy to see that you can say the same!" his friend retorted brightly, blind to the fact that, in all ways but one, his estimation was wholly off the mark. "Everyone was mightily concerned for your safety, you know!" he eagerly continued. "Your sister in particular. Bye-the-bye, I trust you did not mind me agreeing to bring her back to Berkeley Square despite the instructions you left in your letter. She could not bear to sit ensconced at Netherfield and was wild to be home, and gain the earliest intelligence of your return from Brighton. I saw no reason to deny her, so I escorted her and Mrs. Annesley back to town, as your sister had requested."

"I thank you for your kindness," Darcy replied warmly, knowing full well that squiring Georgiana to and fro was not exactly what his friend had wished to be doing, mere days after his marriage proposal was accepted.

He sipped his coffee, twice, feigning great interest in the matter, then sipped again before putting his cup down.

"I trust the family at Longbourn were well when you left them," he said at last, as blandly as he could.

It had been hell to have no intelligence of her – and it did not serve him well to remind himself that three, four weeks were nothing to a lifetime of not knowing how she fared.

There was of course a great deal more to it that merely wondering if she was in good health. Not knowing whether Wentworth had called at Longbourn, or whether he had overcome his scruples and had decided to speak up – *that* was the hell, with all its vicious demons tearing at him with irons and sharp claws.

In lieu of any other answer though, Bingley chuckled warily and, rather surprised, Darcy looked up.

"Well enough, after a fashion," he supplied, then hastily added: "Fear not, they are all in good health – though not so much in good spirits. You see, Miss Lydia and Miss Kitty are not accustomed to having their amusements curtailed, so the weeks after the return from Brighton have been… rather fraught."

Knowing as much as he did of the young ladies in question, Darcy could not doubt that *'rather fraught'* was a marked understatement – which was presumably why Bingley's conscience was not pricked as he related something that sounded so very much like gossip.

Inappropriate as it was to allow it, Darcy could do nothing else. Truth be told, he would have been prepared to allow a great deal worse, from any reliable source of information.

"To add to it all, Mrs. Bennet had become rather impatient with everything that conspired to delay their travel into town," Bingley continued, "for she was quite determined to set off as soon as may be, and visit the warehouses. You know, for the wedding clothes. As you can imagine," he added with a rather touching conscious laugh, "I was all too eager to support her in every scheme of the sort. The sooner the preparations are in hand, the better. Mr. Bennet had observed – rather dryly, I found – that he did not see the need for such great haste, given that I am not likely to change my mind *again*. I daresay there was no malice… That is, I *hope* there was not – just one of those harmless quips that my future father-in-law seems so very fond of… He said that, in his opinion, Mrs. Bennet's maternal instincts would be better employed at home. But then, *he* was the one to change his mind and declared that, upon reflection, it was a good thing that Mrs. Bennet should quit Longbourn for a while, and leave Miss Lydia and Miss Kitty in his sole charge. Thus, deprived of sympathetic maternal interference, they would be more likely to feel the consequences of his displeasure, as well as the error of their ways. Needless to say, the youngest Miss Bennets were forbidden to travel to town," Bingley observed rather sheepishly, "and, according to their father's pronouncements, they are not to stir out of doors even, till they can prove they had spent their morning in a rational manner. There had been some talk, I hear, that they shall not be permitted to attend the engagement ball, unless they stood up with each other, or with one of their other sisters, but Miss Elizabeth had assured me it shall not come to *that*. Speaking of Miss Elizabeth, though," Bingley added, and suddenly all thoughts of the youngest Miss Bennets were driven from Darcy's mind, as his friend casually imparted, "she had inquired most particularly about you. Several times, while we were still in Hertfordshire, and a few times more, since she arrived in town. She had escorted her sister and mother, you see. I understand that Jane – *Miss Bennet*," he hastily amended, "sets great store by Miss Elizabeth's opinion, so of course her advice regarding the wedding clothes would be sought after!"

'Damn and blast the wedding clothes! Will you cease ranting on about them?' Darcy all but thundered.

What did this signify, *'she had inquired most particularly about you'*?

"What did she wish to know?" Darcy asked with forced calm, forgetting to make yet another show of sipping his coffee.

"Oh, all sorts. At first, while she was still at Longbourn… You know, just after the debacle with Miss Kitty's letter. We called upon them the following day, and your sister accidentally let slip that you had set off to Brighton. Bye-the-bye, forgive me for not cautioning her, Darcy, but I had not garnered from your note whether you would have wanted the family at Longbourn left in the dark as to your involvement. But I digress," Bingley stopped short with a casual wave, after a swift glance in his friend's direction.

He might have decided for himself it was high time to cease rambling – or perchance he had caught a dark glare, or some other telling sign of vexation and impatience. Darcy knew not which, nor did he stop to wonder. His steady gaze remained fixed on his fidgeting friend, until the latter finally resumed:

"At first, Miss Elizabeth asked me whether you had given any indication as to *why* you would go to Brighton, or any inkling into your designs. I must say, Darcy, she seemed most perturbed to hear Jane's supposition that you had set off with the intention of calling Wickham out," he added, and this time neither noticed that he had not corrected himself as regards to his betrothed's appellation.

In effect, Darcy could not have cared less if his friend had started openly referring to Miss Bennet as *'my angel'*, *'my sweetest love'*, or anything else that might have caught his fancy.

"How did Miss Bennet know *that* was my intention?" he asked instead, and his young friend shrugged.

"She did not *know*. Jane merely surmised as much, and Mr. Bennet had confirmed it, upon his return. He had learned from Captain Wentworth that it had taken a fair amount of persuasion for you to consent to be his second, instead of challenging the rogue yourself – and, unkind as it may seem, I am jolly glad it was *him* rather than you! Especially when the Captain turned up at Longbourn a few days later sporting an injured arm. I had not imagined Wickham to be such a rotten cad! You have given me hints of dishonourable and dissolute behaviour, but what he had done was beyond the pale! Hiding a loaded pistol in his sling – and him an officer in His Majesty's army!"

"Never mind that, Bingley!" Darcy all but growled, and his friend nodded. "What did Wentworth have to say, do you know?" he asked, with unconcealed urgency this time.

"Of course, of course! I forget myself! As I was saying, Wentworth gave us the full details. That is how we learned that you owe your life to Lieutenant Denny! Thank goodness for the man's quick thinking! Heavens above!" Bingley all but shuddered and walked around the large desk to lay a hand on Darcy's shoulder.

The warm display of friendship could not be ignored – nor could the sentiments behind it – and Darcy would have acknowledged them with a great deal more gratitude, had he not been distracted by the younger man's disjointed and incomplete disclosures and, to some extent, by the fact that he had very nearly overturned his drink over his papers *yet again* as he had perched himself on the edge of Darcy's desk, in dangerous proximity to his full cup of coffee.

"Oh, hang it! Young bull in a china shop, my father used to call me!" Bingley muttered apologetically as he heard the cup rattle behind him and quickly stood aside. "All I wished to say, Darcy," he said warmly, his hand back on his friend's shoulder to give it a tight grip, "I am dashed glad you were not harmed, you know! It does not bear thinking! And I daresay Miss Elizabeth was of the same mind. She seemed exceedingly affected when she heard this part of Wentworth's story. She was horrified to hear that the blackguard fired before the signal and the Captain was injured but, to my eyes at least, she was even more so when she heard the rest. You call me unobservant and you may be right, when I have no interest in the matter, but I tell you this: she had gone deathly pale when Wentworth recounted how Wickham had pointed the other pistol at your back – and I daresay she had stopped breathing altogether until she heard that you were quite safe! Which brings me to the other reason for my call," Bingley added with a rather conscious glance, looking rather taken aback by his friend's stricken countenance, and no less by his stony silence.

He fell silent himself and stepped back to perch on the edge of the desk again, further away from Darcy's cup of coffee. He bit his lip, then swallowed.

"What other reason?" Darcy prompted at last, his voice gravelly, as every form of mental torture known to man was wreaking havoc through him.

"I think…" Bingley offered quietly, hesitantly. "I think you should ask again," he ventured at last and at that, his friend sprang to his feet and pushed himself away from the desk – this time overturning his own drink over his own papers.

With a gasp of dismay, Bingley turned to stem the flow with his kerchief – he had one to hand, on this occasion – but Darcy stopped him with a forceful wave of his hand.

"Leave the wretched coffee!" he burst, his voice ragged, then ran his hands over his face and turned to his friend again. "What are you saying?" he said in an eager, tortured whisper.

"I cannot help thinking she is not indifferent to you," Bingley cautiously offered, slightly perturbed by his friend's outburst which – quite understandably – he was very far from comprehending. "Forgive me, I thought you would be pleased to know…" he added with a nonplussed glance. "I thought you should be told, if your affections and wishes are unchanged. If this is not the case, then tell me so at once! One word from you will silence me on this subject for ever!"

Darcy leaned forward, his palms flat on his desk.

"Continue!" he urged with some sort of deathly calm which, were he to own the truth, Bingley found positively terrifying.

Not for his own safety. He was rather too brave for that – nor did he think Darcy capable of inflicting bodily harm upon his nearest and dearest, regardless of provocation. Nay, it was the said friend's best interest and happiness that Bingley feared for, and he rather wondered whether he might have rushed in where angels feared to tread, as he resumed quietly:

"I had my suspicions even before the incident I mentioned, and a brief talk to Jane has confir– "

If the deathly calm was seen as little short of frightful, Darcy's outburst brought his hapless friend to an entirely unknown realm of terror.

"You have *spoken* to – !" he thundered, suddenly straightening up and gripping the edges of his desk with such force that his knuckles whitened.

Rather glad that it was a wooden desk instead of yet another far too thin a glass, Bingley hastened to correct his friend's misapprehension.

"I have not made any untoward disclosures, I assure you!" he swiftly offered. "That is to say, *she already knew*, Darcy! No one else in their family was informed of course, but Jane already knew of your proposal to her sister. She was adamant that she would not have confirmed my suspicions, nor would she have spoken to me of Miss

Elizabeth's concerns – or yours – were it not for her hope of something good coming from a better understanding between the parties. She seems to think, you see, that Miss Elizabeth has had some time to regret the rashness of her choice, as well as her previous opinions. Jane implied you may have warned her sister of Mr. Wickham's true character and, of course, recent events had only served to vindicate you. As to – hm! – the other matter…"

"My interference in your concerns, that is?" Darcy supplied blankly.

"Jane is still uninformed of your entire role in the affair – or, in her extreme delicacy, she is unwilling to touch upon it, given our connection. Her sister spoke of it, though. We were strolling through Green Park the other day, after their foray through the warehouses and, when she caught a moment alone with me, she asked whether my return to Netherfield last month had anything to do with *you*. I said it did, of course! I did not give details of our… hm!… former disagreement – I merely told her that you wrote me, earlier in the spring, and she seemed very moved to hear it. You may think me a selfish beast, Darcy, carrying on my own courtship and my wedding preparations with no concern for any other living soul, but I can assure you, it weighs on me to see you both unhappy. I know *you* are, and I would do anything in my power to help you – and as for Miss Elizabeth, I can only guess she is distraught at having had misjudged you so grievously in the past. Jane has confirmed as much, and while neither of us can assure you of Miss Elizabeth's acceptance this time round, I – *we* – strongly believe that you should ask again. And you should make haste – before Wentworth beats you to it! He has not spoken yet – he had only visited at Longbourn to announce his intention to visit with his sister for a while, but there is no doubt that he will, and soon! And, to my way of thinking, there is no time to lose!"

Chapter 9

'So, my friend, will you not join me when I call in Gracechurch Street this morning?'

Bingley's warm entreaty tore through him, hours later, tormenting him in ways his well-meaning friend could scarce imagine.

Had he believed in the Oriental religion of reincarnations, Darcy would have been justified in thinking he must have committed unspeakable crimes in each one of his previous lives, to warrant such relentless agony in this one.

Every form of misery he had endured since April paled in the face of a torture such as this. Elizabeth in Gracechurch Street. Elizabeth no more than three miles from his home. Elizabeth wishing he would call. Elizabeth regretting – if his friend was in the right, Elizabeth *perhaps* regretting having spurned his addresses in the spring. Elizabeth willing to make his happiness, in every way that he had dreamt of. Elizabeth's own happiness centred upon *him.*

Elbows on the desk, Darcy dropped his face in his hands, struggling to stop himself from imagining the perfect bliss that *might* have been his, this very evening, if Bingley's suspicions held a grain of truth – and had *he* not been a promised man.

How many times had he advised some wretched other not to make irreversible decisions on the heels of loss and disappointment?

He had thought himself in full command of his reason when he had made an offer to Miss Anne. If anything, it had been an offer sprung from reason and not sentiment – and any sentiment involved had not been of the ardent kind. He had offered for her out of gratitude for her kindness to Georgiana and himself – and out of the candid wish to give her the sort of life and recognition that her excellent nature and elegant mind deserved.

What was he to do now? Break a generous heart that had been already injured by past sorrows? Inflict another wound into a soul that deserved none?

The reverse burned through him with all the searing agony of a branding iron. Keep his word to Anne – marry Anne, when Elizabeth wanted him? Leave Elizabeth to suffer from what she would perceive as a withdrawal of his affections? Make a life with Anne and know, for the rest of his days, that he could have had the best happiness a mortal could be allowed to hope for, had he not been so thoughtless, so full of bitterness, so rash?

A couple of hours had elapsed since the time when Bingley left him, confused and disappointed by his refusal to join him in Gracechurch Street that day, and every second's passing had relentlessly slashed through him as he could not fight the heart-rending thoughts of what might have been.

He could not forsake her! Heaven help him, he could not! Even in the harshest hour of her rejection he could not see her suffer – and *now*, to know that she was perhaps hoping for a renewal of his offer, to choose the path of duty and *leave her behind?*

Every honourable instinct revolted at the notion of *not* doing his duty, every proper feeling shied from the thought of hurting the innocent, but this was beyond honour, beyond reason, beyond self. That he would have gladly laid down his life to spare her a tear was no longer in question – had not been in question ever since the day when he had instinctively rushed off to Brighton, thinking of her comfort above everything else.

In a better world, the prior claim of others should carry the most weight. His duty to Anne. To Georgiana. A better man would perhaps follow the path of duty at whatever cost. Yet the repugnant thought of forsaking every honourable precept drilled into him since childhood lost all its power before the unthinkable notion of forsaking *her*. Not out of passion or selfish desires. He would have liked to think that, had she chosen Wentworth, had she given Wentworth her love and her hand, he would have died by inches at the thought of her belonging to another, but would have carried on, duty to his dependants his succour and support.

This was beyond that duty which the mind dispassionately acknowledged. It was another duty, of a different sort. The utmost duty to protect and cherish something – *someone* – whom the soul recognised as its other half. He could not see *her* suffer any more than he could witness Georgiana's downfall and not lift a finger. He could not protect another at *her* expense any more than he could wilfully set fire to Pemberley House with his own hands!

He had to speak to Anne! He had to! Tell her every shred and facet of the truth and lay himself open to her contempt, perhaps – and hopefully her pity. She *would* see – would she not? – that it was beyond him to do otherwise.

He held no hopes of her forgiveness – indeed, he deserved no such kindness.

The enormity of what he was considering was beyond any meagre worldly satisfaction that, thanks to Sir Walter's inconsiderate injunction, the engagement was not public knowledge and thus would not be binding in the eyes of the world, nor would it impact on Anne's standing, or her prospects, should she find it in her heart to release him from his ill-judged promise.

If she would not… His heart squirmed and twisted, and Darcy chose not to dwell on the unassailable truth that he would then *have* to do the duty that the mind dictated.

Nor did he dare look the other way – towards the hope of having the freedom to offer himself to Elizabeth again; towards dreams beginning with her eyes resting upon him with a look of wonder and of love…

He briskly stood from his desk – no longer marked by the coffee Bingley had spilled – and tugged the left-hand cord with a gesture of determination. He had to see his steward, his valet and his butler – and later Georgiana, to let her know that soon he must away.

She could not travel with him – this was an endeavour to undertake alone and, truth be told, the less she knew about it at this point, the better. He would share the truth with her much later – if, God willing, there were any changes in the future she had reason to expect…

"Ah, Weston! Come!" he said as the door opened and his butler entered – even though the bell-pull he had tugged was destined to summon Hatherley, his steward. "I have to see you in a moment about preparations to remove to Somerset in a few hours' time. But I must see Hatherley first. Would you kindly inform him – ?"

Before he could finish, a knock on the door forewarned of an arrival – and this time it *was* the steward.

"Oh! Just the man! That would be all for now, Weston, I thank you. I shall summon you shortly."

"Sir," the man bowed, and then promptly added, "I came, though, to inform you that an express has just arrived."

"I see. You can leave it here," Darcy indicated the corner of his desk. "Where is it from?" he asked in passing. "Did the rider say as much?"

"Aye, Sir. He has informed me he is come from Somerset. From Thorngrove, near Kellynch."

Darcy cast a cursory glance over the letter sent with such urgency from Thorngrove, while the steward sat across the desk from him, waiting for instructions, but the brief glance was enough to show that Hatherley *had* to be dismissed, along with Weston. Alone once more, Darcy swiftly took up the express again.

It was from Lady Russell, and it was sent that very day.

I must beg leave to apologise, Mr. Darcy, Lady Russell had begun without preamble, *for the suddenness of this message, as well as for having embarked upon a course of action the necessity of which is not as yet in your power to understand.*

Suffice to say, Sir, that I am exceedingly concerned for my goddaughter's welfare. A circumstance which I am not prepared to disclose in a letter has given me great cause for concern and, although I cannot supply a vast deal of detail until we meet again, I will not scruple to say, Sir, that my goddaughter is in great need of your assistance, little as she may recognise it at the moment.

I find it incumbent upon me, Mr. Darcy, to hasten our removal from Somersetshire and I am writing to announce our impending arrival in town. We should set off by midday on the morrow and should arrive at our lodgings in Curzon Street as soon as it could be arranged.

I trust this will find you in town, and that you should be able to grant me a private interview, at your earliest convenience.

I will also add that, irrespective of Sir Walter's ill-judged injunction, I felt it of utmost necessity to reveal the details of my goddaughter's engagement to one person in particular and, as such, I believe you should be informed of the matter, so that the circumstance can be corroborated, if the need arises.

Yesterday, unbeknownst to Anne, I disclosed to a certain Captain Wentworth the circumstances of her engagement to you. It shall be in my power to discuss the matter further, when we are reunited in town. Until then, dear Sir, I remain,

Yours, very sincerely,

E. Lady Russell

Nearly everyone of his acquaintance would have readily vouched for the fact that Mr. Darcy was a temperate man of sober habit and even disposition.

Nearly everyone of his acquaintance would have therefore been most exceedingly amazed to hear Mr. Darcy utter an almighty oath and see him crumple the letter that he had just read and fling it at full force against the door of his study, before storming over to his drinks tray to pour himself a rather large brandy, at an hour as unnatural for this sort of imbibing as half past eleven in the morning.

This is how his cousin found him a short while later, and he was neither unduly shocked nor exceedingly amazed – though he might have been both, and perhaps a touch angry as well into the bargain, had he arrived but a few moments sooner, for then he would have received Lady Russell's crumpled missive fully in the chest.

"Brandy in the morning? Now that does not bode well!" the Colonel affectionately ribbed in lieu of any greeting as he made himself comfortable in one of the armchairs that stood before his cousin's desk. "Can I be of any assistance?" he offered, but Darcy shook his head and took another gulp of the fiery liquid.

"I thank you, Cousin, but I sincerely doubt it!" he all but growled.

Fitzwilliam, however, was not easily deterred – which was after all to be expected of a Colonel in His Majesty's army, who had acquitted himself with honour on the battlefields of Portugal and Spain, and had lived to tell the tale of Torres Vedras and Corunna.

"That is as may be, but from past experience, I can at least listen," the Colonel observed, and was not surprised to see his cousin nod.

And well he might, for there was truth in it. This would not have been the first time when Darcy had derived some measure of comfort from sharing his troubles with the only one of his acquaintance who was not biased by unreasonable expectations, nor by the view that he was never wrong.

"Would you be so kind as to pour me a glass of that selfsame noble liquid?" the Colonel asked as he loosened the top buttons of his coat and, before too long, he had the pleasure of watching the sunlight that brightened his cousin's study through a goblet half full of the warmest amber. He brought the goblet to his nostrils and inhaled. "Tis a great shame that we simply *had* to fight the French, you know," he casually observed. "For my part, I would have been a great deal happier to let them go about their business and create this nectar of the gods, so that it could be smuggled peaceably into the West Country, to everybody's satisfaction, except perhaps the late lamented Mr. Pitt and his tax-men. But never mind that now. Come, Cousin, sit with me – or amble through your study at your leisure – and tell me, what fresh hell is troubling you now?"

Had he been any less distressed, Darcy would have laughed. He did not laugh, but he could not fail to sense the same old gratitude at his cousin's endless and unstinting kindness. He did not *sound* kind, with his incessant prodding and irreverent quips but, underneath it all, the generous concern was there, as was the keen interest in Darcy's own welfare.

In truth, Fitzwilliam was the only one who had shown him concern without burdening him with guilt, or with his pity – and without any expectations of any sort of him.

He ambled for a while – not wholly at his leisure – and later on he sat, and the full truth eventually emerged. To begin with, the ball of crumpled paper had been retrieved, smoothed out and shown and then, when the Colonel candidly admitted that he failed to see the problem, a detailed account of Bingley's disclosures was made known to him, with few explanations and no artifice.

When Darcy had concluded, the Colonel returned Lady Russell's letter to the desk with a deft flick of his hand and took his time in swirling the brandy in his glass.

"Well?" Darcy impatiently asked after a while, forcefully breaking the extended silence.

"Well, what?" his cousin retorted, arching a brow. "I trust you have not given me the part of the Oracle of Delphi – although I *can* provide you with a vast supply of pithy answers," the Colonel smirked at his own questionable sally, then had the grace to apologise. "What are your own thoughts, though?" he asked after a while, and it was Darcy's turn to swirl his drink as he contemplated his answer.

"Before the letter arrived, I had every intention to travel into Somerset and confide in Miss Anne – "

"Lay yourself at her mercy, so to speak?"

Darcy's lip curled in some distaste at the tone, as well as at the choice of words but, in the end, he could not fail to nod.

The Colonel sniffed again at his brandy, then savoured another sparing sip.

"Have you considered, though," he asked after a short period of silence, "that *Miss Anne* might be better suited to you?" He ceased the sipping and the swirling, and lifted his eyes to look his cousin fully in the face. "I, for one, think she is your perfect counterpart!"

Darcy all but winced, then swallowed. He could easily see why Fitzwilliam felt this way. He, too, had considered it, although in a different vein. He could not have failed to notice that they admired the same books. They thought the same about events and people. They even found the selfsame jests amusing. And yet, despite Fitzwilliam's firm opinion on the matter, *this* did not make Miss Anne his perfect counterpart.

She could easily have been the sister his own age that he never had. The friend. The confidante. The respected kindred mind. But not the perfect match, the perfect life companion.

Had they but met a year in the past, he might have offered for her still – and they might have been happy in a quiet, calm and peaceful sort of way, and he might have loved her for it, or might have thought he did, for he would not have known any better.

Now he *did* know better, though – and, at this thought, this time he winced in earnest. It was not merely the passion. The blood rushing through his veins at an arch glance, or the touch of a hand. Not merely that – although it certainly made his life worth living – but the spice, the challenge of a witty repartee. The sparkle of unpredictability. The warm joy of shared laughter…

Just as the thought occurred, he *had* to wonder: had they *ever* laughed together, or had she only laughed *at* him? Had they ever shared an open, candid thought – before the wretchedness of Hunsford, when she had shown more openness and candour than he could ever wish for – at that time, at least?

"And as for Miss Bennet," Fitzwilliam interjected, uncannily in tune with his own thoughts, "forgive me, Darcy, but I *have* to ask! I cannot sit idly by and see you throw your life away! Do you love her for what she truly is, or do you love a figment of your own imagination? And, come to that, can you honestly say, hand on heart, that you know her well enough to love her or, for that matter, that she sees *you* for what you truly are? You told me, a short while ago, of her complete misjudgement of your character. She appears charming, I shall not dispute that, but – I repeat – do you *know* each other well enough for *love?* You have spent virtually no time in each other's company without some strife of sorts, or some misunderstanding. Are you *quite* certain you are not about to set Miss Anne aside – with all the attendant guilt, dishonour and mortification, I might add – for a life based on little more than the misleading stirrings of desire?"

Darcy gripped the armrest. Had this come from any other man – !

It was a useless thought, and he dismissed it. It could *not* have come from any other man, for few other men cared, and none knew him half as well – far off the mark as his cousin might have been this time. With some determination, he released the armrest and, for his part, the Colonel sighed.

"I shall not presume to know your heart – or hers – or Miss Anne's, for that matter. But, Cousin, I would urge you to look before you leap, and look in earnest – for there are times when, much as you might wish it, you simply cannot turn and blithely leap back!"

"I thank you for your concern about my leaps and bounds!" Darcy replied with defensive sarcasm. "I can safely see to that without assistance – "

"Provided no one shoves you as you jump," Fitzwilliam good-humouredly remarked, seemingly without taking offence at his younger cousin's reflex display of temper. "I must confess, it puzzles me though, and I hope you shall enlighten me as soon as you hear more from Lady Russell. Why would she feel the need to communicate the news of Miss Anne's engagement to Captain Wentworth and none other? Do you suppose…? Might there have been some sort of history between them – and Lady Russell is concerned, lest it should be repeated?"

Fitzwilliam's line of reasoning was blindingly obvious and – once he had been able to think beyond the crippling notion of his engagement having been revealed to *Wentworth*, of all people – Darcy could not fail to reach the same conclusion. Particularly as, unlike his cousin, he already had some prior knowledge, from Miss Anne herself, regarding what she had once referred to as *'her lost chance to happiness'*.

Was it Wentworth, then, the man she had alluded to? The one who, eight years in the past, had touched her heart? He certainly had betrayed both knowledge and interest in the area, and in the family at Kellynch! Was his return to Somerset, along with the Admiral and Mrs. Croft, the circumstance that had given Lady Russell such grave cause for concern?

If so, then surely the material point was whether Miss Anne still cared for him, after all those years. Was *that* the reason why Lady Russell felt they had to hasten their removal from Somerset – so that her goddaughter may be out of harm's way, and removed from temptation?

"I must say, Darcy, if that be the case," Fitzwilliam spoke up, once more attuned to his own thoughts, "then it certainly makes your own position a great deal less awkward. You would not be asking Miss Anne to release you – you would be releasing *her* to follow her heart. That is, of course, assuming her heart *does* lean in that direction and, more to the point, assuming *you* would persist on your chosen course of action," he hesitantly added, clearly unconvinced that there was any wisdom to be found in that. "But then, there is also the small fact your interfering friend could not in good conscience brush under the carpet, namely that neither he nor his well-meaning lady could safely vouch for Miss Bennet's acceptance. Would you run the risk of losing Miss Anne and gaining nothing for your troubles?"

"I would," the reply came without hesitation, and the Colonel frowned.

"I see… Well, if this is the lie of the land, then there is nothing more I can say about it, though I certainly wish there was…"

"For my part," Darcy observed quietly, "*I* wish I had your support in this. There will be none forthcoming from the rest of the family…"

"Which in itself should give you pause!"

At that, Darcy stood with a huff of anger and impatience.

"It *had* given me pause – and well you know it!" he burst, turning upon his cousin again, with a glare. "You may remember my wretched mess of a proposal. I assume I *have* given you the full details, have I not?"

"I daresay you have. And although you *could* have shown a great deal more tact – "

"And less arrogance – *and* couch it in less insulting terms!"

"Be that as it may," the Colonel waved dismissively, "your scruples *were* natural and just. You *were* setting a great deal aside in offering for her, and she should have seen it!"

"All she had seen – and she was in the right – was how insufficient were all my pretensions to please a woman worthy of being pleased!"

With a gesture of determination, the Colonel set his empty goblet on the desk.

"Let us be done!" he urged, with undue force. "Forgive me for telling you the reverse of what you wish to hear. My sole excuse is that I want you to be happy – and, having seen you with both, only a fool would fail to notice that it was with *Miss Anne* that you appeared even remotely so!"

"I had not imagined *you* would fail to see the difference between happiness and contentment!" Darcy burst out and, at that, his cousin lost his temper:

"If you call happiness whatever Miss Bennet has brought you so far, then heaven forefend I should ever see you *unhappy!* Pray spare me your avowals and your indignation!" he commanded, raising his hand at Darcy's glare and evident desire to protest. "'Tis your life, not mine, and well I know it! But you would do well to remember that *other* lives will be affected. Georgiana's, for one, and that of any offspring you might have. And I cannot help thinking they would all be a great deal safer in the hands of Miss Anne Elliot, rather than with some unknown quantity of a girl from Hertfordshire, delightful as she may be – and if you were at all disposed to allow your *head* to have a say in the matter, you could not fail to reach the same conclusion! Oh, fear not, I *shall* take my leave!" he added, just as his cousin was opening his lips to forcefully suggest the same. "I will not say I hope you know what you are doing, as there seems to be no purpose in *that!* When the dust settles, I hope you will let me know which lovely lady I am to greet as my future cousin!" the Colonel threw over his shoulder as a Parthian shot and strode over to the door.

He did not open it though, but turned around to face his seething host, who all but sneered as he saw him linger:

"Pray, Cousin, do not hold back now! Surely you can think of something else to say about my character and conduct!"

At that, the Colonel sighed and cautiously walked back.

"Let us not part in anger," he quietly offered. "You are distraught, I know, and I should not wish to add another to your host of demons! Hard as I might have made it for you to believe that, I *do* hope you can secure your happiness, Darcy – one way or the other," he added with a proffered hand which, despite the initial hesitation brought on by resentment and overwhelming anger, the other eventually brought himself to grasp. "You know full well that I *shall* fight your corner before our esteemed relations," came the quiet but earnest assurance. "As long as Georgiana is unharmed by your decisions, you *shall* have my support, as you have always had."

No outward expression of gratitude was expected and he received none – other than a tightening of his cousin's handshake.

"Well, then, you know where to find me, if you think you can digest another bellyful of unsolicited advice," Fitzwilliam quipped and, with another pat on his cousin's shoulder, he bade his adieus in earnest, and *did* leave, this time round.

Chapter 10

Left to his own devices – and to his host of demons – Darcy summarily dismissed his cousin's views and dire warnings. Much as he understood that they had sprung from nothing but genuine concern and brotherly affection, Darcy could not thank him for them, nor could he shake off the lingering anger at the Colonel's wilful obtuseness.

The shreds of doubt that his cousin had endeavoured to instil were shaken in a trice however, without effort. Fitzwilliam *might* have been justified in pointing out that he had scarce been under the same roof as Elizabeth without thinly veiled discord or misunderstanding tainting the air between them. Yet even so, he *had* seen her with others and, despite their own ill-starred interactions, there was not a single thing about her that he had not respected, admired or unconditionally adored. And as for *her*, she had known him at his worst – or at least at what she had perceived as such – and if she had now come to value him and his affections, what better hope was there for a rewarding future?

He did not dare dwell on it though, any more than he had done after Bingley's departure. It was too perfect – and far too premature!

Besides, the very notion of Elizabeth wishing, expecting his addresses brought on not only desperate longing, but also wretched recollections of the last time when he had entertained that thought. When he had marched into the parsonage at Hunsford to deliver the most shameful speech ever uttered by a gentleman. He did not dare dwell on her possible acceptance, least of all *now*, when his hand and honour were elsewhere engaged.

All he could do was to dispatch a note to Curzon Street, to confirm his presence in town and inform Lady Russell that, having received her letter, he would be eager to call upon her and Miss Anne Elliot as soon as they were ready to receive him. That task accomplished, there was nothing left for him to do but wait for Lady Russell's carriage to complete its stately progress towards town, and the enforced inaction, so alien to his wishes and to his very nature, turned out to be one of the worst of his tormenting demons.

Feverish calculations as to how soon he could expect them there, fruitless attempts to deceive himself by saying they could not *possibly* arrive till Friday, and all the while hoping for them twelve hours sooner, were *not* of a nature to inspire evenness of temper – so much so that, were it not for his impeccable training and steadfast loyalty to his master, Mr. Darcy's butler may have gone as far as take offence at the number of times he had been abruptly instructed to send up any note that was received, regardless of the hour.

Mindful of the fact that his master expected a *note* rather than a call, Mr. Weston did not hold too bright expectations of his reception when he walked into the study to announce Lady Russell's arrival but, to his well-concealed surprise, it appeared this was *precisely* what Mr. Darcy wished to hear.

"You have shown her ladyship into the drawing room, I hope!" Mr. Darcy queried and, behind the smooth façade, the butler's disappointment simmered. That it should come to this! After thirty years of service, could he *not* be trusted to fully know his duty?

"Of course, Sir," he impassively confirmed, keeping his voice even – as was expected of him, irrespective of his private sentiments.

"Good. Good. I thank you," Mr. Darcy replied, his countenance betraying his distraction and, at that sight, the butler found it in him to be slightly mollified.

'Peevish old fool!' he chastised himself later. Of course the young master had not intended to imply mistrust! There must have been a matter of great import that he wished to discuss with his visitor – and, having come to this belated understanding, the old butler made

it his particular business to instruct the footman stationed in the hallway to allow no interruption whatsoever, regardless of the source, once refreshment was served.

The exception was unnecessary. Lady Russell did not desire refreshment, as she was only too eager to inform her host, once the young man had remembered his duty and offered it.

"I thank you, no, Mr. Darcy, " she waved with some impatience. "If it does not trouble you unduly, Sir, I would rather get straight to the point."

"Of course," her host felt compelled to answer, anxious to learn the *'point'* her ladyship was so keen to make – although, truth be told, he would have greatly preferred to have a private conversation with the lady's goddaughter. "But first, may I ask, is Miss Anne well? She *has* accompanied you to town, I hope?"

"Of course!" Lady Russell rather forcefully replied. "I thought I have explained in my letter that it was for *her* benefit that we had to hasten our removal from Thorngrove!"

"I gathered as much, though I must confess, I was rather mystified by your note."

"I feared this might be the case – but it could not be helped. I have come here to explain it, and also justify my actions. My goddaughter is still in ignorance of both, as she is of my having called upon you this morning. When the entire business is made known to her, as I know it must, I trust she will ascribe it to the right cause, as I hope *you* shall. But enough with sidelong remarks! The truth of the matter, Sir – and I trust this shall have no bearing on your feelings for Anne – is that, eight years ago, Captain Wentworth had the audacity to make her an offer, at a time when he had no future and no prospects! He had the temerity to expect Lady Elliot's daughter to condemn herself to the adversities of a life as a sailor's wife, with all the attendant risks and privations! I am pleased to say that Anne was swift to see the error of her choice and, thanks in part to my timely intervention, as well as her father's obvious disapproval, she was persuaded to break the engagement! He went to sea soon after, and was never heard of since, even after he had made part of his fortune," the lady added with angry pleasure, soon to be turned into a sentiment of a different kind, as she hastily resumed: "And now he is come to Kellynch, to visit with Admiral Croft who, through the perverseness of fate, has chosen to take up residence there – and I cannot bear to think of the discomfort my dear girl must feel to have *him* living in her home!"

And there he had it now – the full meaning of Anne's confession that, through her own fault, she had lost her chance at happiness. She had been persuaded to err on the side of caution – and had obviously regretted it ever since!

It was *Anne*, though, not Lady Russell, with whom he should discuss the matter – and Darcy knew full well he ought to find a courteous way of telling the lady as much.

Before he could do so, Lady Russell hastened to reassure him:

"Far be it from me to imply that Anne might have wished for a renewal of his attentions, had her circumstances been different – and I can safely say, there is no risk of *that!* They had been in company together no more than thrice since his return to Somerset and on each occasion they had scarcely spoken. He did not approach her – in effect, he had barely said a word over what common civility required but, for my part, I saw no purpose in fostering further interaction. Anne agreed with me that an earlier removal to town would be the better option – so we set to it. As to my decision to inform Captain Wentworth of Anne's engagement when I saw him last, I trust you can see my point. Should they be brought together again until your marriage, I hope this information will serve as sufficient reason for the Captain to avoid her society, and thus my dear girl will be safeguarded from the ghosts of the past. As to Sir Walter's ridiculous injunction, I firmly believe it should be lifted. I shall write him to that effect but, should he disagree, I am perfectly happy to bear the consequences of his displeasure and announce your engagement myself. The sooner the matter is settled, the better – and I have no doubt you are of the same mind!"

The walls of the drawing room seemed to close upon him, just as stifling as the net of his own making that was now tightening on every side, preventing all escape.

What he had hoped for as a liberation has just been shown as nothing but a means to hasten his downfall towards a fate that threatened to be sealed!

Wentworth was *not* about to renew his addresses, and Anne did not wish it. Or, if she did – and was too proud, or too right-minded to let Lady Russell see it, since she was promised elsewhere – she was now suffering in silence from Wentworth's apparent determination to treat her as a common and indifferent acquaintance.

How could *he* then come and deliver another blow? Have her know that she had lost not once, not twice, but thrice over? How could he ask her to release him and know full well that she would go to a worse fate?

More to the point, how could he *not* speak? How could he stand next to Anne before the altar – and hold his peace when charged to confess any known impediment to them being lawfully joined together, as he would have to answer at the dreadful day of judgement, when the secrets of all hearts shall be revealed?

How could he marry her, take her to Pemberley, live with her day after day, night after night – and have every second that they shared branded by the knowledge that, had it not been for his abysmal error, he might have had everything his heart desired?

How could he hide his deep regrets from Anne, year after excruciating year? How could he avoid poisoning her life with the notion that, for all his best intentions and his endeavours to conceal it, it was another that he wanted in his house, in his bed, in his life?

The neckcloth tightened around his throat, stifling him as effectively as the closing net of expectations, and Lady Russell's avowed determination to announce the engagement as soon as may be was not of a nature to help him breathe with ease.

"You are very silent, Sir," his companion finally observed. "I hope that my disclosures have not unsettled you," she offered, and it took every measure of restraint for her host to suppress a bitter laugh at the understatement. "I would consider it a great favour if you can be persuaded not to mention our conversation to Anne as yet. She is still very much affected by the unwelcome encounter in Somersetshire and I was hoping to give her a brief respite to revive her spirits before I disclosed my role in the affair. I trust she will forgive me – she knows I have always had her best interests at heart. I will leave you now, Sir. Should you wish to call in Curzon Street, you shall be most welcome. In effect, I was about to suggest to Anne that we took a stroll tomorrow in St. James's Park, or perhaps Kensington Gardens, and I hope you and your dear sister can be persuaded to join us. Shall we expect you in Curzon Street shortly after ten?"

ꕥ

Too dazed by the onslaught of adverse circumstances, Darcy allowed the decisive matron her way as regards the planned outing and thus, on the following day, he called in Curzon Street, with Georgiana at his side.

His sister's delight in being reunited with Anne could not fail to add to his already unbearable burden of guilt, as Fitzwilliam's words regarding Georgiana's comfort returned to vex him again and again. She was so pleased, so happy, so keen to acquaint Anne with this, that and the other so that – much as she knew she *should* allow her brother some time in the company of his betrothed, and despite Lady Russell's subtle endeavours to orchestrate the same – most of the time it was Georgiana that Anne was conversing with, leaving Darcy to his turmoil and bleak thoughts.

The pattern continued when they left the house; continued as they were strolling through the gardens.

Even now, when the path narrowed to the point of no longer admitting four, Georgiana walked ahead with Anne, telling her of the latest performance at the Little Theatre, leaving him to walk sedately at Lady Russell's side.

It was Georgiana's exclamation of surprise that first caught his attention, followed shortly by Lady Russell's gasp, and he lifted his gaze from the carpet of dry leaves and pebbles – straight into the mesmerising depth of dark brown eyes.

He drew a sharp intake of breath and bowed, too stunned for words. It was Georgiana who cheerfully greeted the other party:

"Miss Bennet! Miss Elizabeth! How wonderful to see you! Anne, pray allow me to introduce our Hertfordshire friends: Miss Bennet, Miss Elizabeth Bennet. This is Mr. Bingley, my brother's longstanding friend and companion, and Captain Wentworth."

Once she had performed the next part of the introduction and presented Lady Russell and Miss Elliot to the others' acquaintance, Georgiana fell silent and Miss Bennet spoke up in her turn, to introduce Mr. and Mrs. Gardiner, who had just joined them, at a slower pace.

Amid the confusion of bows, curtsies, subdued acknowledgement of previous acquaintance and sundry civil greetings, any disturbance of spirits brought on by the unexpected encounter might have had time to abate, had Darcy been able to look away.

He could not – nor did he strive to.

He could not fail to notice that her cheeks were overspread with a deep blush and she was too studiously avoiding any glance in his direction for him to doubt that it was done on purpose.

He sighed. He would have given years of his life – would have traded there and then, without the slightest hesitation, for the chance to know what her thoughts were, at this point in time!

She looked his way again, as though she had heard him sigh, and her glance seemed to hold concern and a million questions – and then she trained her eyes upon the ground and bit her lower lip, her blush even fiercer.

And still he could not look away. Starved for the sight of her, he eagerly took in every detail, every touch of the enchanting picture. The adorable dimple at the corner of her mouth, forming just then, in her left cheek, as she fleetingly smiled to her sister. The long, dark lashes, still screening her expressive eyes from him. The loose tendrils, just above her ear. Those exquisitely perfect lips, smiling again, this time to Anne and Georgiana, then to Bingley – and then suddenly pursing as she looked away.

Every detail mattered, every play of emotion on her beloved features, to be stored for later inspection and doubtless agony – and it was little wonder that, thus employed, Darcy spared neither thought nor glance to Wentworth. He did not catch his long, searching gaze – nor did he notice that it was full of the purest loathing.

"Will you not walk with us?" Darcy heard Georgiana suddenly suggest.

At any other time, he might have shown surprise and cautious pleasure at her increasing ease in larger company – might have dwelt on its cause, with warm gratitude. It did not cross his mind to do so now, as he keenly listened, eager to ascertain the outcome of Georgiana's invitation.

The only voice of polite dissent was Lady Russell's – which was no surprise. The rest were mostly silent – Elizabeth, Anne, Wentworth – and it was Bingley's cheerfulness and Mr. Gardiner's warm entreaties that carried the point.

They struck upon a path that was new to everybody. It was a wide avenue bordered with Dutch elms, leading in a straight line to the water, and they ambled along it, in uneven pairings.

Lady Russell, who had started off at Darcy's side, fell far behind after a while, along with the Gardiners, and her place was taken by Bingley who, for some reason or other, seemed disposed to walk with his friend, while his betrothed was strolling with her sister.

This left Captain Wentworth without a companion, but the gentleman did not seem unduly perturbed. Indeed, he scarcely appeared to notice as he ambled, his hale hand behind his back, some steps to the side of Georgiana and Miss Anne Elliot, so deep in thought that, some time later, Georgiana had to repeat her question twice, before she got his attention. He did not drift so far after that, either in body or in spirit, and although he did not contribute a jot to the ladies' conversation, it was to be surmised he was taking some interest in it.

The other four, who lagged behind, eventually congregated to walk as a group – and it was only when Bingley suddenly offered Miss Bennet his arm and the couple promptly outstripped them that Darcy came to understand their endearingly childish machinations. With a surge of gratitude towards the said well-meaning friend and his all-forgiving betrothed, Darcy found himself falling into step with Elizabeth.

Every shred of reason commanded that he should *not* offer her his arm, all things considered, but he ignored them all, knowing full well that he must have at least the comfort of her light touch on his sleeve – that, or shatter. She *did* take his arm – which only served to show how meagre, how insufficient that comfort was, and how desperately he wished for more.

Every step that they took in silence hung over him with the threat of the impending loss of those treasured moments of illusory intimacy, and all the words he yearned to tell her burned hotly in his throat. He bit his lip.

"I hope your relations are in good health," Darcy said at last, then cleared his voice, for it seemed unwilling to obey him.

"They are, I thank you," he heard her near-whisper, and cleared his voice again.

"I suppose your mother has returned to Longbourn," he observed, then all but winced at his own ineptitude.

Of all the things he longed to tell her – there he was talking of *Mrs. Bennet*, of all people?

"No, she has not," Elizabeth replied, her voice betraying her own surprise at his choice of topic. "I fear that the daily incursions to the warehouses have left her with little energy for touring the parks…"

Nine more steps in silence – nine more steps of wasted privacy!

He could not see her face, hidden as it was by the brim of the bonnet, but her hand was there, in the crook of his arm – the lightest touch that seemed to burn into the smooth dark cloth. Thin fingers encased in crochet gloves.

Behind his back, his own fingers twitched, yearning to hold her hand. Just that, hold her hand at least, entwine his gloved fingers with hers and give her a sign, a wordless indication of what was in his heart. He was not free to do so – as he knew full well – just as he knew that, this time, he *had* to resist the tormenting impulse.

"I am happy to see that you are well," he offered instead, his voice low and intimate and at the sound, she looked up towards him.

The new light in her eyes did something to his breath. His chest was tight, constricted, and he forced a lungful of air in – to no avail. The constriction grew a great deal worse, when he heard her say, in a rushed whisper.

"May I say the same of you, Sir! I have heard a dreadful account of what might have happened, and I can no longer help thanking you for your unexampled kindness to my poor sister. Ever since I have known it, I have been most anxious to acknowledge to you how gratefully I feel it. Not merely I, but my entire family are deeply indebted to you for your generous intervention!"

Darcy did not even register that she had not spoken to him of their even greater debt to Wentworth. That would come later, to painfully suggest to him in the sleepless night to follow that she had understood he did not wish to hear her speak of *him* – not then, not ever.

A different and frightfully worse torment claimed him now. Had he been free to do so, *now* would have been the time to tell her that, if she wished to thank him, it should be for herself alone. That her family owed him nothing. That he had thought only of *her*.

The words choked him, clamouring for release, and he pressed his lips together as the desperate wish to declare himself wreaked havoc through every sense and feeling.

To his further despair, her eyes clouded at his prolonged silence and, with a sigh, she looked away.

He *had* to speak! He had to say *something* – though there seemed to be an embargo on every subject.

"You must not feel any obligation, Miss Bennet," Darcy said at last, his voice laden. "I have done nothing. It was Captain Wentworth who had taken centre stage," he added, the poisoned sentence coming out with a bitterness that was beyond concealment.

"I was told you had insistently endeavoured to prevent him," came the quiet reply, and a different sort of poison coursed through him at her words.

Was *that* what it was all about? *She thought he had aimed to preserve Wentworth? That* was what she was thanking him for?

Shards of ice followed in the wake of the poison, slashing through his heart as they went, forcing up a retort that was instinctive, crisp and prompt.

"I have not succeeded – but, in any case, I must own that my insistence had *nothing* to do with the Captain's welfare!"

She turned a look of undisguised surprise upon him – then suddenly the surprise seemed to twist into horror.

"Of course! I had no wish to imply – "

"Shall we not climb to the top of the Mount? The view must be spectacular from up there!"

At the sound of Georgiana's voice – never unwelcome, until this very moment – they both looked away from each other and Elizabeth swiftly released his arm. Darcy did not even try to hold back a huff of insurmountable vexation at the wretched timing of the interruption.

Wholly engrossed in the stilted and dreadfully unrewarding conversation, he had not noticed that they had caught up with the others. Georgiana had walked back to meet them, leaving Anne and Captain Wentworth a little further ahead, seemingly in some deep discussion, and as for Bingley and Miss Bennet, they were already part way up the artificial hillock constructed from the earth dug up decades ago, in order to create the Serpentine.

Darcy's glance shot towards the other couple. His duty to Anne, to her wishes and present comfort was unsettling enough, without the added notion that her conversation with her erstwhile suitor might have some impact on his own situation.

And then there was *his* conversation, left unfinished at the worst possible spot!

There was but one choice in the matter and, come what may, he instantly took it.

"Excellent notion, Georgiana! Would you care to see the view from the top of the Mount, Miss Bennet?"

The ascent was gradual for the best part, up a winding path flanked by trees and well-established shrubs. It was only for the last few yards that the climb was noticeably steeper and he offered to assist the ladies as they went. Georgiana leaned on his arm with a small grateful smile, but Elizabeth chose to walk on without assistance until the small hillock was conquered, and the wide prospect opened at their feet, resplendent in hazy sunshine, from Kensington Palace ahead, all the way over to St. James's and Westminster, far behind.

At the very top of the Mount stood an ornamented summerhouse which, in the olden days, used to revolve, so that Queen Caroline, His Majesty's grandmother, could sit and admire her garden and domain. It had ceased revolving many years ago, but it served at least to provide shelter from the glare of the sun – and that was where Bingley and his lady could be found.

They warmly welcomed the next ascending party and spent some time admiring the view and the lush shrubs before Bingley, with that same generous intent and unstinting kindness for which Darcy felt he could not thank him enough, offered Georgiana his spare arm and suggested they retraced their steps to rejoin the others.

They could not lag behind for very long – Darcy could scarce doubt it. Still, he could not deny himself the exquisite enjoyment of revelling for a few moments more in the delightful picture Elizabeth presented, her countenance glowing from the sun and the exertion as she looked around at the astounding prospect, the loose tendrils that framed her beloved face swaying lightly in the gentle summer breeze.

With a sigh, Darcy took on the role of the devil's advocate.

"We should return to the others," he offered, and she concurred with a slight nod, then walked back towards him, and they both rejoined the path.

She did not take his arm, nor did he dare offer. Mindful of the precious moments of privacy slipping away from them again, he spoke up, only to discover that they had both begun at once.

"Before we do, though, pray allow me to apologise – "

"Mr. Darcy, I *must* assure you – "

"Pray, continue," he civilly offered, but she shook her head and wordlessly indicated that he should have his say first.

"I beg leave to apologise for my earlier abruptness… I did not wish to offend!"

"Think nothing of it! Mr. Darcy, it appears that in recent times we have done nothing but repeatedly apologise to each other," she added, but the wistfulness was mingled with a trace of the adorable archness of old, and he smiled despite himself to hear it. "For my part," she continued, "I wanted to assure you that I merely wished to thank you for your generous intervention on behalf of a foolish young girl, to whom you owed nothing!"

'Elizabeth, it was for **you**. *For you alone I think and plan! Have you not seen this? Can you still fail to understand my wishes?'*

The forbidden words filled his heart, his senses, and for a moment he thought they had escaped.

They had not – and before too long he would have to utter some half-truth or other, regarding his history with Wickham, and his resulting duty to prevent him from harming other innocents.

It did not come to pass. Engrossed in each other and in the intense moment, none of them looked down to notice the protruding root, nor the stone it had loosened. At her sudden false step and small cry of alarm, Darcy's arm shot out instinctively to steady her, and prevent her from slipping behind the large rhododendrons, down the steep side of the hill.

Later on, he was to make a great deal of effort to persuade himself that he had merely aimed to grasp her arm. That it had *not* been his intention to wrap his own around her waist instead. That it had *not* been his conscious scheme, in any way whatever, if she was suddenly gathered to his chest, warm and safe, and close to him, as close as in his desperate, hopeless dreams. Her eyes intent on his, deep enough for drowning. Her lips mere inches from his own. And everything stood still, even the hazy air full of heady promise, as intoxicating as her warm weight in his arms.

He swallowed, knowing that in a moment it would go to his head.

In a moment, the world beyond the merciful screen of rhododendrons would cease to exist, and his lips would hungrily claim hers, and he would taste at last the sweetness he had dreamt of.

Her breath, her skin, her scent. He would let his lips roam over her translucent skin, glowing from the sunshine and from the deeper, inner glow of a sudden blush. And find her lips again, as he knew he must, and make up for every second of denial, every second of pretence!

The very air between them seemed charged with expectation, seemed to crackle and tingle – or perhaps it was the blood-rush, violent and forceful, that was making him hear things that were not there, as he teetered precariously on this side of abandonment, every drumming of his pulse pushing him closer to the edge.

Perfect, perfect, perfect. Exquisite and perfect. Body and soul his other half, in every way!

Dark eyes with specs of amber searching his in earnest – and softening at something they must have found therein. Her breath coming faster, warm upon his cheek, in small, rapid puffs of air that soothed and burned at once. The scent of her sun-kissed skin filling his senses, close, maddeningly close, and more intoxicating than the finest wine.

He took a deep breath, as though after a long time underwater – and the sound of it shattered the all too dangerous spell. The next moment, dark lashes fluttered over the dark eyes and he felt her endeavour to step back, so he reluctantly released her. His gloved hand lingered on her elbow as he asked – so blatantly unnecessarily that he would have blushed for it, had he been able to spare it a thought:

"Are you quite safe?"

"Yes. Yes, I am. I thank you," came the faltering reply, and they were still close enough for her breath to brush over his face again, sending another rush of fire-needles along already tingling nerves.

His hand tightened on her elbow, this time without intention – and, at her swift glance, he let it drop. She made to carefully step away and resume her descent, but before she could do so, he reached out and offered his outstretched hand.

"Allow me," he said quietly.

She hesitated. Briefly. Yet in the end she placed her small gloved hand in his. And now he had his earlier wish. He was holding her hand, her fingers gripping his now and again, at some occasional unevenness of ground. But it was not enough, not by a fair margin! He wanted more now. He wanted so much more!

He would not speak – he *could not* speak – and the recollection of the heady bliss that had been his, only a few short moments in the past, only increased the agonising dread of the impending separation.

He *could* have kissed her. The overwhelming thought brought back the needles and the rush of fire. Yet, underneath and largely unheeded, reason clamoured that, to have done so without the power to offer his hand in marriage once more, in the same breath, he would have injured her in the worst way imaginable.

It was a while until cold reason could prevail, as the surest way to subdue his disappointment.

Another disappointment lay in store. Half-way down from the rhododendron bush, Captain Wentworth was waiting – and this time Darcy could not miss the sheer hatred in the stony glare. His countenance, however, softened beyond recognition when he turned to Elizabeth and offered his hale hand.

"I must beg forgiveness for my inattention, Miss Bennet, it was most remiss of me. Would you allow me? I thank you, Sir," he added with the scantest bow to Darcy, "for your eagerness to supplant me in my duties. May I observe that I am here now – and I should imagine you might wish to see to your own!"

The man had a horribly valid point and, although seething, Darcy could scarce dispute it. For her part, Elizabeth cast a glance from one of her companions to the other and seemed as though she was about to comment on the Captain's terse words but, for some reason, thought better of it. Before too long, in any case, they had rejoined the others, and found the Gardiners in pleasant conversation with their eldest niece, Mr. Bingley and Georgiana, while Lady Russell stood at the side of a quiet Anne, looking distinctly unimpressed with the morning's outcome.

"Ah! Mr. Darcy! I hope you have enjoyed your walk, Sir," she observed blandly, once he had joined the rest of the party. "Reluctant as I am to trespass on your kindness, I fear I must ask you to escort us home. This walk was a great deal longer than I expected. What say you, Anne? Are you ready to return?"

"If you are in need of rest, Ma'am, then by all means, let us do so," Anne calmly replied, giving no further indication of her own thoughts on the matter.

It was readily apparent which way his duty lay, and Darcy had no option but pursue it.

Adieus were swift and to the point, and there was no opportunity for voicing future plans – not that he could think of any.

The parties separated, each choosing its own path – and Darcy walked away in a daze of longing and despair.

He had caught the vaguest glimpse of *her* upon his departure – a glance, a curtsy – and too many had been in the way, in every sense of the word. Yet it was not merely the parting's bitter sorrow that weighed down his steps and pierced his heart.

The chance encounter in the gardens had suggested that Bingley and Miss Bennet were indeed in the right – not that he ever should have had the folly of disputing the views of Elizabeth's dearest and closest sister. Whatever Elizabeth thought of him these days, she was not indifferent – nor was she irrevocably set against him any longer!

The notion that would have given him cause to fervently thank his maker just four months in the past was now a source of anguish and of the deepest heartache.

It was the cruellest torture to think that, had he been able to offer himself to her again, at that glorious moment on the Mount, by now he might have been engaged to Elizabeth Bennet.

He could scarce bear to walk away from her, that morning.

How could he bear to walk away for the rest of his life?

He could scarce think – and yet he *had* to find a way, *he had to!* Merciful heavens, there *had* be a way of rectifying the very worst misjudgement of his life!

Chapter 11

Another sleepless night – another one of many. It was a wonder he could even function! He had not slept soundly in months – and certainly not now!

There had been no opportunity to speak to Anne and ascertain her own wishes and feelings. She had been very silent and withdrawn on their journey back – and they certainly lacked the privacy such an attempt required.

They had returned to Curzon Street and the Darcys had been invited to remain for dinner but even so, a chance for private discourse had never come – not that he had been able to determine *how* exactly he should approach the matter.

The *'how'* and *'what'* and *'when'* were twisted on all facets over the night-time hours – and it was only in the early morning, as he had cursed Wentworth's name for the thousandth time, that it finally occurred to him it was *Wentworth* he should be approaching first, and gauge his intentions, before he could even broach the subject with Anne.

It would not be an easy task. The man obviously loathed him, but Darcy could not tell whether it was due to Wentworth's feelings for Elizabeth – or because he was championing Anne.

Be that as it may, it was with *him* that he should bring the matter in the open and at the liberating thought of finally having a clear course of action, Darcy felt suddenly refreshed, despite the sleepless night.

He had no notion where the Captain could be found, but it did not take him long to think of the best source of information.

Thus, at an earlier hour than was customary for a morning call, Darcy was pacing the halls of the fashionable establishment in Charring Cross where, for many years, his friend chose to take lodgings on each of his forays into town.

The man sent up with his card returned in a trice, happy to say that Mr. Bingley was ready to receive him, and so the visitor followed him up at a brisk pace.

"Darcy! A dashed welcome surprise! In effect, I was about to set off and call upon you! My sisters will be disappointed to have missed you, though – they were going to join me in Berkeley Square later, as Louisa is keen to secure your acceptance of her invitation. The Hursts' summer ball – if you remember."

Darcy did not – the said event had completely slipped his mind.

"Pray, sit!" Bingley urged. "Would you care for coffee? Or anything else?"

"Do not trouble yourself, Bingley, I am in no need of breakfast – but I apologise to have disrupted yours."

"No matter – I have long finished. As I said, you very nearly missed me. Now, as to the Hursts' ball, I am sorry to say that my sister is not of a mind to divert its purpose and have it in honour of my engagement," he candidly disclosed, to Darcy's slight discomfort at his friend's forthright manner and willingness to discuss his domestic troubles, "but be that as it may! The Bennets *will* receive an invitation. My sisters are about to call upon them later on today. I understand your cousins are also expected to attend. I am quite certain Colonel Fitzwilliam shall, and perhaps Lady Henrietta and Lord Leighton, although Lord and Lady Malvern have declined."

Darcy was not surprised. The Bingley fortune was a great deal too new for Lady Malvern's taste.

"I trust I can count on your attendance as well," his friend continued, "and your sister's of course, and I hope you can be persuaded to bring Lady Russell and her charming niece as your guests."

"Miss Elliot is not Lady Russell's niece; she is her goddaughter."

"Oh! My apologies! But tell me, is there a particular purpose for your call? As I mentioned last time we have spoken on the subject, I would be delighted to assist you in any way I can!" he offered with a hint of a smile, which reminded Darcy to thank him for his earlier assistance, in Kensington Gardens. "Oh, that!" Bingley chuckled. "I daresay I was rather conspicuous with it, but anything to smooth your path, you know! I take it that you have not been wholly successful…? Wentworth seemed quite determined to get in your way!"

"In effect, this *does* bring me to the purpose of my call," Darcy interjected, quick to recognise an opening and unwilling, in any case, to discuss his far from smooth path with his friend. "I was wondering if you knew where I could find the Captain."

A glance of mild surprise crossed Bingley's countenance at that, but of course he was too much of a gentleman to inquire into his friend's reasons.

"I have no notion, I am afraid. I daresay he would have taken lodgings at the Pulteney, or perchance the Admiralty Buildings. I could inquire, if you wish. I am bound to encounter him in Gracechurch Street sooner or later," he mused with a slight grimace, "but I daresay you shall come across him in Hanover Square, at Louisa and Hurst's summer ball."

Darcy suppressed a frown. What he had in mind did not quite lend itself to a ballroom setting. It appeared, however, that a ballroom setting would have to suffice, at least to set the time and place for a more private conversation, since he had no wish to involve Bingley in the delicate negotiations and have him arrange an interview with Wentworth. Much as he held his friend in his affections and esteem, there was no doubt that the late Mr. Bingley's quip about a young bull in a china shop was rather too close to the mark for comfort.

It was therefore in his power to inform Mrs. Hurst and her even more delighted sister, when they *did* call upon him later on that day, that the Darcys would be very happy to attend the Hursts' event of the season.

In effect, Miss Bingley would have been wild with hope, had she but known with what feverish impatience Darcy counted the days until her sister's summer ball.

She did not – which was just as well – but *that* detracted nothing from the lady's felicity when she stood at Mr. and Mrs. Hurst's side in the receiving line to greet her dear friend Georgiana and the young lady's brother.

Miss Bingley was less pleased to welcome the pair that had arrived with them. She could not fail to experience some unease at the notion that Mr. Darcy had been seen more than once escorting Lady Russell's young charge about town.

Only the other day, Miss Grantham had mentioned in passing that she had seen the party of four in the Darcy box, at the theatre.

Then Charles, whom Miss Bingley never listened to, if she could help it – especially *these* days, when he could scarce speak of anything other than his mortifying infatuation – had rattled something about an encounter in Kensington Gardens. Not to mention the morning, at the beginning of the week, when she had come across them herself, admiring the oil paintings at Somerset House!

Her unease notwithstanding, Miss Bingley did not fail to smile brightly as she curtsied to her sister's guests. She was a lady of impeccable upbringing – and if she was able to graciously welcome Charles's insipid ladylove and that odious Eliza, not to mention that dreadful harridan, Mrs. Bennet, and their Cheapside relations, then surely she could bring herself to welcome anyone!

It was most disappointing, though, that Mr. Darcy had not asked her to stand up with him as yet. He *had* asked Miss Elliot, which was a wretched business, but only once, and thankfully Miss Bingley did not have to suffer the indignity of seeing him escort Miss Eliza to the set. It was to be hoped that fine eyes and pert opinions were only a diversion in the wilds of Hertfordshire. Fine eyes indeed! There was nothing extraordinary in them but a sharp, shrewish look that was distinctly unappealing! And she had grown so brown and coarse – which was little wonder, with her revolting penchant for lengthy country walks!

Miss Bingley gracefully made her way through the elegant room, dropping a word of welcome here, a compliment there, as she surreptitiously searched through the glittering crowds for Mr. Darcy.

Ah! At last! She could just about spot him standing at one side, apparently conversing with the rather dashing gentleman who had arrived with the Bennet party. A captain in the Royal Navy, whose name eluded her just now.

Regardless, Miss Bingley allowed herself a long weighing glance towards the handsome captain and could not help wondering whether his fortune was as attractive as his person.

There was every reason to suspect, however, that his temper was rather less than pleasing, judging at least by his forbidding countenance just then – so forbidding in effect that, despite herself, Miss Bingley could not fail to wonder what exactly were he and Mr. Darcy speaking of.

She would have been unable to garner much, even if she had been close enough to hear them, for Darcy merely asked whether the captain would be disposed to set the time and a place for a private interview. *That* was the moment when the captain's countenance had grown sterner and darker.

"Would that be the sort of interview often held on Wimbledon Common?" he asked, arching a brow.

"That was not precisely what I had in mind. At this point in time, I would prefer to speak with you rather than use you for target practice," Darcy replied coolly and the other bowed.

"As you wish. I would gladly oblige with either."

"Would tomorrow be convenient?"

"I am at the Pulteney. I shall await your call."

With a brief exchange of bows, the gentlemen parted and Miss Bingley had the joy of seeing Mr. Darcy walk in her direction. He soon stopped though, then moved towards the line of dancers, and then beyond, in a wide circle around the room.

Miss Bingley wondered whom exactly was he seeking – for there was little doubt that he *was* seeking someone. Not Georgiana, for he did not walk to *her*, to the alcove where she was sitting in conversation with Charles and Miss Bennet. Presumably not Miss Elliot either, for he must have seen her walking to the set with the handsome captain – and yet he seemed to be still seeking, even now.

With a sinking feeling, Miss Bingley wondered if he was looking for Eliza. In any case, she was pleased to see he did not seem to find her, although he diligently walked about the room, for the duration of the next two dances.

When another set began, Miss Bingley had to abandon her discreet surveillance, for Lord Leighton, more mindful than some vexing others of his duty to the sister of his hosts, came to ask for the pleasure of her hand for the following dances so, with a dainty shrug of her shoulders, Miss Bingley left Mr. Darcy to his own devices – for a while at least.

She would have been incensed to *know*, rather than merely suspect, that Darcy was indeed seeking Miss Elizabeth Bennet.

He had only seen her in passing at the beginning of the evening, when he had walked up to her party to greet them – to greet *her* – but, shortly after, the dances had begun, and Wentworth had asserted his prior claim to her hand for the first set.

He had returned then to his own party and asked Anne if she cared to dance – which was of course precisely what was expected of him.

The following half-hour had resembled a strange *melange* of Greek tragedy and Shakespearian play. The intricate figures of the dance required a frequent change of partners between adjacent couples, and malicious gods must have roared with laughter at the sight.

A passing glance at Wentworth's countenance clearly indicated that he was not appreciating the irony of the situation either as, every ten steps or so, he would have to relinquish Elizabeth's hand to receive Anne's and, a few moments later, exchange partners again.

A mocking, painful pattern. Elizabeth. Anne. Elizabeth. Anne. A heart-wrenching reminder of real pain. Of the wrong choice. Of loss.

Darcy's attention could scarce be fixed by Wentworth during the moments when the Captain partnered Anne – he was too engrossed by Elizabeth and everything about her. The touch of her gloved hand. Her shapely form. Her scent. The agonising pain of having to relinquish her to Wentworth every ten steps or so, and watch them walk away along the set together, without a backward glance.

Of course! What backward glance was he expecting? She did not understand! Did she? Did Anne? He could not tell, yet it was plain to see that the ladies were hardly at ease either, and the cheeks of both were blazing in deep shades of scarlet as they turned and walked back and forth between them.

Ten steps with Wentworth, in their intricate pattern. A pirouette. A bow. Ten steps with him, then walking down the line. Back towards Wentworth. Small ringlets at the back of Elizabeth's head, swaying and caressing her creamy neck as she walked away with the other. Oh, *damn him!* And damn all malicious gods, and their cruel sport! Damn them, one and all!

Blessed relief came at last, when the dances ended and, as though by common accord, the gentlemen escorted their partners to opposite sides of the room. In a short while, Anne had appeared to rally, and Leighton had joined them soon after and asked for her hand for the next set, soon to be followed by Bingley, then Montrose, Lady Wrotham's eldest.

For his part, Darcy had busied himself with scanning the crowds for Elizabeth again. He had caught a few brief glimpses of her, but before he could escape the irksome civilities of the number of people who waylaid him, she was no longer in sight. He had espied Wentworth though and had lost little time in approaching him to secure the much desired interview but, ever since the Captain left him, his search for Elizabeth had been as fruitless as ever.

"Darcy!" a familiar voice rang behind him and he turned to acknowledge his cousin – only to be met by Fitzwilliam's sombre stare.

Darcy sighed, dearly hoping that his cousin would have the good sense to see that there was a time and a place for everything and, if he had further complaints about his endeavours and his life in general, he *might* have the kindness to keep them for another day.

His cousin's countenance gave him reason to suspect that he was not about to, so Darcy thought it best to forestall him straight away.

"Can it not wait till the morrow, Cousin?" he tiredly asked.

"I should imagine not. Forewarned is forearmed, as they say, and I believe you ought to be informed of a certain conversation I have overheard."

"It sounds rather ominous," Darcy prompted, and Fitzwilliam humphed.

"Aye – it is that! The long and short of it, Cousin, is that I was exchanging pleasantries with Miss Bennet earlier, Miss *Elizabeth* Bennet that is, and with Captain Wentworth. At some point in the conversation, she casually asked me if Miss Elliot was another relation of ours – "

Darcy all but blanched.

"Pray tell me you have *not* let on more than you should have for the *second* time!" he all but hissed, and Fitzwilliam had the grace to look abashed before blustering, rather offended:

"What sort of a blundering fool do you take me for? Of course not! I merely said she is an acquaintance of my aunt's. *However*, as I was walking away, I overheard Wentworth quietly supplying rather more information… *'I was told she was betrothed to Mr. Darcy'*, I clearly heard him say."

Darcy's heart stopped, then began to hammer. *Of course* he did – devil take him and damn him to the depths of hell, where he belonged!

"You will excuse me, Cousin!" Darcy burst, turning on his heels, but Fitzwilliam hurried after him to lay a restraining hand on his sleeve.

"Do *not* rush into anything foolish!" he earnestly cautioned, but Darcy waved him and his anxiety aside.

"It is not *him* I need to see – not *now!* I know where I can find him!" he threw over his shoulder and was gone, leaving his cousin looking despondent and concerned.

This time he did not even try to be discreet about it, but walked around the room in unconcealed haste. She was not with her sister, nor was she with her aunt and uncle or her mother – and in a flash of inspiration Darcy headed for the large glazed doors that led to the terrace at the back of the Hursts' house.

A handful of people could be seen walking about, but Elizabeth was not amongst them, so he took the marble stairs two at a time, down towards the gardens.

The full moon shone brightly over the wide expanse of shrubs and gravelled walks, and lanterns were scattered here and there, artfully throwing spots of light in places.

Darcy struck upon the nearest path. Despite their carefully contrived beauty, the gardens had not lured the guests into their midst and he could find no one – until, some ten yards further, he heard Wentworth's unmistakable voice:

"You pierce my soul! I am half agony, half hope – "

Darcy froze – but, to his unmitigated shock, it was *Anne's* voice that answered:

"What hope do you speak of? I cannot offer hope! I should not be here, even! We *cannot* continue with these clandestine meetings – there is nothing more to say that was not said already! I have given him my word, and I *cannot* withdraw it! He is a good man, and he does not deserve it!"

"He does not love you! Anne, how can you not *see* that?"

"I *know* he does not love me! We have established that a long time ago! It was not a love match he had offered, and I knew it full well when I accepted his hand! I cannot join the ranks of those who have injured him! I owe him more than that!"

"You owe him *nothing!*" Wentworth forcefully retorted. "But be that as it may! What of yourself? Do you not owe yourself more than a marriage of convenience? Anne, I have wronged you, time and again, in every way! I have been unjust, weak, bitter and resentful! I should have sought you out when I returned to England, in the year eight, with a few thousand pounds to my name! But I was proud, too proud to ask again. I did not understand you. I shut my eyes, and would not understand you, or do you justice. Tell me not that I am too late, that those precious feelings are gone forever! I cannot bear to lose you, Anne! Not now – not again!"

"I must return to the house!" came the reply, in accents of the deepest anguish and, before Darcy could gather his wits about him and retreat from sight, the gravel crunched under hurried footsteps and Miss Anne Elliot burst straight into his path.

He could scarce see her features in the poor light, but her shock and extreme mortification were painfully obvious as she gasped:

"*Mr. Darcy!*"

He had no time to reassure her. Quick to follow, Wentworth was with them before she had even spoken, and rushed to her side, a hand on her arm.

"Perhaps it *would* be best if you returned to the house," he quietly observed. "Mr. Darcy can say his piece to *me*."

As though he had not spoken, Darcy turned to Anne.

"Do not distress yourself," he said with the greatest gentleness. "May I speak with you? It shall not be for long."

"Whatever you wish to say can be said to me," Wentworth repeated. "Either here or on Wimbledon Common, if you prefer," he added matter-of-factly.

"*Would* you desist from constantly bringing Wimbledon Common up?!" Darcy burst out with unconcealed vexation. "Anne?" he asked, offering his hand and, when she hesitantly took it, Wentworth made to speak, but he was forestalled. "Would you kindly give us a moment, Captain? You need not be concerned – and you need not go far."

At Anne's slight nod, Wentworth reluctantly withdrew and Darcy wondered if he was about to stoop to the same ungentlemanly conduct that he himself had inadvertently displayed, and remain well within earshot. The Captain was, however, the least of his concerns, and Darcy turned to speak quietly to the stricken young lady leaning on his arm.

"There is a bench just around the corner. Would you care to sit?"

But Anne shook her head.

"Mr. Darcy, I – "

"Pray, allow me!" Darcy interjected, and there was kindness in his voice, but also keen determination. "I must apologise for many transgressions. For my intrusion just now, and for distressing you, to begin with, though I must confess – "

"Mr. Darcy, I cannot allow *you* to apologise," Anne interrupted hotly, but Darcy pressed her arm.

"And yet I must! Anne, you do not know half of my dishonourable conduct. I cannot allow you to reproach yourself. Pray do not! For over a month I have been battling with the need to confide in you – confess, if you will – that I am finding it… extremely difficult to honour my promise, and beg you to release me. I would have done so the very day when you arrived in town, were it not for… an unforeseen circumstance," he amended at the last minute, not knowing whether Lady Russell had already disclosed her own role or not.

"You have spoken to my godmother, I assume," Anne offered in a voice that was still so stricken so as to fill him with the deepest contrition.

"I have. How did you know of that?"

"Captain Wentworth informed me of her conversation with him, before we left Thorngrove," she added, clearly uncomfortable with speaking to him of the other man. "I can only assume that she approached you as well."

"She did."

"And?"

"Her account made it well-nigh impossible for me to come and injure you further, much as I knew that withholding the truth from you would do greater harm over time."

"And the truth is…?" she gently prompted.

"The truth is that I should not marry you when I love another. It was unfair of me to even suggest it. Unfair, unkind and a gross misjudgement. Can you forgive me?"

To his surprise, all he could hear was Anne laughing softly in the darkness – and then she spoke, but her voice faltered, close to tears.

"We make a sorry pair, Mr. Darcy, with our misguided efforts to protect the other, when the full truth would have served us both a great deal better," she said gently and then, to his even greater surprise, her gloved hand lightly stroked his arm.

"I thank you," she whispered and, when he interrupted to say that *she* deserved his deepest, warmest thanks, rather than the other way around, she suddenly laughed again.

This time the sound was bright and joyful and, when at last she spoke, her voice held so much mirth and was so strikingly different from her usual subdued, almost placid tones that he positively stared – to no purpose, for he still could barely see her face.

"No, Mr. Darcy – I daresay another person deserves the warmest, deepest thanks, and we are all vastly indebted to my father and his request for a quiet engagement!"

The sudden sound of footsteps on the gravel suggested that Wentworth *did* stay well within earshot or, Darcy thought – suddenly filled with charitable feelings for the man he had detested for such a length of time – perhaps he wronged him now. Perhaps it had been the incongruous sound of genuine laughter that had drawn him thither, before he was called.

At his silent approach, Darcy released Anne's hand and bowed.

"I wish you all the happiness you deserve," he said warmly and nodded in wordless gratitude when she responded in kind.

And then he left to search every nook and cranny of the silent gardens, breathless with impatience and – at long last – vibrantly alive with hope.

Chapter 12

The best part of half an hour later, when it became exceedingly obvious that Elizabeth was *not* in the gardens, and there was nothing for him to do but return to the house, Darcy could see Wentworth and Anne reluctantly bowing to the same wisdom and walking up the marble steps, arm in arm. Yet they could not hold Darcy's interest for longer than a moment, and he acknowledged Wentworth's vastly warmer greeting and exchanged a smile with Anne, before swiftly making his way back to the crowded ballroom.

The first person he saw was his cousin, who rolled his eyes in obvious exasperation at the sight of him, then inclined his head with a telling nod towards the far end of the large, brightly lit chamber.

Darcy's own eyes darted in that direction and he walked thither, towards the partially secluded alcove where he could finally espy Elizabeth in conversation with her elder sister. Quite predictably, Bingley was not far and, as he approached, Darcy could hear him say:

"I daresay it is the crush, is it not, Miss Elizabeth? This room is a vast deal too crowded for one such as yourself, with your love for wide open spaces. Would you not walk to the parks with us, on the morrow? It will be refreshing, after an evening such as this! Perhaps we can take another stroll in Kensington Gardens…?"

"I thank you, but *not* Kensington Gardens!" Darcy heard Elizabeth reply promptly, with great determination, then suddenly she appeared to have noticed his approach and blushed profusely, casting her eyes down.

"Ah! Darcy!" Bingley greeted him with obvious pleasure. "Just the man! Can you suggest a more suitable place for a morning stroll? Kensington was, I fear, not to Miss Elizabeth's liking. What say you of St. James's, Miss Elizabeth? Or Green Park, perchance?"

"My apologies, Mr. Bingley," Elizabeth offered as she turned towards her future brother. "I did not wish to cast aspersions on any of those lovely gardens. I suspect, however, that we shall be much engaged on the morrow with preparations for our return to Longbourn. But," she added with a warmer smile, "I daresay I should speak for myself, and not my sister! Jane *might* be persuaded to sample the delights of a lengthy walk!"

Before either Miss Bennet or Bingley could make an answer to that, Darcy took another step closer and bowed.

"May I have the pleasure of your company for this dance, Miss Bennet?" he suddenly asked without preamble, and instantly cursed himself for the shocking abruptness and total lack of finesse.

A moment later though, all such inconsequential thoughts instantly left him for, to his distress, it was plain to see that she did not wish to meet his eyes for longer than the flicker of a second. And then she said with quiet firmness:

"I thank you, Sir, but I must decline. I find myself too fatigued to dance again tonight."

The newly-acquired charitable sentiments towards Wentworth vanished from Darcy's breast as though they never were, and he took a deep breath as he struggled to think of a better way to orchestrate a private moment with her. He could scarce gather his wits about him – and Bingley's constant chatter did not help.

"Miss Elizabeth was just complaining of a sudden headache and, as I said, 'tis no surprise, in this vast crush!"

"A headache?" Mrs. Bennet loudly interjected, at Darcy's right and, his own frustration notwithstanding, he turned to civilly acknowledge her with a bow. "Has your headache not abated, Lizzy? How vexing! You never get headaches – what a wretched business that you should get one now!"

"I must concur with my friend," Darcy spoke up again. "The noise and bustle can do no lasting good! May I escort you to the gardens, Miss Bennet, or to Mrs. Hurst's green room? You may be assured of some peace and quiet there…"

"Oh, it shall be of no use!" Mrs. Bennet intervened. "You have spent an age in the green room – have you not, Lizzy? – and it had no effect! To my way of thinking, we should ask my brother to escort you home. I am quite certain your uncle will not mind! I can join you as well, if you wish, and Mr. Bingley can see your aunt and Jane safely home – there is no reason to curtail *their* enjoyment, is there?"

"No reason at all, and I certainly do not wish it!" Elizabeth replied with great determination. "Pray, do not concern yourselves! I can – "

"May I suggest the green room again, Miss Bennet?" Darcy swiftly interjected, for fear she might see fit to comply with her mother's scheme and disappear from sight before he had the slightest chance to speak to her in private, at least for a moment. "Mrs. Hurst has amassed the most astounding specimens – I should imagine some of them must have escaped your notice!" he added, feeling *gauche* in the extreme and cursing himself once more for his ineptitude and maladroit excuses.

It appeared however that the purpose behind his ill-worded insistence was no longer escaping Mrs. Bennet's notice – for, without warning, the dreaded architect of unfavourable schemes suddenly turned into Mr. Darcy's greatest ally.

"But *of course!*" she brightly exclaimed. "How thoughtful of you, Sir! There must be some, indeed, and Lizzy has the greatest fondness for astounding specimens, have you not, my dearest girl? Go, go and have another look around Mrs. Hurst's green room, seeing as Mr. Darcy so warmly recommends it!"

"Do you, Mr. Darcy? How very gratifying to hear it!" a new voice – another! – was heard at his other elbow and it was with the greatest determination that Darcy suppressed an exasperated roll of his eyes at the most recent unwelcome interruption. "My sister has made the greatest effort in acquiring all manner of exotic plants, and will be delighted to hear they meet with the approval of a connoisseur! Would you care to walk with me, Sir, and point out your favourites? Louisa would be very pleased to know which particular ones have caught your eye!"

Miss Bingley smoothly availed herself of his arm and Darcy swallowed hard in insurmountable vexation, uncharitably wishing each and every one of his current companions – with a sole notable exception – to the other side of the South Seas or, failing that, at least at Timbuktu!

His vexation slid into acute concern at the sight of Elizabeth's countenance. There was little doubt that she was mortified in the extreme by the great fuss made over her – and especially over the excuse she had previously given, in her quest for solitude.

Darcy did not dare hope that it had been the news of his engagement to Anne that had distressed her – yet he was finding it increasingly difficult to dismiss the thought, much as the past had taught him to recoil from misplaced, arrogant confidence.

He was not confident now – he did not dare be – and her visible discomfort could not fail to force his own wishes aside. He would bear anything for her sake – and certainly he *could* bear another sleepless night of torment! Should she wish to walk away from this mortifying debacle, perhaps he would do well to let her do just that!

A small, unruly thought he had not quite succeeded in subduing relentlessly whispered that, if she had indeed been distressed by the news of his engagement, it would be a great deal better for *everyone* concerned, not just himself, to find the means to disabuse her of that notion, but in the midst of this infuriating crowd and with Miss Bingley firmly attached to his arm, he could scarce think of a way to do so. He drew another deep breath and, with a great deal of determination, yet another excuse was proffered – transparent and inadequate as it might have been.

"Perhaps the warmth of the green room makes it a poor choice," he said quietly, then turned towards Miss Bingley as he endeavoured to unobtrusively detach his arm. "I shall be delighted to point out my favourite hothouse varieties to Mrs. Hurst or yourself on my next visit, if it is convenient. Just now, I was about to suggest to Miss Elizabeth Bennet that the fresh air of the gardens might provide some measure of relief and help abate her headache."

"Oh, but of course," Miss Bingley smiled sweetly, clearly pleased by any scheme that would remove Miss Elizabeth from her presence. "Do have a stroll along our lovely paths, Miss Eliza, I daresay the moonlight and the lanterns do them justice!"

"I thank you all, but I would dearly wish you did not trouble yourselves any further on my account! *I am quite well!*" Elizabeth enunciated, having undoubtedly come too close for comfort to the limits of her patience.

Were it not for his manifold concerns, Darcy would have smiled at the belligerent glint in her eyes, which had replaced the subdued look of chagrin.

"What a relief to hear it!" came yet another voice, this time from behind him and, although unable to determine what new form of hindrance the latest arrival would supply, Darcy was at least glad of the opportunity to step aside from Miss Bingley under the guise of making room for Colonel Fitzwilliam into the circle. "Nevertheless, I *would* strongly recommend the gardens, Miss Bennet. They are a sight to be seen, and a credit to Mrs. Hurst's impeccable taste, I assure you. Would you allow me?" he advanced to offer his arm and, when Elizabeth resignedly gave in and took it, he offered the other one to Miss Bingley. "Do join us, Miss Bingley – let us all go!" he urged, leaving Darcy baffled as to what he was about, and half-suspecting that Fitzwilliam's mischievous devils may have had the better of him and enticed him into the fray, purely for sport.

With a reluctant bow, he offered his arm to Mrs. Bennet – to the lady's obvious astonishment – and fell into step with that matron, followed by Bingley, with Miss Bennet by his side.

To Darcy's own surprise, his present companion was uncommonly silent, and the expected tirade of much bustle and little sense did not come, leaving him perfectly able to unabashedly eavesdrop on his cousin's conversation.

He was voicing civil nothings to Miss Bingley regarding the excellence of the evening's arrangements, with Elizabeth painfully silent at his other side, and Darcy cursed the man's unmitigated folly in inviting Miss Bingley to join them on their stroll.

What in God's name was his cousin thinking? How could he be expected to have any meaningful conversation with Elizabeth within Miss Bingley's earshot – or Mrs. Bennet's, for that matter?

"Ah! And there is the valiant Captain Wentworth!" Fitzwilliam suddenly exclaimed, stopping so short along the line of dancers that Darcy and Mrs. Bennet all but stumbled into his back. "Did he mention, Miss Bennet, that he had distinguished himself in the Mauritius Campaign – so much so that his name was known even amongst the rest of us, His Grace of Wellington's landlubbers in the Peninsula?" he quipped, earning little more than a perfunctory smile. "I can only imagine that those naval exploits were rather more thought through than his actions on land," he shrugged. "I could not fathom, for instance, Miss Bennet, *why* would he go as far as suggesting that Miss Anne Elliot might be engaged to my cousin – particularly as he appears more than a little inclined to marry her himself!"

Mrs. Bennet must have missed the quiet remark, for she did not react in any way. Miss Bingley did though, and with such vigour that whatever Elizabeth might have said or done passed wholly unnoticed, under the other's pointed question.

"*Who* is engaged to Miss Anne Elliot, pray?"

"No one, I suspect – unless the good Captain found the opportunity to propose this evening," Fitzwilliam casually remarked.

Not surprisingly, Mrs. Bennet *did* react to that.

"Good Lord! Colonel, how can you tell such a story?" she exclaimed. "Do you not know that Captain Wentworth wants to marry Lizzy? And indeed, why would he not? Anyone would wish to marry my dear girl!" she added, smiling smugly and, with great forbearance, just about managed to avoid a telling glance towards the gentleman beside her.

Predictably, Miss Bingley sniffed. Less predictably though, Elizabeth said nothing, but looked the other way, suddenly taken with an exquisite rendition of Pomona, on the wall behind her. As for Darcy, his glance flew to his cousin, and the words escaped him before he could keep himself in check:

"*How* did you know of that?"

With a crooked smile that endeavoured to look slightly apologetic, the Colonel shrugged again.

"Anyone can be a little blind sometimes, Cousin, but I daresay only those afflicted with the severest blindness can fail to notice *that*," he indicated with a nod of his head towards the spot where Anne was dancing with Captain Wentworth, her clear, open countenance overspread with such a joyous glow so as to make her seem more beautiful than ever. "Which puts me in mind, my dear Miss Bingley! I hope you will oblige me with the favour of your hand for the remainder of this dance. Can I persuade you? Miss Bennet, would you kindly excuse us? My cousin here can escort you to the gardens –

can you not, Darcy? I thank you! Now, Miss Bingley, let us seize this perfect opportunity of dancing a reel!"

Despite her years at the best finishing school, as well as the many years' training in all the spoken and unspoken rules of polite society, Miss Bingley looked well-nigh horrified. She did not wish to dance just now – and certainly not a *reel*, of all the revolting notions – and, more to the point, she certainly did not wish to have Miss Eliza Bennet escorted to the gardens by Mr. Darcy!

However, she could not possibly allow herself to refuse to dance and effectively blast all her chances of standing up with Mr. Darcy later on that night – if he would only awaken to his duties to his hosts and ask her! There was still time, there were at least six dances left, *and* the supper dance! If there was any justice in the world, he might still be seated at her side for supper!

With a fixed smile frozen on her lips, Miss Bingley offered her gloved hand with all the quiet dignity of an exiled queen and allowed herself to be escorted towards the end of the set by the immoderately and – quite frankly – vexingly gleeful Colonel, who hastened her away, leaving behind a fairly stunned party.

Mrs. Bennet was the first to gather her wits about her.

"Forgive me, Mr. Darcy, I must seek my brother and his wife – but, by all means, pray make your way into the gardens! Jane, Mr. Bingley – I daresay you would much better dance! This reel is quite enticing, is it not? I must leave you now. Come – this way, Mr. Bingley, before the dances finish! There, now – I do not doubt you shall like them very well indeed!" she shepherded them away with swift determination, leaving Darcy to the most charitable feelings he had ever experienced for the vociferous matron as he escorted Elizabeth towards the large glazed doors and thence onto the now deserted terrace.

"Would you…?" he gestured in the direction of the descending steps but, after a brief glance at her guarded countenance, he hastily retracted. "Perhaps not. Miss Bennet, pray allow me to thank you for agreeing to walk this way with me," he began, more than a little uncomfortable with the notion that, in effect, she had *not* agreed – rather, she had been ambushed into it.

A sudden tilt of her chin and a flash in her eyes made him suspect she was about to tell him precisely that, yet she said nothing.

His lips thinned into an anxious line of discomfort, and Darcy turned to lean against the stone banister as he endeavoured to order his thoughts – and choose the best words.

No right words came, just a vexed mutter of *"Great Scot!"* as he chanced to glance back into the ballroom, only to espy Lady Russell walking with great determination towards them, the corners of her shawl fluttering belligerently behind her as she crossed the vast expanse of highly polished floor. There was not another moment to lose, before they were interrupted *yet again*, so he said swiftly:

"Miss Bennet, it appears there is little opportunity for a quiet conversation here, tonight! Would you allow me to call upon you on the morrow?"

She glanced up, her lovely lips forming the word *'Why?'* as through of their own volition. She did not say it though, and Darcy added:

"I must speak with you, wherever and whenever you may deem it convenient! If you find the prospect of Kensington Gardens unappealing," he continued, his mien clouding at all the reasons she might have had to shy away from that place, with all the recollections it entailed, "or if you do not care to accompany your sister and Mr. Bingley on their walk, may I call upon you at your uncle's house? Or perchance at Longbourn, if your departure from town is imminent?" he offered, dearly hoping it would not come to *that*. "Anytime – anywhere! It matters not, just name the place and I shall follow!" he pressed on, his eyes intent upon hers, willing her to understand.

The time that the malicious gods were prepared to allow had lapsed just then, and Lady Russell joined them on the terrace.

"Mr. Darcy! I beg leave to apologise for taking you away from your charming companion *yet again*," she sternly observed in a tone of voice that left Darcy in no misapprehension of her feelings at finding him, as she had put it, *yet again*, at Elizabeth's side rather than Anne's, "but I believe Anne and I should return to Curzon Street directly. Would you be so kind to escort us?"

Darcy clasped his hands behind his back.

"May I observe," he said quietly, choosing his words with care, so as not to offend her, "that I believe Miss Elliot is in no haste to go?"

"Which is precisely why we should!" the lady retorted sharply and with great determination.

"As to *that*, Ma'am, I fear that a discussion between yourself and Miss Elliot is decidedly in order. I believe Miss Elliot may have tidings to impart."

"Would that be pertaining to – ?"

"Precisely!" Darcy interjected and at that, Lady Russell's brows arched in exasperation.

"Mr. Darcy, it is *imperative* that I speak with you!"

The pointed request was impossible to ignore, so Darcy was not surprised – merely vexed beyond measure – to hear Elizabeth quietly offer:

"Would you excuse me? I should leave you now."

Lady Russell thanked her with a curt nod – sentiment which Darcy did not share. Past caring, he laid a hand on Elizabeth's elbow.

"Miss Bennet? I shall join you shortly – if you would allow it."

At her silent assent, he took heart and added:

"Before you leave, though, may I have your answer?"

The music from the ballroom, as well as Lady Russell's shocked intake of breath, faded from his hearing as he waited, eyes upon her lips, ears attuned to her and none other. And then at last, thankfully – mercifully! – the reply he prayed for finally came:

"Yes, Mr. Darcy. My relations and I would be happy to receive you in Gracechurch Street on the morrow," she quietly consented, and was gone.

The rest of the evening passed in a manner that could not be conducive to either calm or quiet satisfaction, to most parties.

Lady Russell was most seriously displeased. Not only did Mr. Darcy civilly but firmly refuse to enlighten her as to the night's developments and insisted that it was Anne's place to do so, but very soon left her on the terrace to rejoin his pretty companion.

As for dear Anne, she seemed determined to spend the evening at Captain Wentworth's side. Moreover, she stood up with him for more sets than she should have and, after the supper dance, they wandered off – together, and far away from *her* – to sit and sup at a very distant table!

The supper dance and supper itself, for that matter, was a source of profound vexation to Miss Bingley as well.

Not only did Mr. Darcy fail to solicit her hand for it, but did not ask her to stand up with him *at all* – and then proceeded to escort none other than *Miss Eliza* in for supper!

He did not dance for the remainder of the evening, but persevered at *her* side, in quiet conversation with Charles – foolish, lovesick Charles – and his future relations. He did not look at ease – of course he would not, they were *in trade*, for goodness sake! – yet he never left them, other than for a short while during the last dances, to converse briefly with Miss Elliot and the dashing Captain.

A passing glance in their direction persuaded Miss Bingley that Mr. Darcy's vexing cousin might have been in the right, on more than one count. The Captain *did* seem taken with Miss Elliot and, just as Colonel Fitzwilliam had put it, it made little sense for him to suggest she might have wished to accept another. Miss Bingley could not fail to wonder *which* particular one of the Colonel's cousins were supposed to have been attached to her but, in truth, it did not hold her interest – as long as it was not Mr. Darcy.

As to the gentleman himself, Miss Bingley could not read his thoughts – but then, she never could. Nor could she ascertain that his visible discomfort was not with the present company – or at least, not for the reasons she suspected – but with the long hours till the morrow, when his fate would be decided.

All she could see was that, when the guests began to disperse, he left with the party he had escorted thither – as of course he should – but, to her own good fortune and temporary peace of mind, Miss Bingley failed to notice either the turn of his countenance or the look in his eyes as he bid good night to Miss Elizabeth Bennet.

Chapter 13

"Mr. Darcy! How good of you to call!" Mrs. Bennet warmly welcomed Mrs. Gardiner's guest into Mrs. Gardiner parlour, when the gentleman in question was announced, a mere half-hour after they had finished breakfast.

On this occasion, a smile of smug satisfaction *did* flutter on Mrs. Bennet's lips, albeit fleetingly, at the notion of him calling at such an early hour. Keenness was such a desirable quality in a gentleman – particularly when it pertained to one of her own daughters!

"Would you care for tea, Sir?" Mrs. Bennet offered before Mrs. Gardiner could open her lips to suggest the same.

The gentleman civilly assented and bowed to both before taking the seat his host had indicated – only to stand promptly, eyes darting to the door with poorly concealed anticipation when he heard it open. It was the eldest Miss Bennet though, and he bowed deeply to her, endeavouring to conceal his disappointment.

"My other daughter is in the garden, Sir," Mrs. Bennet obligingly supplied, then proceeded to endear herself to Darcy to an extent the gentleman had never suspected, as she offered the most transparent of suggestions: "If you would care to greet her as well, while refreshment is prepared, then perhaps Jane could escort you – but hurry back, dear girl, for I have a mind to speak to you of a matter of great import!"

Her daughter blushed at the conspicuous excuse and her sister by marriage delicately raised a brow, but none could bring themselves to protest – and as for Darcy, no thought was furthest from his mind.

Had he been able to consider anything other than the impending moment, with all its nerve-racking implications, he would have readily understood at last exactly *why* Bingley could never find it in him to object to his future mother-in-law's ways, mortifyingly obvious as they were.

The shocking lack of subtlety in Mrs. Bennet's machinations could hardly register with him though, much less hold his thoughts as Darcy followed the lady's eldest daughter to the adjoining drawing room.

Miss Bennet's civil comments well-nigh passed unheeded as they walked towards the door that led into the gardens but, miraculously reawakening to his duties, Darcy attempted to make the right response – rather than merely look over Miss Bennet's shoulder, in earnest endeavour to spot her sister a few moments sooner.

He saw her at last, at the furthest end, sitting with her book on a bench shaded by a riot of jasmine in full bloom and he could scarce hear Miss Bennet's quiet remarks about the pleasant ball they had the previous night, as they crossed the small patch of lawn bordered with brightly coloured flowers. He saw Elizabeth look up at the sound of her sister's voice, then blush and stand, when she had espied *him*.

They were beside her in a trice – he must have walked faster, without notice – and he bowed deeply to her curtsy and quiet words of greeting.

"I hope Miss Darcy is recovered, after the late night," he heard her civilly offer a few moments later, her cheeks still of the most appealing rosy hue.

Her beautiful eyes, however, were no longer avoiding his. They were bright and welcoming, holding a warm glow of joyful reunion, and his best hopes soared. He stood in silence, drinking in the mesmerising sight – until suddenly he remembered that he ought to answer.

"She is, I thank you – as I trust are you. You look very well this morning," he added without thinking, and again he saw her blush as she regained her seat, but the smile that fluttered on her lips gave him hope that this time it was with pleasure rather than mortification.

She looked up again, though not to him, but to someone behind him, and Darcy turned to see a young maid advance. She bobbed a swift curtsy when she gained their notice, then walked up to them and stopped before Miss Bennet.

"You are wanted in the house, Ma'am. Mrs. Bennet sent me to remind you she has a pressing matter to discuss," she quietly supplied and left them, and Jane was quick to follow, with an arched brow and a telling glance towards her sister.

And suddenly they were left alone.

Gone were the days when he would have inwardly cringed and censured Mrs. Bennet for her tactlessness, or rather shameless scheming. This time he barely noticed, and he was merely grateful for the privacy she had orchestrated – until the enormity of the task at hand pushed all else to the furthest reaches of his mind.

The notion that everything hung on his ability to say exactly the right words in the forthcoming minutes was nothing short of terrifying, and Darcy took a deep, steadying breath.

It did not help – quite the reverse, in fact. For some unfathomable reason, his mind went blank just then. Completely blank.

Darcy clasped his hands behind his back and swallowed, struggling with the sudden, intense panic. It was a losing battle, and the notion that it was a battle he could not afford to lose did nothing to subdue the crippling anxiety. He drew breath again, slowly, deliberately – then tugged at the front of his coat and needlessly coughed twice.

From her bench, Elizabeth looked up.

"Would you not sit, Sir?" she invited, with both word and gesture, her tones kindly, and it was only her gentleness of address that brought him a modicum of comfort.

'Tongue-tied fool!' Darcy all but muttered. He caught himself in time though and cleared his voice instead, as he nervously brought himself to take the seat she offered.

The sweet scent of jasmine drifted around them in the clear morning air and he sighed, willing his scattered thoughts into some sort of sense, or at least of order. He failed – again – and words perversely continued to fail him also.

All the painstakingly chosen words that he had put together the previous night were gone, forgotten. Just half a sentence here and there sprang to mind, and was instantly discarded, for it made no sense, without the rest.

To beg forgiveness was decidedly the wrong place to start – reviving the abhorrent picture he had once presented to the world, to *her*, was not likely to improve his chances, yet virtually all of his past actions demanded a full and prompt apology, and *that* could hardly be ignored!

To ask if she would ever be prevailed upon to reconsider her original refusal was stark and intolerably blunt! Only a wretched fool would blurt it out, without preamble – and panic welled in him again as all his carefully coined phases still refused to uncoil themselves out of the hazy recesses of his mind.

And above all, it most assuredly would *not* help to allow himself to be distracted by the sight before him. The most enticing sight.

A round cheek, smooth and flawless, a rosy tint creeping upon it, under his very eyes. Auburn hair dressed in a simple yet ever so becoming style, casting glints of copper in the sunshine. Small ringlets round the temple, and a few others framing the most adorably shaped ear. A vein pulsating just behind the corner of her jaw, and another at the temple – a faint blueish line, snaking under the creamy skin towards her eyebrow. The corner of her eye, nothing more than a corner visible from his angle – until suddenly she turned to him, and caught him staring yet again.

She smiled, distracting him anew with a fleeting dimple, the smile reaching her eyes, crinkling their corners, and there was kindness in them, surely he was not mistaken! Kindness and gentle encouragement… was there not?

With another deep breath, Darcy plunged into deep waters.

"I thank you for agreeing to receive me," he began and, with heedless daring, reached out and took her hand. "Elizabeth – Miss Bennet – I had to speak to you," he faltered, words failing him again at the warm glow in her eyes, as well as the simple fact that she had not withdrawn her hand, but lightly curled her fingers around his instead.

"Aye. So you said, last night," she whispered and – *by Jove!* – pressed his hand in silent reassurance. "What did you wish to speak of?" she brought herself to ask, with visible disquiet.

"You," Darcy suddenly blurted out, and recklessly pressed on, before he lost his nerve. "You are always in my heart – have long been… You will always be! Yet, fool that I was, I have failed *dismally* to show it! Elizabeth," he whispered with great urgency, and this time he did not correct himself – indeed, he did not even notice – "there is no joy for me in a life without you, and I have found none, because you have no equal! Would you allow me now to say as much? Would you allow me now to say what I should have said the first time? Can you ever forgive my folly and presumption, and permit me to try to win your heart?"

Under his very eyes, her own filled with tears and his heart suddenly felt as though gripped in a tight fist.

Tight and cold. Cold as ice.

With a dreadful sinking feeling, Darcy leaned away and released her hand.

"I must beg your pardon," he said with great difficulty. "If your feelings are still what they were last April – "

He did not get to finish, as the turn of her countenance robbed him of breath and sent his heart racing. He did not dare hope – yet, surely, if she was determined to refuse him, she would appear sombre, would she not? Her perfect lips would not be curling at the corners, nor would her eyes meet his so willingly, so fully – and would not be brightened by this astounding light that looked so much like love!

Darcy's breath caught again and his fingers curled together, without deliberate intent, around the edges of the wooden bench. Would she not answer? *Why* would she not answer?

His head grew lighter, and it came to him that he had stopped breathing altogether. He filled his lungs and swallowed, vainly fighting for the smallest measure of patience and control. And at last the answer came – and all composure vanished.

"They are not," Darcy heard her whisper and strained to listen, as she resumed, then faltered: "My feelings are… Mr. Darcy, my feelings are so materially altered – have been, for some time – that your assurances… your avowals… are received with gratitude and pleasure… and your willingness to renew your offer is felt as a compliment of the highest kind…"

The dull weight that had oppressed his chest for such a length of time, to the point of becoming part of his very being, suddenly turned into airy nothing – to be replaced by the wildest, most explosive joy.

He could scarce think and, to his utmost shock, words came in a rush now, easier than breathing. An unstoppable rush. And despite his earnest and doggedly persistent endeavour in days, in years to come, Darcy could never be quite certain *what* exactly he had said on the occasion – or indeed whether he had made any sense at all.

Her hand was in his again – had she placed it there? – and he linked his fingers with hers, as he brought them to his lips. And more words came, all woefully inadequate to express the greatest happiness he had felt in his entire life.

She did not speak – she would not look up even, her eyes so downcast that they appeared closed. Yet, somehow, it was easier thus to bare his soul to her; to disclose feelings which might make her see to what extent she had come to rule his heart.

And then she *did* look up, and he fell silent, drawn again into the depths specked with molten amber – and often, in the days that followed, he would be left to wonder, mystified, just *how* had he kept his wits together for long enough to see that leaning forward and yielding to the sweet temptation of her lips would have been, at that point at least, most certainly unwise!

Little as he had known it at the time, it *had* been the right choice, for their privacy was a mere illusion. Ever since Darcy had been escorted to her second daughter, Mrs. Bennet had taken up her post at one of the tall windows that overlooked the garden – and if the curtains did not twitch, it was only due to her mastery of the art.

She frowned more than once, her lips pursed in acute vexation, at the utter lack of encouragement their visitor was receiving for his troubles. Lizzy, headstrong Lizzy! Surely she was not determined to persist in her pointed dislike of the man! Ten thousand a year! The mere though well-nigh made her swoon!

Oh! They were holding hands now? A good sign, surely! It *must* be a good sign!

The parlour door opened noisily behind her and Mrs. Bennet jumped as the troop of little Gardiners burst into the quiet room, their governess following close behind.

"Mamma! Mamma!" the youngest, Emily, piped up. "Miss Harding said we can go into the garden now! Will you come with us and watch me throw the quoits? I am much better at it – yesterday I only missed twice!"

"Now, children – " Mrs. Gardiner began, but her sister by marriage had already taken charge of the situation.

"The garden? Nay, nay, there is no cause for *that!*" she exclaimed with great determination, then cast about her and finally turned a triumphant glance upon her nieces and nephews. "What say you of a game of cup-and-ball instead? Come, let us see who gets the most of twenty! Emily, you first! Aye, hold it just so, then flick the ball into the cup! Oh! Did you hurt yourself? No? I am glad to hear it! You wish to try again? Oh, what a shame! Perchance with more practice you can learn to catch it! Harry! Oh! Three times – what a steady hand, young man, very well done! How about you, Arthur? No? You cannot be persuaded? Let your sister try, then! Come, Mary! Eight? Oh, very good! Very good indeed! Come, Arthur, do you not wish to see if you can do better? Or Edward? Will you have a turn? You think I should? Oh, very well, then! Seventeen, eighteen, nineteen and… *twenty!* And, thus, my dears, is how the deed is done!" Mrs. Bennet concluded with smug satisfaction as, at the far end of the garden, it was plain to see that Mr. Darcy was kissing dearest Lizzy's hand!

"Darcy! Good to see you here!" an unmistakable voice called, rather loudly, and at the intrusion the gentleman in question thought it best to release his fair companion's hand.

Nevertheless, he was not quick enough, judging by the undisguised delight in Mr. Bingley's countenance, and the warmth with which he belatedly greeted Elizabeth showed beyond a doubt that he was making some fairly accurate assumptions regarding their present situation.

"Would you care to return to the house for some refreshment?" Jane quietly interjected, in her turn.

Much as nearly everyone concerned wished otherwise, the privacy on the bench sheltered by fragrant jasmine could not be allowed to endure indefinitely.

Thus, after Mr. Bingley's arrival, Mrs. Bennet had reluctantly instructed her eldest daughter to walk to the gardens and summon the others in for tea. Eagerly escorted by her betrothed, Miss Bennet came to do as bid – and yet the glance directed at her sister gave clear indication that she would have liked to ask a very different question.

The widest smile graced her gentle visage at Elizabeth's swift and bright-eyed nod that seemed to answer the unspoken question rather than the other, and the pair linked arms and made their way across the lawn together, a quick whisper and a warm exchange of glances attempting to make up for the fact that a full disclosure would simply *have* to wait.

For his part, Mr. Bingley had no taste for patience! Thus, it came as no surprise that he took the nearest opportunity to hold his friend back and eagerly ask something. Mr. Darcy's reply was brief and very quiet – whereupon Bingley burst out loudly and with fervour:

"*You are?* At last! Thank goodness! Oh, I am *jolly* glad!"

The ladies could scarce feign either disinterest or selective deafness and turned around at that, in time to see Mr. Bingley warmly clasping his friend's shoulder. Elizabeth's eyes filled with joyful laughter, which bubbled on her lips a moment later, at the unlikely yet ever so endearing mix of profound delight and undeniable vexation in Mr. Darcy's countenance.

Their happy tidings could not be shared with all and sundry yet; ought not be openly shared with their relations, even, until Mr. Bennet's consent was sought and – hopefully! – granted.

Yet somehow Mr. Bingley's affectionate concern made small work of niceties and conventions, and the four regrouped for a few brief moments to shake hands and rejoice in their future close connection, before returning to the house with the cheerfully conspicuous air of co-conspirators in a secret known, or at least guessed, by nearly everybody.

Much as Mr. Bingley's expressive countenance rather gave the game away, his presence was also of invaluable assistance for, shielded by his readiness for conversation, the unacknowledged lovers could remain undisturbed in blissful silence. Darcy was not of a disposition in which happiness overflows in mirth and Elizabeth, agitated and confused, rather *knew* that she was happy, than *felt* herself to be so.

As they partook of their refreshment, Mr. Bingley proceeded to endear himself even further to his companions with a suggestion of a lengthy walk. He did not dare mention Kensington again, after Elizabeth's flat refusal to consider it, the previous evening – but she made a point of withdrawing all objections and so, less than an hour later, it was precisely *there* that the party determined they would go.

A small party of four it was set to be for, unsurprisingly, Mrs. Bennet declared she was too fatigued to walk, after the late night and the ball's exertions. As for Mrs. Gardiner, she smilingly informed them that, much to her regret, she could not be spared from her maternal duties. The Gardiner landaulette was gladly put at her nieces' disposal however, ready to take them on their outing, with the two gentlemen as riding escort.

During those times when the busy road compelled the gentlemen to ride behind the carriage, rather than each on either side, the journey to West End gave the sisters ample opportunity for hushed and delighted confidences.

At such times, Mr. Bingley might have been inclined to seek some answers of his own, had he not seen that his companion was too far above the clouds for conversation. With a knowing glance, he left him to his own devices and rode on, inwardly delighted to see his best friend frequently smiling to himself for no apparent reason, so clearly distracted that he might have ridden past Bonaparte himself, and still failed to notice!

Mr. Bingley made no effort to suppress a grin and shook his head in wonder. Seemingly, love was apt to make playthings of stronger and much wiser men than he!

Unlike the other time, Kensington Gardens were not bathed in sunshine that morning, but none of the happy four were disposed to complain. The Gardiner conveyance was left to await them at the gates, along with the coachman and the gentlemen's horses and they soon drifted away, to wander in pairs along the paths, sparing no thought to their direction. There was too much to be thought, and felt, and said, for attention to be drawn to their surroundings.

As they walked on, lagging far behind Jane and Mr. Bingley, the newly engaged couple spoke of everything that came to mind – retrospections and mortifications, dreadful errors and good principles badly put in practice.

"Such I was, from eight to eight and twenty; and such I might still have been but for you, dearest, loveliest Elizabeth! What do I not owe you! And your kindness in still hearing me out, despite my appalling conduct – "

A rueful chuckle interrupted his earnest declaration and, affectionately pressing his arm, Elizabeth shook her head.

"Nay, nay, I cannot in good conscience allow you to give me any credit for it! I have point-blank *refused* to hear you at first, if memory serves – though I daresay my foolish obstinacy was not the only nuisance thrust upon you, yesterday evening," she added, finally able to find humour in the chain of vexing interruptions that kept occurring on the night of the Hursts' ball. "Indeed, it was as though an entire army of spiteful little creatures led by Puck himself had conspired to delay our better understanding!" she laughed again, and this time Darcy joined her, delighted beyond words to see her spirits raising to playfulness once more.

For many months, she had been altered beyond recognition. Heavy silence had replaced the witty repartee, and arch looks had given way to downcast eyes and fierce blushes. A painfully unnatural transformation that had filled him with dismay and longing, particularly as he had thought himself responsible for it – one way or the other! And now the woman he adored was returned to him again; had promised herself to him that very morning – and there was more happiness in that single thought than most men were allotted in a lifetime!

"As we have previously determined," Elizabeth resumed, her voice still light with laughter, "it falls on me to teaze you as often as may be – and I shall begin at once, by asking what made you so unwilling to come to the point at last. I should have imagined you would disclose your feelings on the Mount. A much better setting, in every way – do you not think? – than Mrs. Hurst's green room, her terrace, or my uncle's garden!"

Darcy bit his lip, then swallowed – and, taking a deep breath, he jumped head on into what *had* to be done, with fearful, yet strong determination.

"You must have seen how much I wished to! Yet I could not. I was not free to do so. At the time, I was…" he faltered, then took the plunge at last. "At the time, I was engaged to Miss Anne Elliot."

"You were –… *I beg your pardon?*"

Her shock was unmistakable, and Darcy sighed.

"Elizabeth," he offered quietly, "Captain Wentworth was in the right, though of course he only knew half the story – if that. It was… I can scarce explain the enormity of my misjudgement, other than by saying that it had happened at a time when I was past caring or, at least, past sound reason. After April…" he whispered, and stopped as her other hand came to rest upon his sleeve, then drifted slowly, in a gentle, light caress.

He glanced at her and smiled, soothed beyond words by her affectionate offer of comfort, and then resumed again:

"After April, when I knew full well that what I wished for would not come to pass, I was resigned to make a match that would at least benefit Georgiana. She had befriended Miss Anne Elliot over the intervening months, and Miss Anne had been uncommonly kind to her – had helped her greatly to overcome her shyness and the lasting effects of the… ghosts of the past. As for Miss Anne herself, she seemed in need of a better home, and more appreciation than her nearest relations were prepared to give her. I was… willing to offer that, in exchange for her friendship, and as thanks for her unremitting kindness to my sister… and to me. You see, she knew that I did not love her, although of course I had not disclosed any of the details. And she herself had been willing to inform me that her heart was otherwise engaged – by Captain Wentworth, as it eventually transpired, some weeks later. But at that time, we were both prepared to make a match of mutual understanding and support, rather than affection. It was, of course, a gross misjudgement on our part – mine more than hers," he chivalrously added, although perhaps it was not strictly true. "To our great fortune," he eventually resumed, "her father had insisted on a long, quiet engagement, to give her elder sister a chance to marry first. We did not dispute it – neither cared enough to do so – and the only one who fought the scheme in earnest was Lady Russell, Miss Anne's godmother, who was determined she should make a better match than the one Captain Wentworth had once offered, several years ago. At Lady Russell's persuasion, Anne had refused him then, and had regretted it ever since. And then they were reunited, when Admiral Croft, by some odd twist of fate, had happened to lease Miss Anne's family home, of all places. As to the twists of fate," he laughed, rather harshly, "you can perhaps imagine how I felt, when it became apparent that Captain Wentworth was courting *you*. How it had tortured me, to think of you belonging with another!"

Her hand pressed his arm again, for longer this time, and a warm glance encouraged him to continue – which he did, with another laugh, much brighter this time. In effect, it held a small measure of wicked satisfaction.

"It was, of course, through no fault of the good Captain – though I daresay he later had a taste of the same bitter medicine, when he learned that the lady he still loved had promised herself to *me*. It was Lady Russell who had informed him of it, no doubt with the intention of warding him off. *Why* would he mention it to *you* though, I cannot begin to fathom. He had some suspicion of my feelings for you long before – they had emerged, too obvious for concealment, around the time of the… events in Brighton. I can only assume he was endeavouring to protect Miss Anne's interests, whom he believed attached to me in earnest – or he was merely determined to extract some strange form of revenge, purely out of jealousy and frustration, when it became apparent that, through a mistaken sense of duty, Miss Anne would not relinquish me. In any case," he added with a long sigh of relief, "this convoluted tangle of misunderstandings came to a head on the evening of the ball. Miss Anne and I found the opportunity to talk, and finally disclose our real sentiments and wishes. From then on, it was the work of a moment to relinquish all claims on each other, without reservations. It was very fortunate indeed that the engagement was never made public – and it would have been of course preferable if Fitzwilliam had not been compelled to refer to it in Miss Bingley's presence, but I cannot fault him for it!" Darcy added, with the warmest smile. "In effect, I owe him a vast debt of gratitude for his unorthodox assistance!"

"When you *do* thank him, pray convey my gratitude as well," Elizabeth smiled in her turn. "I was too overcome at the time to do him justice!"

Darcy winced at that, and his countenance turned deeply remorseful.

"I have a great deal to answer for, Elizabeth, and it weighs heavily on me. There is so much pain I have caused – so much to beg forgiveness for! Before April *and* after."

"Pray do not speak of forgiveness – or if you do, you must allow me to ask for yours, for having so readily believed all aspersions cast upon your character, and for abusing you so dreadfully, so abominably – "

"What did you say of me, that I did not deserve? For, though your accusations were ill-founded, formed on mistaken premises, my conduct throughout – and on *one* occasion in particular – was unpardonable. I cannot think of it without abhorrence! I cannot change that, much as I would wish to, nor can I dispense with the wretched time that followed. I can only thank you for entrusting me with your hand and your heart – and for allowing me to cherish you, for as long as I live!"

"And I can say the same… " she said softly, her gaze suddenly filled with such boundless love so as to root him to the spot, overcome anew with his amazing, undeserved good fortune.

"Elizabeth… he whispered, his eyes intent on hers.

The whole world – *his* whole world – seemed encompassed in their depths and he stood, falling deeper and deeper still as they drew closer without notice – and yet with unspoken common accord.

Her hand slipped from the crook of his arm as they turned to face each other, and Darcy reached to hold it, palm on palm, fingers interlacing.

He *hated* gloves, he instantly decided. Hated *all* gloves – there was no doubt about it! His, hers – perverse, frustrating barrier between them!

He found her other hand, and his hold tightened. His thumbs moved up, to rest upon her wrists, then slowly stroke them, in light, caressing motions.

Faint brushing of his thumbs against gloved wrists, in circles; slow, tantalising circles. Faint brushing of his thumbs against the exposed skin above her gloves…

He heard her draw breath sharply at the touch and swallowed hard, his movements frozen for the briefest moment, before his fingers tightened around hers again.

Their eyes did not waver. They would barely blink as they stood there, perfectly still, their clasped hands the only points of contact. And then he released his grip on her fingers, and his hands slid up along her arms, thumbs kneading in small, caressing circles until, without warning, the amber-specked depths were fringed with long, dark lashes, and she sighed. A small, barely perceptible sound, half shy consent and half anticipation – and he could hold himself in check no longer. He could not keep his distance any more than he could have stemmed the tide and, slowly, irreversibly, his head bent lower, until his lips found hers.

The lightest kiss, the briefest touch – or, at least, that was how he had intended it at first, before delicious softness and the enticing flavour of all dreams fulfilled made small work of his best intentions. And all dreams faded, surpassed and muted by a reality so wonderful, so perfect – and so much sweeter than any tortured dream.

His hands slipped to her shoulders and then across her back and his kiss grew deeper. Impatient. Insistent. Claiming without restraint what he had craved for, through endless months of anguish. In his arms at last! His. Forever. Tender, pliant, warm. Soft lips yielding to his, their exquisite flavour sending his desire spiralling wildly into depths that he had not imagined; into a whirl that he could scarce control.

A sense of *déjà vu*, hazy and confusing, seeped gradually through his scattered senses, too vague for recognition – he could not concentrate on *that*, as wave after wave of overpowering sensations held him in their thrall.

And then it came to him, the reason for the puzzling *déjà vu*.

The dream. The all-too-vivid dream, that distant night, on the way to Brighton.

The same – yet somehow not. The molten fire that he had imagined was but a pale reflection of the blaze that consumed him now – but it was not his own response that clamoured for immediate attention. It was hers.

In his tormenting dream, the tantalising figment of his imagination had clasped him to her with unbridled passion. Had tangled her fingers in his hair and brought him closer, consumed as much as he by the same yearning.

Reality was different – conspicuously so. She was in his arms, eagerly responding to his kisses, yet her shy acceptance, tentative and unpractised, was a sobering reminder of her innocence – and somewhere, beyond the sound of his own racing heart thundering in his ears and drowning out every form of reason, a small and very vexing voice rang out, stern and persistent, warning him against frightening her with his untoward ardour.

That she loved him, there was no longer any doubt – little as he had ever done to deserve it! And yet love blossoming into desire was not something that life had taught her yet – and the unwelcome voice declared in no uncertain terms that the time of their first kiss was *not* the time to start!

The ignored voice grew louder with every passing second – louder and increasingly more irate – until at last he grudgingly obeyed and drew back with unspeakable reluctance, his senses swimming, his breath ragged. He did not release her from his arms though, but pressed his lips against her cheek instead, lightly this time, as he fought to temper his ungovernable wishes and his need, his mounting, almost terrifying need of her.

"Elizabeth… " he murmured against her skin, softer than velvet blossoms and fragrant, more fragrant than he ever had imagined, and his need rose sharper, fierce and compelling – and this time he forced his arms to drop down to his side before he crushed her to his chest; before he got carried away beyond the pale, into the realms of wholly intolerable conduct.

"Forgive me…" Darcy whispered softly, penitently, linking his fingers with her gloved ones once again, willing her to excuse the inexcusable.

She smiled faintly with a soft murmur of *'There's nothing to forgive'*, her eyes still closed – until suddenly they opened, fastening themselves to his, glowing, verily glowing with unacknowledged passion, sending his blood rushing and his unruly senses ragingly aflame.

"We should find the others," he whispered hoarsely and passed his other hand over his face, struggling wildly for the last shredded vestiges of self-control.

"Oh, without a doubt!" she readily concurred, making him search her countenance in panic for signs of regret or, worse still, reproach.

Mercifully, he found none and, to his incommensurable relief, she suddenly laughed – a breathless little sound – as she took the arm he offered and they resumed their amble, wild emotions under some measure of tenuous control.

"Would you not share the source of your amusement?" Darcy tentatively asked after a while, only to see her blush and shake her head, leaving him disconcertingly in the dark as to the substance of her thoughts, just as he had been so many times before then.

At least, judging by the turn of her rosy countenance and the smile on her lips, her thoughts were not unpleasant and, reassured by that, he did not press the point.

They walked in silence till they reached the water, at the very spot where the Queen's Temple stood, reflecting its straight, unadorned lines into the smooth surface. Nor far from there, just above the treetops, to their left, the summerhouse could just about be glimpsed atop the Mount, towering over the surrounding landscape.

Their wide path ended in a knot, where several avenues were joined together, and on the one leading to the Mount, they could espy the others. The happy pair they were – or at least, they knew they *should* be seeking.

"Would you like to walk up to the summerhouse again?" he quietly asked, and a sharp shock of desire coursed through him again as he caught her glance, the warmth in her eyes already giving an unspoken answer.

And then she spoke, only to wreak further havoc through his senses.

"Very much! There is no other spot where I would rather be, just now," Elizabeth owned with a very private smile, and breath caught in his chest at her declaration.

The first thought was unsurpassed delight. The second – unsurpassed vexation, at the thought of having Bingley and Miss Bennet as unintentional chaperones as they returned to the poignant spot and climbed back up the path sheltered by rhododendrons.

Recollections of that heart-rending day flooded through him – the near-embrace, the near-kiss – stirring a compelling wish to return there *now*, this very moment, unencumbered by former obligations, to erase the memory of abject hopelessness and replace it with one of perfect joy.

It will not come to pass. Not today. Not with Bingley and Miss Bennet present. Yet, despite the sudden stab of disappointment, it occurred to him that perhaps it was just as well. They *would* return. Someday. But now, given the past half-hour, for his own enduring sanity, perhaps he should be *very* glad of chaperones!

A fleeting smile fluttered on his lips, and this time it was Elizabeth's turn to ask – and not be told – what was it that amused him.

"Oh, idle thoughts!" he shrugged, then turned towards her. "Elizabeth? Would you allow me to speak to your father as soon as may be?"

Chapter 14

"You are to leave for Longbourn *on the morrow?*" Georgiana asked in disbelief.

'Why would you, though?'

The query, clearly visible in her expressive eyes, remained nevertheless unuttered, for Georgiana had never been in the habit of questioning the motives of a brother she regarded almost as a father.

"I am! My dearest girl," Darcy offered gently, coming to sit beside her on the sofa and taking her hand, "there is something you need to know."

He took a deep breath and his lips curled into a smile that made his younger sister stare, for she had never seen the likes of it before. Not in her brother's countenance – her temperate, solemn elder brother.

"This morning I have asked Miss Elizabeth Bennet to marry me, and she has accepted. I leave for Longbourn at first light, to ask for her father's consent."

Despite his own burning impatience to settle the matter, he had in effect considered postponing the journey into Hertfordshire until Elizabeth, her sister and their mother were ready to depart from town themselves but, during their stroll, Elizabeth had smilingly observed that he ought not wait that long.

She did not doubt that their own journey will surely be postponed, as recent events would rekindle her mother's interest in wedding clothes and warehouses.

From her seat, Georgiana all but gaped.

"But… what of Anne?" she whispered in something very much like horror.

"Miss Elliot has had a change of heart. She is to marry Captain Wentworth."

The words were ill-chosen, he determined. It had not been a change of heart – quite the reverse, in fact, but there was no reason for Georgiana to learn all the details, and particularly the rather mortifying one that the people she held in such regard – her best friend and her brother – had been prepared to marry without the right sort of affection.

"But… was not the Captain supposed to marry Miss Elizabeth?"

"He might have wished to, until he understood that she was in effect attached to *me* – and I to her."

Brows arched in a delightful picture of confusion, Georgiana said nothing. With some measure of nervous impatience, Darcy prompted:

"Will you be pleased to have her as your sister?"

"I would have preferred Anne!" Georgiana burst out without thinking – but then anxiously clasped his hand. "Forgive me, Brother!" she urged, full of remorse. "Of course I shall welcome any lady of your choice, and I am convinced Miss Elizabeth is in every way delightful, although at times quite painfully shy!"

Her brother laughed immoderately at that.

"Dearest," he felt he should explain, a moment later, "you have made her acquaintance at a time of disquiet and confusion. At a time when Miss Elizabeth was far from her usual self. *'Painfully shy'* is certainly *not* how I would describe her – but I daresay you shall see that for yourself."

Georgiana nervously toyed with his fingers.

"Are you quite certain that Anne is no longer attached to you?" she whispered, loyalty for her long-standing friend urging her on.

"Absolutely certain. She is deeply attached to Captain Wentworth, and they are very happy!"

"Did she say as much?"

"There was no need for her to put it into words. But I am persuaded you shall catch my meaning as soon as you see them together."

"And when would that be, do you know?"

"I do not, dearest. From what I understand, they have returned to Somerset to seek Sir Walter's blessing."

'For what it was worth.' But that, he did not say.

"So… they will marry soon?"

"I believe so."

"And you?"

"I?"

"When will *you* marry?"

'The morrow would not be soon enough' – but he did not say that either. Instead, he smiled again in the same carefree, almost boyish fashion that had made her stare in wonder a short while ago. She stared again. Then, at his reply, this time she gaped in earnest.

"Earlier today, Bingley had proposed a double wedding and E – … Miss Elizabeth and her sister were both delighted with the prospect. As you may have noticed, they are very close."

"So, pending Mr. Bennet's consent…?" Georgiana began, but did not get to finish.

Her brother interjected, his eyes very bright.

"Aye, dearest. If all goes well, we shall be wed by Michaelmas!"

"And so he is to marry?" Lady Malvern earnestly inquired, her eyes intent upon her second son.

"He is, Ma'am. In three weeks or so, from what I hear."

"Heaven help us! Then he *has* lost his head!"

Colonel Fitzwilliam could not fail to laugh – there was a great deal of truth in that! – and her ladyship resumed the inquisition.

"Who is she, then? Is she of tolerable stock?"

"She is the daughter of a small country gentleman from Hertfordshire," the Colonel selectively supplied as he walked over to refill his glass, then returned to pace before the mantelpiece as he continued: "By your way of thinking, he *could* have done better, in some respects at least, but not in others. He *has* found his match, Ma'am. In more ways than one!"

"Do not presume to know my way of thinking, Richard, and pray cease this infernal pacing!" her ladyship commanded. "Found his match, has he? I shall thank you for letting me form my own opinion. I trust he will have the grace to arrange for us to meet her, while she is still in town."

"Your trust is misplaced, Mater," the Colonel offered with something of a smirk. "The young lady has returned to her father's house and, to the best of my knowledge, Darcy has followed her post-haste to Hertfordshire."

This time, Lady Malvern's shock was readily apparent.

"He would lodge at an inn for three weeks, merely to pay court?"

"Oh, fear not, 'tis not as bad as that! To Darcy's great fortune, his friend Bingley's house in the country is but two miles from Miss Bennet's doorstep. It *would* be fair to say, though, that he is sufficiently besotted to have settled for the inn, if it came to that."

"Cease smirking, Richard! You are long out of the school-room!" Lady Malvern ordered, then sniffed: "Bingley? Is that the coltish young man whose sisters suffer vastly from delusions of grandeur?"

"The very same," the Colonel laughingly confirmed.

"Well! At least Darcy did not offer for that young man's sister – *there* is a small mercy! – or the Grantham chit, *or* your cousin Anne!"

Colonel Fitzwilliam knew better than to laugh this time – just as he knew full well there was no love lost between his mother and her husband's sister.

In effect, it could safely be said that they heartily detested each other, which was no surprise, knowing Lady Catherine's ways and Lady Malvern's disposition. Lady Malvern had always frowned at Lady Catherine's pointed references to Darcy's tacit engagement to her daughter – as she generally frowned at nearly everything that Lady Catherine said.

Rallying for subtlety rather than open battle, Colonel Fitzwilliam schooled his features into something very much like solemn horror.

"If I may say, Ma'am, it *has* been a close call! Had Miss Bennet not caught his eye last Easter, Lady Catherine might have been skilled enough to wear him down before too long, and carry her point!"

"Do not flatter yourself for a moment that I do not know *precisely* what you are doing," Lady Malvern dismissively observed. "I would suggest you employ those tactics on your *father* – though you would be better advised to think of other ways to frighten him. He favoured the de Bourgh match, if you remember!"

The Colonel could not help laughing at that.

"I beg your pardon, Mater, I *should* have known better – after all, I have not conjured up my celebrated wits just from thin air!"

"Your celebrated wits!" his mother scoffed. "I daresay young Bingley's sisters are not the only ones affected by delusion! Sit, Richard!" her ladyship sternly intoned. "I shall not crane my neck to watch you any longer!"

With brisk, matter-of-fact motions, Lady Malvern poured his tea, and then her own.

"Sit with me," she asked her favourite son, her tone of voice a great deal less belligerent this time, "and tell me, what do your celebrated wits have to say about her?"

The Colonel crossed his legs and reached for his cup of tea. Then, choosing his words with utmost care, he proceeded to relate the very best he had ever known of Miss Elizabeth Bennet to the most honourable and astute lady of his acquaintance. A lady of keen discernment and kind heart, underneath the bluster, who might be persuaded to understand her dearest nephew's choice and wishes. Who might indeed become the future Mrs. Darcy's most powerful ally, rather than her critic. Who might – just might – be turned into her staunchest champion.

If she chose to listen. If *he* played his cards right!

He could not sleep – again – yet the vibrant restlessness that now banished slumber was as far from former anguish as can be.

He took a long, deep breath, his chest expanding – and, somehow, it was still too narrow to contain the overwhelming happiness he felt.

Fulfilment – absolute fulfilment of every wish, of every hope – spread, warm and glorious within him, and Darcy's arms tightened around the sleeping form he cradled.

Breath caught in his chest as fleeting moments of their night of passion swirled in a haze, too exquisite for words.

His, now, in every way – as he was hers, forever.

He swallowed hard, his fingers moving over her silky skin in a cautious, light caress, so as not to wake her, and turned his head to brush his lips against her brow.

For some reason of her own, which he could not fully fathom, she had rejected his suggestion that they spend their wedding night at Netherfield and, with a charming blush, she had smilingly informed him that she would much prefer they travelled to the house in Berkeley Square, once it was time to leave the wedding breakfast.

Her choice was a surprise. He would have thought that, at a time of such momentous changes in her life, she would seek the reassurance of more familiar surroundings, and indeed the comfort of being near Jane. She did not – and her willingness to leave them all behind her, to start her life with *him*, was yet another source of gratitude and wonder.

Still, she had been pensive and very often silent on their journey into town – which could not surprise him. It merely made him wish he were more skilled with words, so that he could bring comfort at this unsettling time, and dispel any unease she might have felt at the unknown future.

He was not skilled with words – he never had been. All that he could offer was the comfort of his embrace, and was reassured in no small measure to see her nestling into his arms rather than shy away, in self-consciousness or blushing discomfort.

Self-consciousness, however, turned out to be the order of the day – for both – when they arrived at last in Berkeley Square, and it had scarce abated by the time they sat for the elaborate repast that Mrs. Herbert, his housekeeper, had arranged for them – too lavish for two, particularly as they had barely picked at it.

He had wondered briefly whether having Georgiana with them might have improved matters – or whether the reverse might have been true. There was no way of knowing, for Georgiana was from home, conspicuously invited by Lady Malvern to visit with her family for a se'nnight or two, right after the wedding.

By the time Weston had returned to announce that the tea things were laid out in the library, he could not bear another moment of surreptitiously watching her toy with her food upon the plate, her countenance a kaleidoscope of unreadable emotions.

He yearned to hold her – nothing more, just hold her and find a way to set her troubled heart at ease. Make her believe there was no need to fret; that, alien as this new life must surely be, he will be kind, she will be cherished, and they will be happy.

He had not known quite *how* to say those words a short while later, when the butler and the footman had withdrawn and they were left alone at last, in the cosy quiet of the library.

Unnecessary as it might have been in view of the mild weather, a merry fire burned within the grate and, glad of it, he spared a thankful thought to the wise soul who had ordered it lit, for the warmth it brought went beyond the mere realms of temperature.

"I suspect I might have found my favourite room," he heard her say, her lips curling at the corners and he smiled effortlessly back, self-consciousness well-nigh forgotten as he asked if she would care to have a look around.

They ambled round the room, her hand in his, the candlestick he held casting a glow over the surrounding shelves, over the dark panelling and the stern old portraits.

"Have you found anything you liked?" he asked, and her response was to laugh softly.

"Great many, aye. I should imagine this room might keep me out of mischief for a while!"

Smiling again, he stroked her hand, immensely reassured to hear the laughter in her voice; to see her drift away from the awkwardness of earlier hours.

"Would you like me to read for you?" he offered, grasping at anything that might help keep the unease at bay, and her eyes warmed as she looked up towards him.

"I daresay I have not had the chance to tell you that I love your voice… Well, now you know," she said matter-of-factly, with an impish glance and a delightful little shrug. "I would like that very much," she added, her tone and mien altered, "but… not tonight." She stopped, then swallowed. "Come, let us sit," she urged at last. "Would you care for tea?"

He did *not* care for tea – not by a fair margin! Truth be told, *tea* was the last thing on his mind! And if a *beverage* was the only option, he would have gladly gone for something much stronger than tea!

He bit his lip though, allowing that in this instance tea will *have* to do.

"Tea would be good," was what he brought himself to say and they returned to the table by the fire, where the small urn was set, along with all the other tea things.

He watched her pour, the picture adorably domestic and then she set the cups before them. She did not pick hers up, but turned to him instead.

"How is your hand?" she asked in quiet whisper.

"My hand?" he wondered, baffled by the question, until comprehension dawned, and with it came a flood of wholly unnerving recollections.

He had not quite got around to answer and assure her that his injury was by now well-healed, before she took his hand without hesitation, just as she had the last time, and turned it over in her clasp, palm up. Her fingers reached to stroke the thin white scar, and then the palm around it – and his own fingers twitched again, clasping hers this time, just as his other hand came up to cup her cheek.

There never was a hope for *this* kiss to be tame! There was too much history, too much borrowed tension, and a great deal too much longing carried all this time, ever since that distant day, at Longbourn. And yet the same old demon, or perhaps guarding angel, returned to warn him against untoward haste – *Festina lente*, and all that! – so, with a great deal more reluctance than a month ago, in Kensington Gardens, he drew back again, his breath just as ragged.

"Shall we have some tea?" he brought himself to offer, his voice low and conspicuously uneven.

The look of stark surprise she shot him was as unmistakable as it was delightful.

"*Tea?*" she whispered, with a throaty chuckle, her fingers still tightly clasped on his lapels.

He smiled and bent his head to drop a light kiss on her nose.

"No tea, then?"

"No. No tea."

He chuckled in his turn.

"Oh. Just as well. I hate the blasted stuff!"

They laughed – more or less breathlessly – together, and he put an arm around her waist as they settled back into the sofa and against each other, and then he turned his head to brush his lips against her temple.

"Just so you know," he whispered, a hint of boyish laughter in his voice, "this is *precisely* what I longed to do, when you finished drying the spilled tea off my hand!"

She turned to him, her laughter warm upon his cheek.

"Perhaps you *should have!* It might have saved some time – and spared us all a fair amount of trouble! Or perhaps not."

No. Perhaps not – as he was still engaged to another at that time. His eyes narrowed and he all but winced at his destructive folly. He chose not to go down that path though – not now, not in this happy moment – so he laughed mildly in his turn instead.

"I should imagine our relations might have had a thing or two to say of *that!*"

She laughed again.

"Oh, aye! I daresay I quite forgot about them!"

And so had he – to some extent, at least. He smiled at that.

"But… what exactly are you saying?" he grasped her meaning at last, if only in small part, and he pressed on, eager to know more. "Are you by any chance suggesting you were no longer set against me, *even then?*"

"No, I most certainly was not!" she whispered softly.

"*You were not?*" he all but gasped. "But… you were so quiet! I thought you were resenting my intrusion into your life – yet again! I thought you were shocked to see me at Longbourn!"

"Oh, I *was!* I could not imagine *why* you would give yourself the trouble to return! And when I heard you speak to Jane the way you did – and later on, when I learned you would have risked your life to protect Lydia, that was when I knew, beyond a shadow of a doubt, that you were the very best of men!"

"That I am not, my love, but I am very gratified you think so."

"Oh, we shall not argue over this! I must give you fair warning, I shall brook no opposition! I had my suspicions, long before, but – "

"*Long* before? Since when, exactly?"

"It has been coming on so gradually, that I hardly know when it began. But I believe I must date it from my first seeing your beautiful grounds at Pemberley," she smiled.

He laughed at her obvious jest, and pressed on, regardless.

"I wish you would tell me. 'Tis all in the past – *thank goodness!* – but I *would* like to know."

She raised her eyes at him.

"And yet I am in earnest. My mistaken views were already altered by your letter, but it was only there, at Pemberley, that I fully understood at last. Understood *you*. Who you were – where you came from. What you have set aside – to come to me. And as for – " she raised her hand to his lips to forestall the interruption, and gave a little misty smile when he kissed her fingertips. "As for the praises Mrs. Reynolds did not hesitate to heap upon you, they had helped me see what sort of man you were. What sort of brother, landlord, master. How many people depended on you, for their happiness and welfare. How much pleasure or pain it was in your power to bestow – and how judiciously you have used that power."

He made no answer, not quite knowing what to say to that. They settled back against each other and silence fell, peaceful and intimate, barely broken by the sound of her even breath and by the distant crackling of the fire.

He turned to brush his lips against her cheek again.

"Are you quite comfortable?" he whispered.

"Quite. I thank you."

"You *will* let me know – will you not? – when you have grown tired…" he tentatively offered, not knowing how to phrase it better – and more than a little mortified by his own *gauche* approach.

And then she whispered back:

"I am not tired… but… I believe I am now ready to retire…" she shyly offered in her turn and, at that, he cautiously searched her eyes.

"You are?"

She would not look at him at first, but then she did, her eyes warm and sparkling in the candlelight, and her hand reached up to caress his cheek.

"I am," came the quiet whisper, and he swallowed.

"Would you care to go up, then? Your maid must be waiting. I will summon a footman to show you – "

She shook her head, then laced her fingers through his.

"No. Do not summon anyone."

"Shall *I* show you to your chambers?" he asked, very quietly.

"If you would…"

"Of course. I can do that…"

They stood and walked up together, hand in hand, to the floor above, and thence to the door a few yards down from his own bedchamber.

She went in, with a soft endearment and a swift brush of her lips against his chin – and he was left in the darkened hallway, his heart hammering wildly in his chest, until he suddenly turned and walked to his own chambers.

He could scarce remember what Lydford might have said – if anything – as he prepared him for the night.

He had not been so nervous in his entire life, not even on the day – or *days* – when he had offered for her!

He cast a glance at the glass of port Lydford had left on the nightstand for him and considered it briefly, then promptly dismissed it. It would not do – the taste, the scent of it on his breath. Best not!

He chose to pace instead, in his dressing gown, for something that felt like an inordinately long time – and also like a flicker of a second. He checked the clock on the mantelpiece, twice, but *that* served no purpose, for he had no notion how long ago they had retired to their chambers.

He determined he should allow another quarter-hour, just to be safe – and chances were he must have left it for a great deal too long for, when he finally walked up, with a deep, steadying breath, to knock on the door between their chambers, it was opened at once, as though after a long wait.

She was exquisite. A vision in a long, white, flowing garment, her hair tumbling in glowing auburn splendour to her waist. She looked up at him, biting the corner of her lip in the same endearing fashion, and the touching mix of innocence and acquiescence moved him more than he could ever own.

His heart went out to her – as did his arms. He led her into his own chambers, some scattered sense advising it was for the best, so that, if she chose to, later, she could leave him and seek her comfort in her own apartments – although he certainly preferred she found it in his arms.

He would have liked to think he had been kind. Patient. Careful. Subduing his own wishes to her comfort – for tonight was hers. And, if he was to judge by her responses, and the simple fact that she was still content to remain here, asleep in his arms, her slender limbs entwined around him, he might be justified in thinking that he *had* got it right.

He smiled – if a trifle smugly – and, with a happy sigh, he settled against her and closed his eyes at last.

Quite suddenly, she moved, nudging him rather painfully with her elbow as she did so, and he all but laughed to discover that she was a restless sleeper – though *why* he had ever imagined otherwise, he really could not tell!

He slowly eased her elbow from his ribs and wrapped her in his arms again.

His nose skimmed along her jaw line, inhaling her sweet scent, dropping feathery kisses as he went – and then she stirred, with a soft sleepy murmur, very much like a contented purr. She brought him closer, and her lips sought his. Translucent skin glimmered in the moonlight as her arms came out from underneath the counterpane to wind around his neck, her fingers tangling in his hair, and her lips parted under his suddenly hungry kiss.

"I love you," he heard her whisper later, when his lips had drifted to her throat, and he stopped from tender ministrations to hold her very close.

"And I love *you!*" he whispered back.

The one truth that would never alter.

He loved her. More than life itself.

Epilogue

The sound of laughter intermingled with disjointed but cheerful strains of music drew him from his papers, and Darcy put the pen down, a smile fluttering on his lips at the interruption. He pushed his chair back and promptly left his study to walk towards the drawing-room instead. He stopped in the doorway, his mien softening as he beheld the delightful picture they presented, sitting together at the pianoforte. They were still practising the duet they had chosen – a lively, jaunty piece – and the fact that it was not going well was apparently a source of undisguised amusement. They laughed together, even then, as hands collided over the same keys and landed on the wrong ones, sending up sharp, discordant notes, followed by more laughter.

Seeing Georgiana thus had long ceased to surprise him. There were many months since his reserved young sister had begun to open up to his wife – many months since they had grown so fully, so completely at ease with each other; since Georgiana's shyness had been cast aside, as she had flourished under the influence of her affectionate new sister.

It was no longer a surprise to see them thus, merely a source of profound joy, and Darcy smiled again as he leaned against the doorframe, unwilling to come in and disturb them.

A moment later, though, he had been spotted, and Elizabeth turned towards him with an airy little laugh.

"Forgive us! I daresay we were rather loud."

"*Rather* loud! Elizabeth, we could be heard from Lambton!" Georgiana giggled – a clear exaggeration – then stood from the pianoforte and tapped her hands upon its top with some determination, while Darcy walked in to take a seat on the nearest sofa. "We are not to be defeated by this troublesome little piece," Georgiana smilingly declared, "but, to my way of thinking, we ought to hide behind closed doors in my sitting room and practice on the pianoforte there, at least until we can contrive to sound a little less discordant!"

"A tall order, that," Elizabeth laughed in her turn, then walked over to sit at her husband's side and place her hand in his – a natural motion, which Georgiana was by now accustomed to seeing, every day.

She had grown accustomed to see them seek each other, sit together, touch, as they shared their thoughts and laughed and chatted – as though they could not bear to be apart for a moment longer than their respective duties unavoidably required.

It had come as a great shock to her at first, this uncommonly strong bond that her brother and his new wife shared – and, were she to be perfectly honest, Georgiana had begun by resenting her for it. Nay, perhaps not, perhaps resentment was too strong a word! But she had felt uncomfortably excluded or, worse still, supplanted in her brother's affections by this dark-eyed stranger who – Fitzwilliam was in the right, of course – could not be described as *'painfully shy'* by any stretch of anyone's imagination!

The discomfort had not lasted long, nor had her cool reserve. They were soon melted by Elizabeth's warm affection. Her obvious devotion to Georgiana's brother had put Elizabeth onto the quickest path towards the young girl's heart, as had the happiness she very clearly brought him, but it was the genuine interest and warmth she had constantly shown Georgiana herself that had helped form the sisterly bond between them, closer now than the strongest ties of blood.

With another swift glance at the endearing picture on the sofa, Georgiana chose to turn towards the windows and cast a glance outside.

It was still snowing. In effect, it had been snowing, with brief interruptions, for three days together, and the grey, dreary landscape had become pristinely white. It was not gentle snow, not now, but something of a fierce blizzard, and Georgiana sighed.

"I hope our guests arrived home safely, and did not met with *that!*" she whispered wistfully, almost to herself.

The quiet words nevertheless reached the others and, on sudden impulse, Elizabeth came up to press her younger sister's hand, knowing full well that it was the safety of *one guest* in particular that concerned her the most.

Captain St. Lawrence had arrived with Anne and Captain Wentworth to spend Christmastide at Pemberley, to add to the number of family and friends already gathered there – and also add to Georgiana's enjoyment of the season.

Nothing was said between them yet; it was perhaps too soon for that. Merely subtle hints, such as the Captain's openly avowed intention to return to Derbyshire after a long-overdue visit to his family, and seek to lease or purchase an estate in the area, and settle there, as soon as may be.

Georgiana had blushed profusely at that – particularly as it had appeared at the time that, although mentioned to the entire company, the words had held a message for her, and her alone.

She was not the only one to decipher the message – for, after all, the young lady's brother had never been deficient in his understanding. It had raised no particular concerns, however. His prejudices against naval captains long discarded, Darcy saw no reason to object to his courtship, nor to his sister's choice.

Much like Captain Wentworth, Captain St. Lawrence was an upright gentleman of good principles, good standing and independent fortune – and if he had gained his sister's heart, then Darcy would not be the one to break it, much as Lady Catherine would undoubtedly say, to anyone who would care to listen, that none of her departed sister's children had troubled themselves to make a suitable match.

That was of course a matter of opinion – but then again Darcy knew full well he could not expect her ladyship to comprehend the joys that were daily brightening up his life.

The twelve days of Christmas certainly could not have been any brighter. Happiness and laughter had constantly filled the halls teeming with visitors from many quarters.

Mr. and Mrs. Bennet had come to Pemberley of course, along with their two as yet unmarried daughters, as had Bingley and Jane, who did not have quite as far to travel, from their newly acquired estate in Staffordshire.

Of the Bennet sisters, it was only the youngest who could not join the cheerful family gathering, for she had recently taken to travelling the world at her husband's side, shortly after their very unexpected wedding the previous summer.

To everyone's surprise, she had gained the affections – or rather, she had healed the broken heart of one of Captain Wentworth's friends, a certain Captain Benwick, whose first love had succumbed to a pernicious fever, while he was at sea.

Mr. and Mrs. Gardiner and their family had joined them at Pemberley as well, tipping the balance heavily in favour of Elizabeth's relations for, on Darcy's side, it was only the northern contingent of his Fitzwilliam connections that had arrived to see the New Year in, just as they had the previous one.

It was to be suspected that Lady Malvern had accepted the first invitation to Pemberley largely to see how was her nephew's new wife deporting herself, in her position. The fact that she had returned, time and again, and brought his more reluctant lordship, told its own story, as did the staunch support the newly married couple had uniformly received from her in town.

To Elizabeth's relief – and no less Darcy's – Mrs. Bennet had somehow avoided attracting Lady Malvern's censure, presumably because she stood in such awe of her eldest son-in-law and his exalted connections that she hardly ever ventured to speak in their presence, unless it was in her power to offer them any attention, or mark her deference to their opinions.

As to Mrs. Darcy's Cheapside relations, it eventually emerged that Lady Malvern was not so much objecting to money made in trade, as to the untoward airs and graces of those who would endeavour to forget precisely *where* was their present comfort coming from.

The opening door tore Darcy from his ruminations and he looked up to see the youngest day nurse enter.

"Ma'am, I am come to say that the young master is awake now, and clamouring for his mother," she cheerfully informed her mistress, bobbing a prompt curtsy.

A warm smile brightened Elizabeth's countenance at that and she excused herself directly, with Georgiana quick to follow. The young maid dropped a curtsy to the master of the house and returned to her duties, closing the door behind her – and suddenly the drawing-room was unbearably quiet.

Darcy stood. He consulted his pocket watch as he walked to the window. Weather permitting, in another hour he was supposed to ride out with his steward.

He cast a glance outside. Apparently he would not. Well, then, perhaps they should sit together and go over the plans for the refurbishment of the alms houses in Kympton. Work was due to start in February – or as soon as the spring settled in earnest. As to the drainage of the eastern meadow…

He gave a little rueful chuckle and put his watch back in its pocket. It really served no purpose to dissemble, and much less to attempt to deceive *himself!* The truth was that he cared very little about the drainage of the eastern meadow now, nor did he wish to return to his study and his papers.

With a light shrug, Mr. Darcy determined that if following his heart was a sign of weakness, then he *was* weak – and glad of it!

His heart made him follow Elizabeth to a room on the first floor, in the south wing. A room that, after nearly two decades of disuse, was no longer empty, and very far from quiet!

The door into his old day nursery was already open and Darcy walked in, only to see them sitting on the floor, amidst an army of toy soldiers and stuffed animals of all shapes and sizes.

The days spent aligning those very same toy soldiers into neatly ordered regiments and marching them to the sound of the well-worn drum in the corner of the room were long forgotten, as carefree days of childhood were wont to be.

He could see several other old favourites scattered among shiny new toys as he picked his way towards the spot where Elizabeth and Georgiana sat, gleefully clapping once his son and heir succeeded in clambering onto his old rocking horse – and did not roll off down the tail end this time!

A look of immense self-satisfaction spread over the soft features which, despite the round cheeks and very tiny nose, strikingly resembled his own. The determined rider dug his fingers into the horse's mane in an endeavour to retain his balance as he glanced from one adoring admirer to another, then stretched a chubby little hand in his direction.

"Papa! Papa come! Papa on hosey too!"

"Now, George, I think we might need a slightly larger horse," Darcy smiled as he crouched down beside him, his heart brimming with love for the three of them, his family – and above all, for his darling wife.

He caught her warm glance, over their son's head – and it was strange that, in such a private moment, it should be *Wentworth's* words that suddenly sprang to mind.

It still went against the grain to own it – much as he had come to like the man at last – but the Captain had the right of it with something he said to him the other day, as they companionably sipped their port together.

"There is nothing to be done about it", Wentworth had cheerfully observed. "We must endeavour to subdue our minds to our good fortune: we must learn to brook being much happier than we both deserve!"

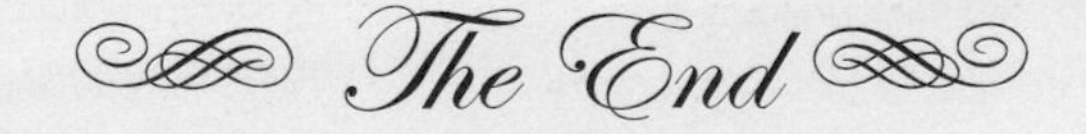

BY THE SAME AUTHOR

FROM THIS DAY FORWARD
~ THE DARCYS OF PEMBERLEY ~

"A thoughtful and discerning sequel about the Darcys"
Austenesque Reviews (September 2013)

On a crisp winter morning in a small country church, Miss Elizabeth Bennet married Mr. Darcy – and her quiet, tame existence abruptly changed.

The second daughter of a country gentleman is now many different things, to different people. Beloved wife. Mistress of a dauntingly great estate. Reluctant socialite. Daughter. Sister. Cousin. Friend. And as the days of her married life go by, bringing both joy and turmoil, the man that stands beside her is her shelter and comfort in the face of family opposition, peril and heartbreak.

Three very different Christmas seasons come to serve as landmarks to their lives and there are blissful days and times of sorrow at the old English country house. And before too long, a time would come when Darcy must decide if he is prepared to risk everything for the sake of a full life together - or succumb to the collection of his fears.

"Quiet footsteps, eerily quiet, drew him from his trance. He looked up – and followed. The ghostly sound faded as he reached the eastern staircase and he took the steps two at a time, down to the very bottom. A madman's quest for he knew not what pushed him to the gallery. In the light of the moon, from her portrait, his grandfather's first wife looked down upon him with the deepest compassion. He dug his fingers in his hair. A long, dry sob racked his chest as he pounded the frame of the unfortunate woman's likeness, and broken gilt plaster fell to the floor. He covered his mouth with his fist, stifling the groan. And ran."

Researched in great detail and mindful of the language and manners of Jane Austen's time, *'From This Day Forward'* sensitively explores life at Pemberley after Elizabeth Bennet's marriage to Fitzwilliam Darcy, as well as the turns their fates might have taken, in a context that the creator of *'Pride and Prejudice'* could have recognised.

'From This Day Forward' is as much a story about the fortunes of the Darcys as a journey back in time. Christmas traditions are revived, as well as real-life events and titbits of eighteenth century gossip. Against this backdrop, we witness Elizabeth Bennet grow from a pert young miss who loves reading and long country walks, into a strong, confident woman, who can run an imposing household, help Georgiana overcome her past, and become the mainstay of Darcy's life, in every way.

'From This Day Forward' is available at Amazon in paperback and Kindle format and in other ebook formats at most online retailers.

COMING SOON

THE SECOND CHANCE

A 'Pride & Prejudice' ~ 'Sense & Sensibility' Variation

Soon after the Netherfield Ball, a troubled Mr. Darcy decides to walk away from a most unsuitable fascination. But heartache is in store for more than just him, and his misguided attempts to ensure the comfort of the woman he loves backfire in ways he had not expected.

Excerpt from the opening chapter :

Absentmindedly, Darcy returned his watch to its pocket and strolled down the corridor to the left side of the house, to the predictable sanctuary of his choice. The library would be deserted at this time in the morning. At any time of day, to be precise. Bingley, for all his other virtues, was not an avid reader, and neither were his sisters, despite the eldest's protestations to the contrary – which, to own the truth, suited him very well indeed.

He opened the panelled door and entered, closing it quietly behind him. *'Sparse'* would be the kindest way to describe Bingley's collection, and Darcy wondered what could he choose today.

He slowly wandered in, aiming for the furthest shelves where, a few days earlier, he had found a tome about some intrepid explorers and their perilous travels to the far-flung reaches of the Orient – and suddenly stopped, frozen in his tracks.

The library was *not* deserted at that time in the morning.

Previously hidden by the high back of the sofa she reclined upon, the occupant was now revealed to him, and Darcy all but gasped.

A book loosely resting in her lap, her thumb still keeping her place between the pages, Miss Elizabeth Bennet sat before him, oblivious to his presence – and for a moment Darcy contemplated the wisdom of a swift retreat. But nay, she was bound to notice his withdrawal, and deliberate rudeness was not a trait Darcy had ever wished to cultivate – except towards those who clearly deserved it.

He drew breath to greet her – but, as his slow footsteps brought him at last in full view of her countenance, the civil words faded on his lips.

She was asleep. She must have come down in the early hours of the morning for a brief respite, after tending to her sister for the best part of the night, and tiredness must have overcome her, as she read her book.

It forcefully struck him that, for the very first time in their acquaintance, he did not have to swiftly look away, for fear that she would notice he was staring, and the unhoped-for chance to take in every detail of her appearance rose to his head, with all the heady effects of a fine wine.

Beautiful? He had taken great pains to make it clear to himself and to his friends – impudent dog that he was! – that she hardly had a good feature in her face. Yet he had scarce persuaded himself of the fact, before that very face had begun to draw him, with the beautiful expression of her eyes, with every play of genuine emotion over the less-than-classically-perfect features, with every smile for her eldest sister, with every arch look towards *him*.

Whether she was beautiful or not to other eyes no longer mattered. It was *she* who drew him, more than any reputed beauty. Her warmth, her artless charm, her smile. She was smiling now, her lips ever so slightly turned up at the corners, ever so slightly parted, allowing quiet, tranquil breaths, softly in, softly out.

Her nose – small and endearingly perfect. The stubborn little chin, often tilted up in a playful show of defiance, as he could often witness, the latest instance no further than the previous night.

'I have therefore made up my mind to tell you that I do not want to dance a reel at all – and now despise me if you dare!'

He smiled despite himself as he remembered, the delightful mixture of archness and sweetness in her manner more bewitching than anything he had ever come across.

She had very long lashes, he suddenly observed. He had never noticed this before, too mesmerised by the mirth in her eyes to pay any heed to something as mundane as lashes. They were thick, dark, and curled up at the ends.

Her head was tilted to one side and the auburn ringlets that framed the oval face were now in disarray – she obviously intended to slip out for a moment from her sister's chambers, and had not readied herself for anybody's company, and certainly not his.

He ought to leave – *that*, he knew full well. He ought to turn on his heels and leave her, before the lashes fluttered, her eyes opened and she caught him in the unpardonable act of spying on her in her sleep – and yet he could not, would not move.

It took all the restraint he still possessed to *not* drop to one knee by the arm of the sofa and reach to brush his fingertips against the rosy cheek. He slowly flexed his unruly fingers into a tight fist, one by one, pressing his thumb against them, in forceful endeavour to ensure that he would not succumb to the inconceivable temptation – yet, even then, in defiance of his strict control, tantalising thoughts began to weave ever so slowly through him, spreading subtle, delicious poison in their wake.

To have the right to do so! To have the right to reach and caress her cheek, as she would lay asleep in his bed beside him. To see her eyes flutter open and crinkle at the corners as she would smile to him. To be allowed – encouraged – to lean towards her and taste the sweetness of her lips, to feel them soft and pliant beneath his own, as he would take her in his arms, her warm, lovely form cradled to his chest. Tender. Loving. Beautiful. His.

He swallowed hard, his mouth suddenly dry and drew a ragged breath, so loud to his own ears that he feared it would wake her.

She did not wake and, mindless of the dangers of exposure, he still stood exactly where he was, drinking in the sight of her and recklessly courting disaster. If she should wake, this very moment…

Seconds passed, one… two… three… a number. And every shred of reason cried out at him to leave, no longer merely to avoid detection and the attendant mortification, but to preserve himself from an enchanting vision that would most likely haunt him from now on, in all his sleepless nights…

At long last he obeyed and walked back to the door, on mercifully sturdy floorboards. The hinges did not creak – another mercy – and he noiselessly closed the heavy door behind him – just as the thud of a book falling to the floor could be heard from the room that he had quitted.

Darcy took his hand off the door-handle as though the intricately moulded metal burned and, exhaling in sudden gratitude at his own narrow, far too narrow escape, he hastened away from the blasted spot – and from the strongest of temptations.

'The Second Chance' will be available at Amazon in 2014, in paperback and Kindle format and in other ebook formats at most online retailers.

ABOUT THE AUTHOR

Joana Starnes lives in the South of England with her family.
A medical graduate, over the years she had developed an unrelated but enduring fascination with Georgian Britain in general and the works of Jane Austen in particular.

You can find Joana Starnes
on Facebook at www.facebook.com/joana.a.starnes
on Twitter at www.twitter.com/Joana_Starnes
or on her website at www.joanastarnes.co.uk

Printed in Great Britain
by Amazon.co.uk, Ltd.,
Marston Gate.